PENGUIN BOOKS

THE DARTS OF CUPID AND OTHER STORIES

Edith Templeton was born in Prague in 1916 and spent much of her childhood in a castle in the Bohemian countryside. She was educated at the French lycée in Prague and left the city in 1938 to marry an Englishman. During her years in England she worked in the Office of the Chief Surgeon for the US Army in Cheltenham and then became a captain in the British Army, working as a conference interpreter. Her short stories began to appear in *The New Yorker* in the 1950s. Over the next several decades she published a number of novels as well as a popular travel book, *The Surprise of Cremona*.

Edith Templeton left England in 1956 to live in India with her second husband, a noted cardiologist and the physician to the king of Nepal. *Gordon* first appeared in 1966 under a pseudonym and was subsequently banned in England and Germany, and was then pirated around the world. In 2003 Viking brought the novel back into print in Britain. The author has lived in various parts of Europe and now makes her home in Bordighera, on the coast of Italy.

The Darts of Cupid

and other stories

Edith Templeton

PENGUIN BOOKS

PENGUIN BOOKS

Published by the Penguin Group
Penguin Books Ltd, 80 Strand, London WC2R ORL, England
Penguin Group (USA) Inc., 375 Hudson Street, New York, New York 10014, USA
Penguin Group (Canada), 10 Alcorn Avenue, Toronto, Ontario, Canada M4V 3B2
(a division of Pearson Penguin Canada Inc.)
Penguin Ireland, 25 St Stephen's Green, Dublin 2, Ireland (a division of Penguin Books Ltd)
Penguin Group (Australia), 250 Camberwell Road,
Camberwell, Victoria 3124, Australia (a division of Pearson Australia Group Pty Ltd)
Penguin Books India Pvt Ltd, 11 Community Centre,
Panchsheel Park, New Delhi – 110 017, India
Penguin Group (NZ), cnr Airborne and Rosedale Roads, Albany,
Auckland 1310, New Zealand (a division of Pearson New Zealand Ltd)
Penguin Books (South Africa) (Pty) Ltd, 24 Sturdee Avenue,
Rosebank 2196, South Africa

Penguin Books Ltd, Registered Offices: 80 Strand, London WC2R ORL, England

www.penguin.com

First published in the United States of America by Pantheon Books 2002
First published in Great Britain by Viking 2004
Published in Penguin Books 2005
1

Grateful acknowledgement is made to *The New Yorker*, where the following stories
originally appeared: "The Darts of Cupid," "Equality Cake," "Irresistibly," "The Dress Rehearsal,"
and "Nymph and Faun."

"A Coffeehouse Acquaintance" originally appeared in *Three: 1971*.
Copyright © 1971 by Random House, Inc.
Published by Random House, Inc., New York, 1971

Printed in England by Clays Ltd, St Ives plc

Contents

The Darts of Cupid

and other stories

The Darts of Cupid

Sometimes I wondered whether he had not chosen the Merry Widow because she had crinkly red hair, freckles, a bony face, and small dark eyes, the same as he—just as people choose dogs whose masks resemble their own features. But I knew this was an idle conceit of mine. He had obviously wanted a mature, well-bred, and decorous woman for the job, and he could not have taken anyone else from our crowd, because the Merry Widow was the only one of us who, owing to a perverse whim during one phase of her life, had learned to be competent in shorthand and typing. The Merry Widow was also known as the Secretary, because she was the Brigadier General's secretary, and the Brigadier was the only one in the Office of the Chief Surgeon, U.S. Forces, who had a personal secretary to himself. According to the law of irony, which states one thing while implying its opposite, the Merry

Widow was neither merry nor a widow; she was married and grieved for her absent husband, who was doing service overseas, and in this she was the exception in our crowd, who were none of us single and had all a history of ill-starred marriage behind us.

It was fortunate for all of us women who worked in the U.S. War Office in Bathdale in those days of the war that Claudia Carter and the Merry Widow were both "old girls" of the Bathdale Ladies' College, and had been in the same house at school. Thus, through Claudia, we were guaranteed our supply of the very best quality gossip, fresh and untainted by later distortions. The Merry Widow, sitting in the anteroom of the Brigadier General's office, was not easily accessible; she did not take her tea break, nor was she given to dawdling in the ladies' rest room. Yet there were certain occasions when she could be drawn into talk, because it was she who dished out the remedies for hangovers, coughs, and headaches. With the cough mixture—a sinister-hued, muddy green liquid of early Victorian vintage—she had the greatest success, because she never failed to comment, "Only a teaspoonful, mind you. It's got real dope in it—it's dangerous, you know. It beats me how they allow it to be sold across the counter."

In the beginning, I had made attempts to draw out the Merry Widow—like, "I say, Gwendolyn threw a frightful tantrum and weeping fit in the ladies' rest room again. Is it true that the General took the Osborne woman to a party?" And she would reply, "Never you fear, Prescott-Clark; he's merely widening his field of operations." This was quite witty, because he was, like most of the officers in the department, a doctor, and he was a Regular Army man, too, but it was an unsatisfactory reply, and I resigned myself, like the others in our crowd, to leaving it to Claudia, whose claims to intimate gossip were further strengthened by the fact that both she and the Merry Widow were natives of Bathdale and had remained in that town. We, the others who were employed as civilian labor in the U.S. War Office, had merely happened to be living there at the outset of the war, owing to various circumstances in our lives.

While the Merry Widow dealt with such unspectacular complaints as coughs and headaches, it was Sergeant Parsons who was called in on those dramatic occasions when it was imperative to remove grit from under the eyelid or a splinter embedded in the hand. He was the only man who was allowed to enter the ladies' rest room, where, on an electric hot plate, he boiled his surgical implements in a tin that had once contained condensed milk. He had "golden hands" and a way of saying, "Don't worry, ma'am. I won't do anything yet. I'm only going to have a look-see," while adding, a few seconds later, "Here, that's what's been bothering you, isn't it?" To shrieks of "It's not possible. I never felt a thing," he would reply, "Do you want me to put it back again, to convince you?"

He was a short, narrow-chested man with graying hair, rather older than the other soldiers, with deep-set eyes of the same muddy greenish color as the cough mixture. He came from somewhere in the South—Arkansas or Texas, I think. He had a small, thin mouth, and when pondering important decisions he would compress his lips, making them still thinner. His other features were small and thin, too, as though his Creator had applied the mold in a hurried, slapdash way, intending to finish the job more thoroughly at a later date. It was not only in applying first aid that he was remarkable. In emotional upheavals, too, he was excellent— better than women friends, who found nothing better to say than, "Pull yourself together, Gwendolyn—the General is too old for you anyway," or, "Don't be silly; no man ever is worth it," or, in an affected stage accent, "Men are deceivahs evah." Whereas the Sergeant would remark, "You women are so stupid. When will you understand that because a man prefers another girl to you it doesn't mean that the other girl is prettier or wittier or smarter. It doesn't mean anything at all." I thought how this was exactly the right kind of comfort for Gwendolyn, because in her case it was not a matter of sensuous desire but of vanity and ambition.

Gwendolyn was a young girl and not a part of our crowd, and the Sergeant dealt with her for soothing purposes only. He had to deal with us all the time, because he was responsible for our work and responsible to the Colonel, who was the chief of our department. He was efficient in this, too, probably because in civilian life, before the war, he had been a schoolteacher, and his manner of treating us certainly was flavored by his peacetime calling. When trouble arose, he never interfered straightaway. He approached the offending person about an hour later, for a quiet talk: "Now, ma'am, I thought you'd like to know, I used to know a little girl called Claudia—isn't it strange? Claudia, just like you—and little

Claudia never could be bothered to check over her work and always relied on other people to pull out her mistakes, although her father and mother . . . ," and thus he continued, relentlessly, toward the final catastrophe of fire or drowning, till Claudia grew suitably remorseful and promised not to be slapdash in future.

It was Sergeant Parsons, too, who improved my manner of dress: "A nice girl who works in an office, now, she doesn't slop about in odd skirts and woollies and cardigans. She shows her respect for her work by wearing a coat and skirt and a blouse, and the blouse is always freshly laundered, and she presses her skirt every night. And a very nice girl wears shoes that match her purse, but being English she'll call it 'handbag.' I thought you'd like to know."

"And how does the nice girl manage with the clothes rationing?" I asked.

The Sergeant said, "She doesn't get herself evening dresses for parties, because that would look bad in these days of austerity, and she spends all her coupons on good tailor-mades and doesn't worry, because the war will be over before her suits wear out."

He did not drink and he did not smoke. He had no favorites among us and seemed to have no friends among the army personnel, either. When we received visits from the Big Bad Wolves, he tolerated their presence without joining in the horseplay. Sergeants Kelly and Danielevski, the Big Bad Wolves, were greatly liked by us. They were a couple of highly intelligent young men who, in guarded isolation, in rooms situated at the end of a separate passage, serviced the mechanical tabulators and the coding machines, which transformed long medical histories into rows of ciphers for the records. The Wolves came to pay homage to us, to offer the incense of flattery, to bear gifts, and to spread the spirit of peace and goodwill among men. Each of them had a permanent joke, like a leitmotiv in an opera. When Kelly entered our room, he did the rounds, saying, "Do you still love me, Buttercup? Give your daddy a kiss." Danielevski displayed his "tidiness." "Allow me, ma'am," he would say as he approached the woman nearest the door. "I perceive you have a speck of fluff on the front of your dress. May I dust it off?" and he fluttered his hand against her breast. "There, ma'am." Then, approaching the next one, "Now, you, ma'am. I perceive that you, too, happen to have a tiny speck . . . ," and by the time he had "dusted off" each of us, the office resounded with shrieks and giggles. Then the two distributed cigarettes and spilled onto our tables those flat round American sweets that look like the coins of an exotic country, and Kelly would remark, "No girl nowadays needs to go hungry, because there is always a wolf at the door." It was mainly from them I learned American army slang, like "wolf," which meant seducer of women, or "goldbricking," which meant avoiding work, or "polishing the apple," which meant currying favor.

If Sergeant Parsons tolerated these uproars, the Colonel pretended to ignore them, though he could hear them, working as he did in an office opposite ours, across the passage. I think he ignored them partly from weakness and partly from laziness and partly out of solidarity—because two of our crowd, June and Betty, were united in ties of close friendship with two officers, both doctors like himself. Claudia's lover, whom she hoped to marry after the war, was an officer in our department, too, though, not being a doctor, he belonged to Medical Administration. He was said to be rich, and managed to look it, despite being in uniform. The Colonel contented himself to show his zeal by making us assemble from time to time with the entire staff of the department in a vast, unused ballroom, where we had to listen to talks that sounded like a course in idiomatic English for the benefit of advanced students; we were urged to pull up our socks, pull our weight, toe the line, pep up our work, show our mettle, show the stuff we were made of, and, once having seen daylight, consider this a feather in our cap.

Usually after such a talk, the Big Bad Wolves entered our office with a look of worry and preoccupation. "Ladies," one of them would announce, "the Colonel wants you to know there is just one obscure but vital point he did not touch upon . . . No, not what you think. Quiet, please . . . It has now been put down in this memorandum, which you will please read and sign and return to us." We never showed Sergeant Parsons the yellow paper slips they distributed. One, to give a sample, read, "This young lady got out of bed in the morning, put her robe and slippers on, pulled the curtains, took the cover from the parrot's cage, and put the coffee on the boil. Then the telephone rang and a voice said, 'Honey, I'll be over in ten minutes.' So the young lady takes the coffee off, draws the curtains, puts the cloth on the par-

rot's cage, takes her robe and slippers off, and just as she gets
back into bed she hears the parrot mutter, 'Christ, that was a
short day.' "

When the Colonel was posted away and the new Major
arrived to take his place, we all took pains to assure him how
fond we had been of the Colonel and how we regretted
his departure. This was untrue. It was because malice, even
senseless malice, is the luxury of underlings, and we thought
this an easy opportunity to distress the new Major. We were
not easy to deal with. We were women, and we reveled in the
knowledge that it is embarrassing for a man to be the head
of a female staff. And though this was also the case with the
other civilians in the Office of the Chief Surgeon, we were a
choice collection of troublemakers, more unpredictable and
harder to control than those in the other offices—docile
young girls who would have gone into employment in any
case, war or no war, and who did not feel they were doing
anyone a favor by going to work. Whereas we in the medical
coding department had never had to earn our living. We
all had that expensive education which, being useless for
monetary gain, is meant to be, like virtue, its own reward,
and we had been chosen for our familiarity with medical
terms. We were doctors' wives, doctors' widows, doctors'
divorcées. In my own case, though I was married to a
nonmedical husband, I had been recruited because I had
studied medicine for two years. I was by far the youngest
of our crowd—twenty-four as against their forties. Yet I
was accepted as a full member because I could say with the
best of them, "Aren't husbands ghastly?" and "It doesn't

matter whom you are married to—after a year, you feel like kicking him down the back stairs." I could also remark pleasantly upon the Merry Widow's plaint of not having seen her husband for the last two years, "That won't keep you warm in bed."

One month after I joined the U.S. War Office, my husband had been posted for service abroad. Thus we would have been apart in any case, but I had made it clear that this was a final separation, and I had given up our flat, sold the furniture, and taken up lodgings with my friend Beryl, a woman twice divorced, in a house owned and still occupied by her former lady's maid, where we allowed ourselves to be pampered shamelessly. Apart from this comfort, there was Beryl herself, who exhorted me to keep my resolve and to be a "stiff upper lipper." She said, "Marriage is a bloody institution, and some get stuck in it, being miserable worms, and put up with it forever. The decent women have the guts to stick up for their rights and clear out."

"Yes," I said, "but clearing out doesn't put an end to it. At night, when I can't sleep, I go over and over all those rows and scenes we've had. It's like having a mill in my brain grinding away, and I can't find the switch to turn it off."

"I know it," said Beryl. "We all go through it. It will stop after a year."

"Do you think it's a form of bad conscience?" I asked.

"Don't talk rot," said Beryl. "You didn't run away with another man. But that's what husbands can never understand. They could understand it if you wanted to leave them because you'd fallen for someone else. What they can't grasp is that you walk out simply because they themselves are the way they are."

I FIRST HAD a glimpse of the new Major through his half-closed door as I walked past his room. Seeing that large, square-jawed face and the strong shoulders, I would have expected him to belong to the breed of men who give a promise of impressive authority when seated and who turn out to be small, squat, and insignificant when they stand up. Then, later, I saw him walking away from me, with his back to me, down the passage, and I glanced up at the full height of the heavy-boned, magnificent physique of what the French call *un homme de poids.* And along with my surprise there passed through me a shudder of fear and admiration. There was no telling whether his weight would be used for protection or menace. Then there occurred to me yet a third possibility, the most likely and the least flattering of all— that he would pass by with indifference.

Two days after the new Major's arrival, we were moved from our little room, where we had sat side by side on old benches wedged against old school desks, into the empty ballroom where we used to gather for the Colonel's talks. We were provided with metal tables and metal chairs painted pike gray, loose-hinged for folding and stacking up. "The Major doesn't want to stew in his office all on his little lone," Sergeant Parsons told us. "He wants to move in here with you ladies. He is pining for company."

"And what are these in aid of?" I asked, pointing to an

incalculable number of stacked chairs, rising close to the walls like skeletal towers. "Is he going to sit every five minutes on a different chair, or what?"

"You'd better ask him yourself, ma'am," said the Sergeant.

On the following day, I had the answer to my query. Regimented in rows and lanes, like the beds in a nursery garden, were not only our crowd, as promised, but three more departments of sorters and checkers and filing clerks, all of whom we knew by sight only. With each group were their sergeants, like undergardeners. The Major, being head gardener, had his desk close to the first window as one came in through the door, thus having a full view of all his flowers. It was a master stroke. It was also a blow to us. Henceforward, there would be no more raids from the Big Bad Wolves, no more giggling over funny medical histories passed from hand to hand, no more poring over fashions, and no more savory tidbits read out from the newspapers. And it had been achieved without a single word of chiding.

When I returned from luncheon that day, I followed Claudia to her seat and sat aslant the corner of her table and talked. The Major came in and sat down at his desk.

"I say, Prescott-Clark, he's looking at us," whispered Claudia.

"Let him, Carter," I said.

"I say, Prescott-Clark, you'd better skedaddle back to your place."

"In a minute, Claudia," I said. "I'm not a maidservant who picks up the broom and the duster as soon as the master shows up."

"Come here, Miss P.," called the Major.

"What did I tell you? Now you're in for it," said Claudia. "And he knows your name, too—that's bad."

I went up to the Major.

"I wanted to consult you on an important question, Miss P.," he said.

"Yes, Major," I said in my most dutiful voice.

"As you know, I'm now privileged to be in charge of you ladies. My greatest worry, of course, is to know if you are happy with your work. But in your own particular case, how am I to put it? If I asked you, 'Are you happy with your work?' it would be a joke, wouldn't it? So I'll just ask you if you are happy." And he laughed loudly. I could still hear his laughter as I walked back to my place.

During the tea break, Claudia said, "How on earth did you do it? All merry laughter. And I could have sworn he'd put you on the carpet."

"He didn't. Because there is no carpet," I said.

Later on in the afternoon, I got up, gathered two pencils, and strolled at a leisurely pace to the far end of the room, where I devoted a good deal of time to sharpening them in the machine. I had barely returned to my table when the Major called, "Come here, Miss P." For a while, he looked at me in silence, smiling. He had excellent white teeth, too small and dainty for that square-jawed face, and they gave him an air of youthful eagerness and of guilelessness.

"Efficiency above all," he said.

"Yes, Major."

"Now, I'm afraid you are falling down in efficiency. If I

were in your place, I'd take one pencil to be sharpened first, then go back, pick up the other, and do the second walk. Get the idea? Bear it in mind, will you?"

"I will. Thank you," I said.

He left the office soon after this, and I worked steadily during his long absence. When he returned, I saw him glance questioningly at me, with a smile. Furious, and intent on emphasizing my state of not being a maidservant, I got up and with deliberate speed did the round of several tables, searching for a refill for my stapler, which I could have got straightaway by asking the Sergeant for it.

"Come here, Miss P.," called the Major. "You are looking distressed," he said. "I hope nothing went wrong during your search."

"Nothing," I said.

"I thought maybe you are lamenting the late departed Colonel?"

"Certainly," I said.

"And will you lament me, too, when I'm gone?"

"Certainly not," I said.

"How's that?" he asked.

"Because you are just a slave driver," I said.

"Sure."

"And that wouldn't be so bad," I continued, "but on top of it, you enjoy it."

"Sure," he said. "Now I got you. You don't like watching me having fun, is that it?"

I nodded. "You are uniting the useful with the beautiful, as Goethe would have put it," I said.

"I knew you'd be worthwhile to talk to," he remarked. "But what the hell. I must get some pleasure out of this damned office. I'm a surgeon. Damned office job."

"But isn't it interesting—for you, I mean?" I asked.

"It is interesting," he said, "but in the wrong way. For instance, we'd like the tabulators to throw up results like two hundred men sprained their ankles when getting out of landing barges. Then we'd know there's something wrong with the design of the boats. Instead, we get saddled with statistics of how many troops in Africa got jaundice after the yellow-fever vaccine, but the hell of it is that it's nearly all officers and no enlisted men. Now, why? And the Germans have exactly the same problem."

"Drink," I said.

"No," he said. "Among the fighting corps out there, there's no difference with the booze. They all live the same way. It's a mystery." And as I gazed at him silently he added, "That took your speech away, all right. I didn't know it could be done."

I nodded.

"Now, tell me, since we are getting on so famously, that Colonel before me—light colonel, wasn't he?"

"Yes," I said, "he was a lieutenant colonel."

"Where are the light colonels of yesteryear?" And he laughed loudly. "Now, tell me. What was so good about him, a quitter like that? No fight in him."

"There was some fight in him, but not enough," I said.

"Was he a choleric? Did he rave and rant at you when you went to sharpen your pencils?"

"He never did," I said. "He never interfered. But I know he would have liked to have power, too, only he couldn't get it. But he'd never admit it, of course."

"Then what the hell—how do you know?" asked the Major.

"Once I had to go to his office with some papers," I said. "And you know the War Office rule—no door must ever be closed. He was standing with his back to me; he didn't see me. He had a—it's quite sickening—a fly, with a thread tied round its middle, and he let it fly away from him at arm's length and then he'd pull it back by the string."

"And what did he say when you interrupted his idyll?" asked the Major.

"I didn't," I said. "I never went in at all. I sent the Sergeant."

"Pity you didn't go in, Miss P.," said the Major. "He might have tied a string around your waist."

"I'm not a flirt, you know," I said.

"I know you are not. But you are giving a very good imitation of one." And he laughed so loudly that when I left, Claudia said to me, "How do you do it, Prescott-Clark? You seem to be getting on with the Major like a house on fire."

"I don't, Carter," I said. "Besides, one has to get used to his what-the-helling."

On the following day, the Major was absent during the morning and looked in at the office for some ten minutes in the late afternoon. On the next day, Sergeant Parsons said to me, "I thought you'd like to know, ma'am. The Major won't come in today at all. But he'll want me to report about the work. He said I should keep a special eye on you. Now, I wonder why."

"So do I," I said.

"I told him you'd been very, very good yesterday, which is true," said the Sergeant. "I told him you are like the little girl with the little curl in the middle of her forehead. And do you know what he said? He said, 'That suits me fine. And when she is horrid, I'll be horrid, too.'"

"Charmed, I'm sure. Much obliged," I said.

"I thought you'd like to know," said the Sergeant.

"That's big of you," I said.

I continued "very, very good" during the Major's absence. When I saw him entering the office the following morning, I decided that I was not going to expose myself to any more of his taunts. By working diligently during his absence I had proved myself to be the opposite of a maidservant. This praiseworthy state of mind did not last long, however, and I grew steadily more enraged at the sight of the Major, who was also playing the game of not being a servant and sat tilted back in his chair, reading the *Times*. I rose and left the office and went to the lavatory, where I dawdled for a while. On my way back, I met the Major in the passage, walking in the direction of the General's office. I repeated my excursion once before and once after the morning coffee break. On that last occasion, I met the Major once again in the passage, this time coming up behind me. "Miss P.," he said. I stopped and turned around.

"How is it," he asked, "that every time I happen to pass by I meet you outside the office?"

"If you didn't run around so much yourself, you wouldn't meet me so much, Major," I said.

"May I inquire where you've been?" he said. "Was it a case of the lady glowworm who told her boyfriend glowworm, 'If you've got to glow, you've got to glow'?"

"Vous tombez mal," I said. "I went to get a drink of water."

"Oh, we speak French when we are on our dignity, do we?" he said. "But tell me, how did you manage to drink? Are there any glasses in the ladies' room?"

"Oh, yes," I said, "there are some tumblers."

"And you drank it out of a tumbler?" he asked.

"I did," I said.

"That's bad," he said, with a pretense of being grieved. "I thought you'd be quicker on the uptake, after what I told you the other day." He paused. "Next time you're thirsty, Miss P., drink with a spoon. One spoonful at a time. Go back, return—another spoonful. That should work out at fifteen journeys." And I walked away, followed by the sound of laughter.

That day, in the late afternoon, the Major came in carrying a sheaf of papers. He stopped in the door and informed us that it had been decided to spread the free days and to carry on with the work on Sundays. "Now, ladies, which of you would like to work on Sunday?"

The idea appealed to me greatly; it was nice to be free during the week, when the shops were open. "I'll work," I said.

"You mean, you'll be here, Miss P.?" said the Major.

In the week that followed, I worked steadily, irrespective of the Major's presence or absence, and I was quieter, too, during the tea and coffee breaks, and somewhat morose during the lunchtime gatherings, which made Claudia remark, "You are losing your sparkle, Prescott-Clark. You aren't going to run round as a reformed character, are you?" And June said, "How now, brown cow? Let's have a real orgy today, shall we? He won't be in all day. He's gone to London, I hear." And I said, "But he'll pick on me when he gets back, and I refuse to be his court jester and office clown, you know." When she said, "Shame on you, Prescott-Clark, to let yourself be got down by our beloved Major," I hinted that my dejection was due to a certain Captain's having been posted abroad.

Beryl liked to declare that she was "sick and tired of men" and couldn't be "bothered anymore with that rot," but I, on the contrary, felt willing to be bothered, and even if I admitted to the rot, I found it worthy of indulging in, because it was never quite the same kind of rot. Since entering the War Office, I had had two affairs with American officers, each lasting for several weeks. I finished the one by provoking a quarrel and withdrawing in a pretense of huffiness. In the second case, there had been no need for such subterfuge, because the officer had been posted away. In each case, I had been bored. And in each case I might have been willing to carry on for longer if it had not been for the attitude common to both men; they were both married, and they gave me to understand that they were fundamentally faithful. It boiled down to the joke of the wife in America writing to her husband-soldier overseas, "I hear you got yourself a mistress. What has she got that I haven't got?" and his replying, "Nothing, except she's got it right here." I could not stand this. I did not want to be second best. I wanted to be the one and only one, even if it was for a short span of time. Amazed and disgusted at the blockheadedness of the men who failed to perceive this, I was able to agree with renewed sincerity with Beryl's utterances concerning the selfishness, the insensitivity, and the lack of curiosity of men when dealing with women.

As I watched the Major day by day, I found that he was double-faced; his countenance bore one character when seen full front and a different character when seen from the side. Talking to him, looking him full in the face, I noticed that his square forehead and square jaw made him seem straightforward and reliable, and the fair glossiness of his coloring, the smooth blond hair, the evenly pink skin, the gray eyes, and the well-shaped teeth, which gleamed whenever he parted his long lips, lent to his person an air of unspoiled youthful candor, an eagerness to please that seemed almost simpleminded. When I observed him from across a distance, the beguiling coloring was dimmed by gray shadows, and his profile stood out against the windowpane as if stamped out of a sheet of steel. There sat a charmless, blunt-featured man, looking older than his years—clever, stubborn, unkind though given to joviality, unsubtle and yet capable of deviousness.

I was at that time doing the most difficult of the medical coding work involving the Zone of Interior. In military parlance this name designated the United States of America, and my work dealt with the cases of soldiers whose condition was so serious that they had to be returned to the States for further treatment. Among the checkers, whose work was much easier and subordinate to mine, was a dentist's widow, a Mrs. Dicks, with the face of a garden-statuary dwarf. She clearly came from a ruling-class background, of which she never spoke, and had lived long years in Ceylon, of which she spoke often. She had tried to be admitted to our crowd and had not made a success of it. Mrs. Dicks had already exasperated me on two previous occasions, when she had come to me with queries couched in such Edwardian terms as "fearful bloomers" and "someone came a cropper," and I had treated her with arrogance and bad temper, cutting her short with, "Go back to your knitting," and, "Get out of my sight." She had retreated, indignant, convinced that I was in the wrong, and that I was "afraid to face the music" or "afraid of losing face." Now, on the third occasion, perhaps because I was feeling more downcast than before, I did not cut her short, and we had a row. Sergeant Parsons came to visit me an hour later.

"I just thought you'd like to know, ma'am," he began, "I used to know a little girl and she was called Eve—isn't it strange? Eve, just like you. She was only six years old at the time, but she was already very clever, and this would have been fine, only little Eve was conceited about her cleverness and she wasn't clever enough to understand that it isn't clever to be clever when it upsets other people."

I said, "Widow Dicks should have jumped onto her husband's funeral pyre and committed suttee," and the Sergeant said, "This is not done in Ceylon, and we are not talking about Mrs. Dicks, we are talking about little Eve," and he went on relentlessly till I promised to keep my peace with Mrs. Dicks in the future.

On the day after this, the Major called me: "Come here, Miss P." When I stood by his side, he handed me what looked like a poem, beautifully set out on a sheet of hand-made rice paper with those carefully irregular edges that look as though they have been nibbled by a well-behaved mouse. "You're welcome to see it," he said. He watched me, smiling, as I read:

> I now leave the Zone of Interior,
> Where everyone was my superior;
> Henceforward the body's exterior
> Is all I'll endeavor to know.

It went on for six more stanzas.

"What do you think of it?" he asked when I had put it down.

"It's awfully impressive," I said. "Very smooth. The paper, I mean."

"Mrs. Dicks has resigned," he said, "and this is her Parthian arrow."

I said, *"Mea culpa, mea maxima culpa."*

"Oh, we speak Latin when we are humble," he said.

I nodded.

"Sergeant Parsons was already here," he continued, "buzz-

ing into my ear. Wondering if you are worth it. Worth keeping. He says you're a demoralizing influence. But what the
hell. As long as you demoralize me in the future, instead of
the others. How's that?"

I did not speak.

"May I take it that since you did not say no you mean yes?"
I nodded.

"What's troubling you, Miss P.? You don't look happy
about it."

"Why do you always call me Miss P.?" I said. "You deny
me my status and my full name."

"I just can't think of you as married," he said.

"How do you mean?" I asked. "Do you mean that you
can't imagine it, or do you mean you cannot bear to think
about it?"

He looked at me, silent, till I cast my eyes down.

"We'll get around to this another time," he said, "but in
the meantime, as a stopgap, I'll give you another reason.
'Mrs. Prescott-Clark' is such a mouthful. 'Miss P.' is a matter
of convenience. I'm kind of lazy, I suppose. You of all people should know how I feel." And he laughed loudly.

From that day on, the Major, when he was present, made
me come and talk to him at least once a day. But it was never
for the purpose of chiding me, and he dispensed with all
forms of address. He called, "Come here to me."

He had no cause for chiding me, either. I would have
despised myself if I had now traded on his apparent goodwill toward me, and thus, in order to show that I was not a
maidservant, I was forced to be on my best behavior.

Though the Major did not engage in talk with any of the others, none of my crowd was resentful or jealous. They had, from the beginning, given him his due as "a fine figure of a man" and as "having a presence," but had made it clear that they did not consider him attractive. June, Claudia, and Betty went through their days with amorous blinkers, being devoted to their lovers, and the others rather inclined toward the frigid indigo in the rainbow of the emotions and, like Beryl, were "sick and tired of all that." Sergeant Parsons refrained from comments. And the Big Bad Wolves, who had become tame wolves and could now talk to us only during the tea and coffee breaks, contented themselves with slight, inoffensive chaffing. "If you were a soldier, Buttercup," said Sergeant Kelly one day, "you'd be polishing the apple. But being what you are, it's a sheer waste of your time singing duets with that big blob. Why don't you ask him what kind of tree he is—if he is a son of a birch or a son of a beech?"

"Never you mind, Kelly," said Claudia, who had just joined us. "Keep your filth for another time. Listen, you lads and lasses, great news from the home front. This new wench who came yesterday into filing. The Major asked her out that very night. Straight off the bat. Aren't you staggered?"

"She looks anemic," said June.

"Someone should tell her to get rid of that mustache," said Betty.

"And she did accept?" I asked.

"She did," said Claudia.

"And what happened?" I asked.

"I'll tell you exactly," said Sergeant Danielevski. "She has this speech defect. And by the time she told the Major she was a g-g-g-good g-g-g-girl, she wasn't anymore." We screamed with laughter.

"No, but seriously, what happened?" I asked.

"Nothing," said Claudia, "as far as I can make out. She hasn't got a stammer, but she's got a boyfriend on a firm tether, or he's got her on one, and she was transferred here because he pulled strings, and he's Quartermaster and works in the PX. The Major gave her a chaste drink and then they separated. He didn't even see her home to her place."

I was convinced of the truth of the story, especially because I knew that our crowd would have taken great pains to keep me informed of the Major's amorous exploits. And yet, an hour later, when the Major made me come and talk to him, remarking, "I just don't feel like work today. I'm tired. I worked hard all day yesterday and then some, late into the night," I could not restrain myself from saying, "Yes, on the mattress. On the human body."

"First wrong, second right," he said calmly. "I'm taking an additional degree as a surgeon, the F.R.C.S. What the hell, I'm in England anyhow, I might just as well. That's why I sometimes go up to London—for the coaching."

"I didn't know," I said, "and I shouldn't have made that remark. It was frightfully *mauvais genre*."

"You are never *mauvais genre*. You couldn't be if you tried," he said. "What the hell, you are like a little princess—you even have long hair and put it up like a crown."

I thought, And what's the use being like a princess if you

ask out the common floozies? and to cover my embarrassment, I said hastily, "But isn't it an awful strain on you?
Working here and then cramming on top of it?"

"No," he said, "for me it's easy, with the kind of training
that I've got. I've done the first part already. It's in two
parts."

A few days later, Claudia came with more news. "I say,
you lasses, he's doing the rounds. He must be frantic for a
woman. There's this new girl, come in to work for the Merry
Widow, and he asked her out. Again slap on the very first
day; her bottom had hardly touched the chair."

"What's she like?" asked June.

"Usual stuff—common as dirt, trained shorthand-typist.
What'd you expect?" said Claudia.

"And what happened?" I asked.

"Wouldn't play," said Claudia. "Gave him the cold shoulder, and he retreated to previous position according to plan,
as they give out in the war news."

"Very odd," said June, "when you come to think of it.
He's been here two months now and still hasn't got himself
a steady."

"Perhaps he doesn't want a steady," said Claudia. "Let's
ask Prescott-Clark. She's an expert on the Major."

"I haven't got a clue," I said.

"But he's an expert on you, Prescott-Clark," said Betty.
"Do you know, the other day when you took the half day off
he cast round for you and got at Sergeant Parsons. 'Where is
Miss P.? Why isn't she at work?' And Parsons said, 'I let her
go home, she wasn't feeling well.' And the Major said, 'This

must have been a great relief to her.' The Sergeant went away blushing, I swear to God. And, Prescott-Clark, now you've blushed, too. Golly."

"He's a beast," I said. "And you know I never make a fuss over my curses. Besides, he's barking up the wrong tree, what with my blameless life, as you know. Besides, I had such a cold I shouldn't have come in in the morning, either."

"Keep your shirt on, Prescott-Clark," said Claudia. "You go and tell him how blameless you are. But you've got to hand it to him, he's awfully good at repartee."

"Mostly of the hand-me-down ready-made variety," I said.

We went on speculating as to why the Major had not got a woman friend. I thought it was because he did not wish to be distracted from his studies for the Royal College of Surgeons, but I kept quiet about it, just as I kept quiet about all our talks. When we came to learn the answer, I was as astonished as everyone else.

"Shame on you, Prescott-Clark, you really haven't got a clue," Claudia a few days later. "Yap-yapping at him, day in, day out, God knows what drivel, and if I hadn't had a hangover and gone screaming for an Alka-Seltzer, you'd still be in the dark, the lot of you. And all this time, here we were worrying if he really is a man, only because he looks like one. But now we've caught him with his pants down."

"Speak for yourself, Carter," I said.

"You pipe down, Prescott-Clark. You're a washout," said Claudia. "The hat at the gate. That's her."

For two nights running, upon leaving work, we had seen a young woman outside the wire netting, a few paces away from the guards at the main gate. We had noticed her mainly because of her elegance, which was underscored by her large, soft-brimmed summer hat. During those war years, ladies' hats had fallen victim to the prevailing fashionable shabbiness, and were replaced, though in cold weather only, by turbans and woollen large-meshed snoods. Glancing from the hat downward, I had seen that the stranger wore a sky blue dress with inset panels of pleating, of the unfashionable and expensive kind favored by elderly and rich clergymen's wives—a garment belying her youth and her tall, voluptuous figure. And glancing upward once more, I saw that she was a pretty blonde, with a tip-tilted nose in a long oval face. Her prettiness was of the kind that is entirely pleasing and entirely forgettable, and if she had appeared by the gate on the second evening without the hat, I might not have recognized her. Though standing alone, obviously waiting, and looking into space, she was smiling. I suspected that this was not so much due to happy thoughts as to her willingness to display her pretty teeth.

"She's come down from London," said Claudia. "That's why he's been flitting Londonward all this time. And now he's brought her down here to share his bed and board. He's left his hotel and moved into a flat. And she's flung her bonnet over quite an expensive windmill, never you fear; the flat's in a house in St. James's Square—superb situation, high living and low thinking. The Merry Widow knows exactly what it cost, too, because she did some of his ordering for him. And the woman in the hat's a lady, because she called him once over the telephone while he was in the Brigadier

General's office, and, you know how it is, two words are enough and you know where you are. Not like with the Yanks, where you never can tell from the way they speak. And she's called Constance Ray. Mrs. But then, over that I wouldn't put my hand into the fire. Altogether, if you ask me, apart from the Mrs., the name is too good to be true."

"Sounds made up to me," said June.

"Rather eccentric of him, bringing her down here. Coals to Newcastle," said Betty.

"She is a Gainsborough type," I said.

"Harken to Prescott-Clark, standing up for the Major," said Claudia.

"Perhaps she's an actress," said Betty. "What with that name, and not at all out of the top drawer, and it's been the good old elocution lessons for her all the time."

"Never you fear, we'll find out," said Claudia. But they never did find out.

For days, Sergeant Danielevski went about saying, "Have you seen the Major's mistress? She's got lovely big blue eyes," and he accompanied these words with a most suggestive mime, holding his cupped hands in front of his body and shaking them up and down as though weighing two out-size oranges. I joined in the laughter, experiencing a kind of relief, as one may feel relief when at last receiving the punishment with which one has been threatened for a long time.

Once more, I could not master myself and made a remark to the Major. He called me to him one day and threw on his desk a stack of snapshots, facedown, with a gesture of contempt, as though after having started on a game of cards he had found himself holding a bad hand. "Look at them," he said. "I just got these, sent from home."

I gathered them up and turned them over. I did not like being shown photographs "from home." I always found myself embarrassed when confronted with pictures of scraggy or sagging wives and overfed, grinning offspring, and I had learned from June and Betty to overcome this embarrassment and to say, "Now, it beats me how a ghastly man like you managed to hook himself such a divine wife and produce such angelic children."

But this time there was no need to brace myself. "What a beautiful woman," I said.

"Part of her profession. She used to be an actress," he said.

In another snapshot, immediately recognizable, like the winged lion on things Venetian, was the baby's scowling face, stamped with the square jaw and square forehead. "How old is the little girl?" I asked.

"Three," said the Major.

"Really, Major," I said, "with a lovely wife like this, I cannot understand how you can even as much as look at another woman."

"I don't look. So what the hell are you talking about?"

As I turned away and his laughter followed me, I thought how odious it was of him always to laugh at his own jokes. And yet I always came when he called, "Come here to me," and by now no one took the trouble anymore to remark that "Prescott-Clark and the Major get on like a house on fire." Sometimes it was related to me that he had been at a party with Constance Ray, and that they both had been very animated, and I was given descriptions of her dress. Once, I saw them at a dance, but only from afar; they were leaving as I arrived.

ONE DRIZZLY MORNING in the autumn, I slipped as I got out of the bus in front of the gate, fell on the mud-sodden fallen leaves, and grazed the heel of my hand. It did not bleed when I looked at it, but after I started work I saw that I had stained my coding slips. I went to Sergeant Parsons. "Better than having a torn stocking," I said, "what with clothes rationing being the way it is."

"I'll clean it up for you," said the Sergeant.

"I thought you'd say you'd give me a pair of nylons," I remarked. "They do exist, don't they? And is it really true that they last longer than silk?"

The Sergeant said, "The harder you work, the sooner the war will be won and the sooner you'll find out, ma'am. Come along now and get it over with."

"Get over what?" asked the Major, who had just entered.

"I'm off to the slaughterhouse, euphemistically known as the ladies' rest room," I said.

"Stop clutching your hand," said the Major. "Come over here to the window and show me."

"I'll cut off the rough edges, sir," said the Sergeant, who had followed us, "and fix it up with iodine and a bandage."

"No," said the Major. "No iodine. With that skin of yours, you'll get an eczema and no end of trouble. Iodine is all right for the sheep and the cows and the horses. But you are too delicate. I won't have it. Wash it with soap and cold water and let it dry in the air. Let her be, Sergeant."

When I was coming back from luncheon, Sergeant Parsons approached me. "You women are so stupid, you'll believe anything. I just thought you'd like to know."

"How do you mean?" I asked.

"Telling you you are so delicate. Routine treatment is all right for others but not for you. Because you are so delicate. And you fall for it."

"He's a surgeon," I said. "He should know."

"He knows, all right. He knows only too well what he is after," said the Sergeant. "And if you don't, it's about time you did. He's broken you down so he's only got to whistle and you come. And he won't let you go. If I say a word, it's always, 'She's our most brilliant coder, and even if she weren't, what the hell, I've got to have her around, she does me good.' But what good is he doing you? If I were you, I'd get myself moved. You needn't raise a finger. I'll fix it for you."

I did not speak.

"Look at it this way," said the Sergeant. "You are only twenty-four, aren't you, and you are married?"

"Not fearfully, not frightfully," I said.

"I know," said the Sergeant, "but you want to think ahead. Maybe when the war is over you'll want to go back to your husband."

"What's all this got to do with the Major?" I said. "You go drown yourself in your iodine. You are barking up the wrong tree. He doesn't . . . You know quite well he's never even asked me out. He's got other fish to fry. He's got his mistress, with the big blue eyes. And a wife and child in God's own country."

"He's been after you from the very first minute he set foot in this office," said the Sergeant. "First, I thought it would blow over, but it hasn't. Now you are in it up to your neck, and before long you'll burn your boats. If I were in your shoes, I'd run for dear life."

I did not speak.

"Don't say I didn't warn you," he said.

"Charmed, I'm sure. Much obliged, Sergeant," I said.

It was after this—only a few days after, it must have been, because the blood crust on my hand had not yet fallen off—when the Major said to me, "I'd be very pleased if you'd come to dinner with us tonight. Constance—what the hell, you know my setup—she'll be delighted to have you, and there's a friend of mine, a colleague, just come over from the States, and he's staying with us. I told her you are such good company."

"Thank you, Major, I'd love to come," I said.

"Then why do you look so sad about it?" he asked.

"I didn't know it showed," I said.

"It does," he said. "It doesn't matter what you say, I can always read you in your large brown eyes. Now, what is it?"

"It's only—," I said. "Only that it makes me feel so ghastly respectable. Promoted to the position of the trusted family friend, like the maiden aunt. But I feel greatly honored, of course."

It was agreed that he would fetch me from my place at

half past seven that evening, and when I started to explain how to find the house where I lived he cut me short, saying that he knew it anyway.

I did not tell anyone of the invitation, but my first thought was of Sergeant Parsons, and how ridiculously wrong he had been with his warning. To me, the invitation had been like a slap in the face.

It is not often in life that things turn out as one has expected them, but when I saw the Major's flat it was exactly as I had pictured it beforehand; this was not remarkable, because I knew the square, and I knew that Bathdale, apart from its colleges, is famous as a retiring place for colonial servants. It was situated on the first floor, in the corner of the house of one of those Regency terraces whose pilasters counterfeiting Doric columns and gables give the town its make-believe air of Greek temples. Above these, incongruously, the Chinese-style green copper roofs curving upward over the narrow iron-railed balconies draw an ever-recurring pattern of Oriental fantasy across the eggshell white façades. The big drawing room had the customary three tall windows and stuccowork ceiling, and was furnished, as I had visualized, with easy chairs and settees whose ill-fitting loose covers of faded flowered cretonne partly concealed sagging springs and lumpy stuffing. There were banal ivory carvings, the cloisonné plaques, the brass Benares tray tables, and the dancing Krishna in bronze with which the army officers, the tea and rubber planters, and the civil servants who had once lived here recalled their former life in the Far East.

Whenever I enter a room, I can tell at a glance whether I

am attractive to the men who are there, and when I saw the
Captain, who stood by the fire, glass in hand, I was glad to
feel that I pleased him. It would, I thought, provide me with
a measure of consolation for being made to witness the
Major's loving ménage. The guest looked clever, restless, and
dissatisfied—an uncomfortable person to be with. In his
early thirties, about the same age as the Major, he was thin
and narrow-faced, with black curling hair, small eyes, and a
strongly jutting nose and chin. His deeply sunburned color
proclaimed his recent arrival in England and gave him a perhaps spurious air of vigorous health.

"How do you do it? Where did you get this peach of a girl
from?" he asked as soon as he had been presented to me.
"Say, what kind of an office is this where she comes from?"

I did not pay much attention to their chaffing. It was
along the same lines as, "How can a ghastly man like you get
himself such a divine wife?" and as I sipped my drink of gin
and lemon I thought what a pity it was that it was night and
that the blackout boards had been fitted over the panes; I
would have liked to stand by the window on a fair evening,
looking at the sunset sky from perhaps the very spot that
Beau Nash had done the same.

Constance came in. It was not her easy, beautiful smile
that I saw first of all, nor the kind of dress she had on. It was
her figure. She was certainly six months pregnant.

"How nice of you to have come, Eve, and at such short
notice, too," she said, and I noticed that she, the stranger,
called me Eve, when the Major had never done so, and I fell

to wondering what he had told her about me. I also gave full praise to the Merry Widow's judgment; she was genuinely well bred.

"It was awfully good of you to ask me," I said. "Simply thrilling nowadays to be asked to dinner, the cheese ration being what it is."

"I'm so glad, Eve, you didn't say, 'I hope you aren't going to make anything special,'" she cried. "Because when people say that, they expect you to do something special, and to trouble like mad."

The Major several times made hearty allusions to her state, laughing loudly. Addressing her, he would say, "Now, what will you have to drink, the two of you?" and, "Sit yourselves down, the two of you," and, "Let's get up—shall I hoist you up with a crane?" Each time, she would first seek my eye, as though waiting for my approval, before joining in the laughter, and then say, radiantly, "Isn't Calvin silly?" And while I forced myself to smile, too, my heart tightened each time I heard her pronounce his Christian name; I had never heard it spoken before.

We went into the dining room—narrow, ill lit, and chilly, despite two burning electric stoves. This, too, was furnished as expected, with the usual shield-back imitation Hepplewhite chairs and bowfront sideboards. It was hung with dilettante oils depicting Asian women in their native costume, and these provided the Major with further jokes about Constance's condition, and the danger of her "taking fright."

The meal was lavish, by wartime standards. The fish was

cooked with mushrooms and shrimps, both unrationed and expensive, and there was cold tinned turkey, which was a present from the Captain, and the American tinned fruit was served with those little domed cakes smothered in chocolate shavings that were the hallmark of Kunz on the Promenade, the best pastry cook in town.

After the meal, Constance went out to make the coffee. The Captain rose and, despite my offers to help, began to stack up the plates. "I'll clear away," he said, "and you two go back to the fire. I'll cough three times before I come into the room."

We went to the drawing room, and the Major, after having put more coals on the fire, came and sat on the arm of my chair. "Sad again?" he asked.

"Not exactly," I said.

"Because of that remark?" he asked.

"Oh, rot," I said. "That was just silly and *mauvais genre.*"

"Then what is on your mind?" he asked.

"Wondering what's going to happen," I said.

"There are two possibilities," he remarked. "Either it's going to be a boy or a girl. It isn't twins."

"And what then?" I asked.

"Nothing," he said. "I suppose she'll get herself a pram. What the hell, she's got money of her own."

I did not speak.

He said, "What the hell, I didn't want it to happen. But she was all set for it. And besides, what was done could have been undone. I offered it to her ten times over. It would have been child's play, I have so many friends among my colleagues. But she wouldn't hear of it. She wants to have it and she is going to have it, and I'll leave her to it. She knows it. She knew it from the beginning."

"Dreadful," I said.

"No. It's what she really wants."

"It's dreadful just the same," I said, "and she is really and truly a sweet girl."

"Oh, what the hell. She's sweet. All right, sure, she's sweet," he said in a weary voice.

"She isn't married?" I asked.

"There's a husband floating about. English. He's a major in India now. She'll never go back to him. She was off him already before I met her, so I didn't grab her and break up a happy home, if that's what's worrying you."

I remained silent.

"Have a drink," he said.

"Not just now."

"Come on, behave like a guest. You didn't come here for the pleasure. Just a tiny drop. Do you know what the old lady said to the bishop when she went bathing in the sea? 'Every little drop helps.' "

I forced myself to laugh.

"Oh, Eve, you two make such a lovely group sitting there by the fire," said Constance from the door.

"Sure we do," said the Major. "We are used to making a lovely group. We are old friends by now, aren't we?"

"Or old enemies," I said. I watched the Captain coming in; he was pushing a trolley. While setting out the coffee cups on their saucers, he said in a distracted tone, as though intent on his task, "Do you know what the Chinese call a lover? They call him one's preordained enemy."

"The Chinks do give me the creeps," Constance said. "Don't they you, Eve?" And she gave me a cordial smile.

"Not me," I said. "I always think I'd like to go to bed with a Chinese. And failing this, with a plumber. There's nothing I wouldn't do to get in well with a plumber. He is the only man a woman can't do without."

"Oh, Eve, aren't you naughty? Isn't she dreadful?" cried Constance with a delighted smile.

"Now I know what made me think of the Chinese," the Captain said to me. He had remained grave and preoccupied. "I've been trying to figure out all along why you are so fascinating, and who you look like. And now I've got it. You look like Luise Rainer when she played in *The Good Earth*. That's set in China."

"I didn't see it," I said.

"Oh, Eve, he's right," said Constance.

"What the hell, stop buttering her up," said the Major. He seemed annoyed, but Constance did not see his vexation. The Captain did, though, and he appeared to enjoy it.

After we had drunk the coffee, Constance brought out an album and made me sit next to her on the settee. I thought she was going to show me photographs, but when I opened it I saw it was a book of remembrance. "You must write down something for me, Eve," she said, "because this is such a nice get-together, and nice people are always ships that pass by night."

I glanced at her sideways. She was smiling, her hands folded over her breast.

"You mean here today and gone tomorrow," said the Captain, watching her, too. Then his eyes flashed on me, and I bit my teeth together and returned his look.

The Major gave me his fountain pen. "Make it as good as Widow Dicks's," he said.

"Don't remind me of that," I said.

Then I wrote quickly, feeling embarrassed because they were all watching me in silence. "Here," I said, handing the book to Constance. "As a souvenir of Bathdale."

"Oh yes, of course, how clever of you," she said. "But they won't get it, poor lambs."

"Let's have it, what the hell, then we'll say whether we've got it or not," called the Major. And Constance, who had closed the album, recited:

> Miss Buss and Miss Beale
> The darts of Cupid don't feel.
> How different from us,
> Poor Beale and poor Buss.

The Major said, "Good, clean English fun. It's always beyond me. Come on, unbosom yourselves, the two of you."

"It's to do with the Bathdale Ladies' College," said Constance.

"The Merry Widow went there, and Claudia," I said. "That's why they are so pally."

"You tell them, Eve," said Constance. "You are heavier in the brain than I am," and I told about the birth of the poem, which was and still is famous and to which no one has ever owned up as being the author. In Victorian times, when the school was at the height of its fame, the principal, Miss Buss, invited Miss Beale, headmistress of a girls' school in north London, to look over the college. While touring the empty classrooms they found the poem chalked on a blackboard.

"Well, this is my swan song," I said, "and now I'm going home." I got up hastily.

"Oh, Eve, look here—you can't—," began Constance.

"Take her to the bathroom," said the Major.

When I heard Constance's voice calling, "Are you all right, Eve?" I was looking in the mirror, dabbing my face. "May I come in?"

"Yes, do," and I opened the door. "I'm frightfully ashamed of myself, Constance," I said. "I thought I could hold my liquor like a gentleman, and I never felt a thing all along, till it was too late. I didn't know I'd drunk so much."

"Oh, but Eve, you didn't drink half of what I had. And I know exactly how it is. It suddenly hits you out of the blue, and it was Calvin's fault anyway. When he puts the gin into the lemon, you can't feel the kick, and it's like drinking lemonade."

"Yes," I said, "and I felt stone sober all the time, too, I swear to God."

We walked past the elbow in the passage and came into

the hall. "I'll be all right now," I said, "as soon as I get out into the fresh air."

The Major came out of the drawing room. "Put her to bed, Constance," he said.

"No, but honestly, this is too—," I began.

"You heard me," said the Major, and he went in and shut the door behind him.

"I'm sure he is right, Eve," said Constance. "You are in no fit state to leave. And we've got lashings of spare rooms. And it's no trouble, really." Linking her arm with mine, she walked me back past the bend in the passage and into a bedroom.

"It joins the bathroom, anyway," she said, "in case you feel queer again." And seeing that I was standing about, undecided and awkward, she added, with her most cordial smile, lowering her voice to a whisper, "And I'll give you a really super nightie, Eve. Look." She opened a door in the built-in cupboard that ran the length of one wall. "I've never had it on," she said. "It's prewar stuff, and it will suit you marvelously."

It was a gown of tea-rose yellow crepe de Chine, the square neck bordered with roses of ivory and fawn lace.

"I'm quite overcome," I said. "First I disgrace myself, and then this—it's much too good."

"Come on, you'll look lovely in it," and she glanced at me with a winning smile. At the door, she turned and smiled at me once more.

THERE WAS a double bed in the room, close to the window, and it was made up and opened, with the spread folded over the high foot rail of brass. There was a single bed close to the opposite wall, obviously not in use, because several blankets were stacked side by side on the bare mattress. I wondered briefly if I was going to occupy the bed that had been got ready for the Captain, and whether they would not want now to take out the other bed and carry it into the drawing room, or whether there were other bedrooms in the flat. Then I was possessed once more by dizziness, and my limbs grew chill, as though they were enveloped in snow, and I undressed speedily, slipped into the nightgown, and got into bed. I felt better as soon as I lay down.

Constance came in again. She was now in partial undress, in a dressing gown which gaped open over her petticoat. "Calvin says that you are to take these," she said. "Not to chew, just swallow." She extended her hand, on the palm of which lay two white glazed pills. "And here's some water." When she had taken the tumbler from me, she began to unpin my hair. She ran her fingers underneath the twisted tresses and shook them loose. "You look simply heaven, Eve," she said. "I knew you would, with your black hair on the yellow silk. You look like a mermaid."

I said, "Mermaids always drink and never vomit."

"Oh, Eve, you are the greatest fun!" she cried. "Just as Calvin said you'd be."

"I don't feel it, though," I said.

"You poor lamb, of course. Do you think you'll be all right now?" After several inquiries of the same nature, and reassurances on my part, she left and turned the light out. I cannot fall asleep while lying on my back, but I did not dare yet to turn on my side; I remained stretched out flat, taking deep breaths. The light went on and the Major came into the room and, wordless and without giving me a glance, passed into the bathroom.

I thought, Oh, God, how awkward. I suppose they've got another bathroom that's occupied, what with everybody going to bed now. I saw him coming back, and again he did not look at me. He was in shirtsleeves and carrying a towel over one arm. I saw him standing in front of the cupboard and rummaging among the shelves, and I closed my eyes, thinking, I suppose this is his dressing room and now he's looking for some pajamas. I'm hanged if I want to know what color pajamas he wears.

I heard a hinge creak, and then the light was turned off. The next moment, he was in bed with me, with one side of his body covering mine, and taking hold of my shoulders and hurting them in his grip. I turned my head away. "I must be sick again," I said.

He sat up, passed one arm under my waist and one under my back, drew me to a sitting position, propped me up, and tore apart the blackout curtains on the window; he slid the sash up. "Here, go right ahead," he said. He steadied me against his chest and laid his arms round me while I was shaken by my violent heaving.

Unlike the tall elegant windows in the front part of the house, this was a modern low window, with the sill about a foot beneath my head. It was a moonlit night. And while I was being sick I noticed, with that part of one's mind that remains lucid and observant in any calamity, a pair of motoring gloves laid on the outside ledge. They were of an expensive make, with backs of pigskin and palms of crocheted yarn, and I was furiously ashamed when I saw that I had spattered them with my vomit.

"Finished?" he asked, laughing loudly.

"Yes, thank you," I said.

He propped me up against the pillows. I heard him moving about and I opened my eyes when I felt the light through my closed lids. He brought a basin and sponged me with warm water, gave me a lotion for rinsing my mouth, and dried me. Then he laid me down flat. I saw he was wearing nothing but his open pajama coat.

The light went out and he was in bed with me once more, extended over the full length of my body once more, with his virility pressing against my closed thighs while he grasped my wrists, raised my arms, and forced them to close round his neck.

"I've got to be sick again," I said. He released me and straightened up, and held me and supported me as he had done before, and as before I soiled the motoring gloves on the ledge and was desperate with shame at their sight. My shame was mingled with fury and indignation toward him for having wanted to make love to me, and at the same time I was flooded with gratitude.

This time, after he had cleaned me and put the lights out, he did not cover me with his body but came and lay by my side. "No more, worse luck," he said. "You are too weak now. There is nothing to think about and nothing to worry about. Go to sleep."

He turned me on my flank and pulled my nightgown up under my armpits. He placed my head against his chest and slid his arms about me and entwined his legs in a bewildering, complicated grip with mine, till my body was entirely enwrapped and enclosed and imprisoned in his, and as I drew a trembling breath and tried to stir he pressed me yet more closely to him and held me in utter captivity.

Mrs. Dicks had on one occasion, when she had tried to ingratiate herself with our crowd, brought to the office a valuable collection of prints drawn by the most famous Japanese masters between the fifteenth and the eighteenth centuries. They showed men with men, men with women, and women with women, all partly clothed, in the greatest variety of voluptuous pleasures. I had looked through them hastily, ashamed of my interest and reluctant to admire the possession of the woman whom I disliked. The only picture I remembered clearly forever after was one unlike any of the others, perhaps because it was fantastic and thus lacked the realism of the others. It was starkly timeless; it had a fairy-tale quality. It was a naked woman, dead, floating in the sea, with an octopus, larger than man-size, fastening round her and holding, caressing, and penetrating her with his many arms. Her face was serious, with that air of deep abandon and satisfaction that may be given to those who have been granted their most heartfelt desire. Her spread-out tresses, the waving algae, the undulating water—black, whitish, gray, and suffused with green—now appeared to me, as though floating toward me out of the moonlit night behind the window, and I knew that this was the rendering of love as it should be: trapped inescapably, secure and fastened, drowned in bed and water, both cradle and grave. I gave a sigh of contentment and fell asleep.

WHEN I WOKE UP, it was daylight, and I saw the Major standing behind the brass bars at the foot of the bed and looking at me over the top rail, like a keeper in the zoo who has come to look after his charge. He was in socks and underpants and vest. "I'm getting dressed," he said, "but I think I'll undress again, now that you're up."

"No," I said.

"Why not?" he asked, gripping the bed rail with one hand and pulling off his socks.

"Even if you are a beast," I said, "I couldn't possibly. Think of Constance. I couldn't look Constance in the face anymore. And she's so sweet. She even gave me her best nightie to wear."

He said, "We've had Constance and her sweetness last night. She's sweet—you said so, I said so, ad nauseam. Perhaps that's what made you throw up." He rested both arms on the bed rail and leaned over it, looking down at me.

"I don't understand you," I said, avoiding his eyes.

"You have that marvelous cold skin," he said. "You can lie for hours in bed with a man and you never get sticky and sweaty."

I did not speak.

"You are so exquisitely made," he said, "I could break every bone in your body."

"Go to hell," I said.

"I shan't go to hell," he said, "but I may go to the office."

"Yes, do," I said. "Go to the office."

"I needn't go," he said.

"You look so revoltingly clean and healthy it makes me ill just looking at you," I said.

"Yes. I suppose so," he said. "You are exhausted, but you're looking very pleased with yourself just the same. So be it. Relax. I'll put you down as a case of battle fatigue, but not incurred in the line of duty."

It was only when I heard his laughter that I knew he had strangled his desire.

I lay back on the pillows and nestled into the covers. I heard him come and go, opening and shutting doors and drawers, and felt reassured at these sounds. Once, I heard his voice and laughter outside in the hall, but I could not hear anyone answering. He returned, stopping in the door. He was fully dressed and carried his cap in his hand. "I told Constance not to disturb you," he said. "Go to sleep now, and when you wake up she'll give you a nice breakfast." Once more, I heard his laughter outside, then the muffled slam of the front door.

When I woke up, I felt bright and light-headed and hungry. I went first of all to the window and looked out. The ledge was empty, the mortar dirty and eroded by many craters, and my heart tightened with remorse and shame and gratitude at the thought of the soiled gloves lying in the leaden moonlight. I took the Major's dressing gown from a hook on the door and stepped into his bathroom slippers, plaited of raffia and lined with Turkish toweling, and made my way along the passage, around the corner, past the open door of the kitchen, past the closed doors of the dining room and the drawing room. I knocked at a couple of narrower doors and opened them. In one room I saw an ironing board surrounded by chests and boxes. The other was a bathroom. I went back to the drawing room, walking slowly and with a shuffle, trying to stifle the slapping noise the outsize slippers made at every step. From the dining room I heard Constance's voice: "Is that you, Eve?"

"Yes, Constance, I'm afraid so. Outstaying my welcome."

"Do come in, you poor lamb."

I opened the door. It was not the dining room, as I now realized; I must have passed that before or after the kitchen. I saw the wide bed in the middle, well away from both walls, and in it Constance, half sitting up, facing me, and I thought again how pretty and how forgettable she was. Only then did I see more. Leaning against her shoulder was the Captain's head.

"Do come right in, Eve," she said, giving me her delightful, cordial smile. Running her fingers through his hair, she added, "Doesn't he look sweet with his curls? Just like a little boy."

"Yes," I said, forcing myself to look pleasant.

"He's such a lamb altogether," she said. "We'll be sorry to lose him, shan't we? He's got to leave tomorrow."

"Yes," I said.

I did not know what sickened me most about the sight of the pair—whether it was her pretty, unconcerned ease at having broken faith with the Major, or the sheer physical fact that she had lent her body, growing the seed of one man, for the use of another, or whether I was revolted by his clever, grinning face, tanned and with the jutting nose and chin, recalling those evil masked puppets carved of wood by the peasants of some Alpine regions. I felt that I might not have been pained so much at her betrayal if at least the Captain had resembled the fair, square-faced, masterful Major.

As I watched her smiling and caressing his curls, I realized that she was truly sweet "ad nauseam," as the Major had expressed it. It was just because she was so kind, so good-natured, and so welcoming that she found some attraction in every man and some reason for indulging him. Like a whore, she consorted choicelessly, and yet she was the opposite of a whore. A whore hires herself out for money and as an expression of contempt and hatred toward men, but Constance did so without heed of monetary gain, out of admiration.

"You needn't dress yet, Eve," she said. "We'll all have breakfast together. Calvin told us we should wait for you."

"He went to the office," I said.

"So he did," she said. "It's the Calvinist in him. Aren't these American names ghastly, really? This one here is a horror, too. He's called Dallas."

I said, "What can't be cured must be endured."

"Oh, Eve, you do come out with the screamingest things!" she cried, and, turning to the Captain, she said, "Look at her, standing there in Calvin's dressing gown, and so serious. Doesn't she look heartbreaking? Like a poor little orphan?" I recalled how she had coaxed me to accept the splendid nightgown, how she had loosened my plaited hair and admired it, how she must have known, and taken a pleasure in knowing, of the Major's wish to lie with me, and I marveled at her goodness.

"What would you like to have?" she asked. "Bacon and eggs?"

"Oh, Constance," I said, "what a question. You must be joking." It was truly a hardly creditable question at that time, when one got one egg a week and the bacon ration was two ounces.

"I get it and I never ask where it comes from," she said. "Calvin does know his way around. And you know, I must hand it to the Yanks. They're like Father Christmas."

"Not entirely," I said, "because Father Christmas only brings gifts for good little children, and everyone knows that good little girls never get to wear nylons."

"Oh, Eve, aren't you dreadful," she cried. "I wish I had known you before."

"You are easy to please," I said.

"Promise we must see a lot of each other, now," she said.

"Of course," I said. I never saw her again.

"GOT OVER IT all right?" the Major said to me on the following day.

"Yes, thank you," I said. "And I want to thank you for your kindness. Yours and Constance's. Please tell her."

"But you're shocked, aren't you?" he asked.

I did not speak.

"Yes, I can see it in your eyes. Why are you so shocked?"

I said, "It's—to me, it is revolting. And unforgivable. How could she?"

"You are looking at it the wrong way," he said. "What the hell, why shouldn't I lend her to a friend? Hospitality." And he laughed loudly.

I said, "I'm not—please don't think that I am judging her. She really is a lovely person. It's just that I can't understand it. And I can't understand you, either."

"I know you can't," he said. "You are like a princess—I've said so before—and like a princess you are intolerant and won't make compromises, and if you can't have everything, you want nothing. To me, it's a matter of convenience, what the hell. And the same with her."

"Convenience, like your calling me Miss P. because you are lazy?"

"Yes," he said. "That's it. I'm kind of lazy."

"Yes," I said, "and it's dreadful."

"It isn't dreadful," he said. "It's just not in your nature."

For a while, we were silent. Then he said, "What are you going to do with yourself? Will you go back to your husband?"

I was bewildered. Just as he had never mentioned his marriage before or after that time when he had shown me the photographs, I had never talked about my marital situation. "Sergeant Parsons must have been yapping at you," I said. "He did it to me, too. I told him he should go and drown himself in his iodine."

"But I can't drown myself," he said, "because I don't hold with iodine," and I waited till his laughter had ceased.

"Well?" he asked. He bent his head. He was fondling his key ring and caressing his bunch of keys. I watched his massive broad hand with the thick fingers, smoothly pale and showing no bones, and thought how curious it was that his hands were not pink like the rest of his body, and how I had never yet seen a surgeon fulfilling the myth of possessing long, sensitive, tapering fingers. And then I thought of how my husband had asked me every day, "Do you love me? Are you glad you married me?" and how I had always answered yes, though it had not been true, and how, despite these words, my husband in all of our married life had never so much as fetched me a glass of water or brought me a cup of tea when I was not feeling well or had a cold, and how this man, this stranger, to whom I meant no more than the value of some amusing talks, had washed me and nursed me and cleaned me, good-humoredly and without disgust, and taught me the meaning of love in the course of one night, which I had not learned in those four years from my husband. The Japanese picture came swimming before my eyes, in moonlit tints of white and gray and green, and I closed my eyes for an instant and passed my hand over them.

"No," I said, "I'll definitely not go back to my husband."

"And where do I come in?" he asked.

"Nowhere," I said, "because to you I was just someone in your bed one night. And by mere chance, too."

He said, "You are on my mind all day long and all the time."

I forced myself to laugh. "Did you think this up by yourself, or did somebody help you?" I asked.

"You know it is true," he said, "and you know it was true from the first minute I saw you."

"Yes, I know," I said.

"And with you, too," he said.

"Yes, with me, too," I said. "And now that I've told you, you can go to hell."

"You are making it very difficult for me," he said, "because yesterday when you told me to go to hell I went to the office. Now I'm here anyhow. So where am I to go?"

I watched him in silence.

He said, "I will go to hell if you will come to hell with me. Will you?"

"I don't know," I said.

"You do know, and you are afraid," he said. "But it's useless being afraid. It's got to be."

He did not come in for the next two days. Upon his return to the office, he called me as usual: "Come here to me."

"Where have you been?" I asked, trying to sound friendly.

"London," he said, "and I've moved back to the hotel. I've given up the flat."

"And Constance?" I asked.

"She's gone and joined a girlfriend of hers, in an apartment. High time she did anyway."

"It's all such a pity," I said.

"I didn't turn her out because of you, if that's what's worrying you," he said.

I did not speak.

"You are not talkative today, are you?" he said.

"No," I said.

"That suits me fine," he said, "because I have a lot of work to get through."

"Yes, I know—on the mattress," I said, and watched him laughing.

On the following day, he did not come in till late in the afternoon—half an hour before it was time to leave. He put his briefcase on the desk and called Sergeant Parsons, and talked to him for a few minutes, remaining on his feet. Then he came over to me and sat on the corner of my table. He had never done this before.

"Eve," he said.

"Yes?"

"I've got orders to leave," he said. "Overseas, tomorrow morning."

"Yes," I said.

"Look at me," he said. "You are not weeping, are you?"

"Only a little," I said, "because you never called me Eve before."

"I want you to stay the night with me," he said.

"Yes," I said.

"And I won't ask you out and give you dinner," he said. "I can't stand sitting for two hours opposite you at a table."

"Yes," I said.

"Go home now and eat," he said, "and I'll come round and fetch you at eight o'clock. Will that suit?"

"Yes," I said.

"I'll take you to the flat tonight," he said. "I passed it on to a colonel, but I shoved him out for tonight. We'll be on our own."

"Yes," I said.

I did not speak during that night at all, and he spoke only three times. Once, he said, "Human relationships are the most interesting thing in life." Then he said, "Never mind the past and never mind the future. You are warm, you are safe, you are here." The third time, he said, "You are my one and only love. Go to sleep now, my love. I want you to be asleep when I go."

ABOUT A MONTH after the Major had left, Sergeant Parsons stopped by my table and said, "I thought you'd like to know, ma'am. The Major is in the north of France. And he isn't a Major anymore, because his gold leaf has turned to silver."

"Charmed, I'm sure," I said. "That makes him a half colonel. I've always wondered, you know, why in the American army silver is above gold."

"Why don't you write and ask him?" he said.

"I may," I said.

Though I did not show it, I was glad of what the Sergeant had told me, because the Major when he had written had only told me of his being "somewhere in Europe," and he had not mentioned his promotion. This was late in 1944, and he was in charge of a hospital for German prisoners of war.

Soon after this, it was decided to move the Office of the Chief Surgeon to London, together with other branches of the U.S. War Office, and this brought about a split in our crowd. Claudia, June, and Betty were going to London as a matter of course, to be united with their lovers, but Beryl said she was "sick of the Yanks" anyhow, and did not see why she should forsake the safety of Bathdale for the bombing raids of the capital. I was pleased at the chance to get to London; the mild, heavy, wind-still climate of Bathdale, called "relaxing" by the inhabitants, had never suited me. I would have moved, in any case, with our office, because the Major had written that he wanted me to do so; thus he would always be able to find me, no matter what might happen. There were many other losses, too—among the most regretted the Merry Widow, who stayed behind, and the Big Bad Wolf Danielevski, who was posted for service overseas.

Thus we restarted the Zone of Interior in London with only four of us, headed, as before, by Sergeant Parsons. I found a room off the Bayswater Road, a district of imposing residences, stretching along one side of the park, fallen into neglect and converted into private hotels and lodging houses. It was the first time that I took up life in a bed-sitting-room, where the bed was represented by a narrow couch called a "divan" and the sitting by a tub chair of wicker. It was the first time, too, that I had to obtain heating by dropping a sixpenny piece into the slot of a meter, and that I experienced the fear of missing being called on the telephone if I went to the bathroom. But I could always still my dejection by repeating to myself the phrase with which the Major had closed his last letter to me, which was the one he had used on our first night together: "There is nothing to think about and nothing to worry about."

I had chosen Bayswater for two reasons. It was a cheap district, with a still decent address, and there were three buses coming from Notting Hill Gate down the Bayswater Road and going in a straight line to Marble Arch into Oxford Street, with a stop at Selfridges. Our office was situated nearby. The entrance was a shabby, narrow doorway—an entrance of the type used by cleaners and messengers. Once inside, one descended into a basement and into a still deeper basement down two more flights of stairs, where our office spread into majestic proportions and took up the whole floor of the building. It was safer from air attacks than any shelter, and the heated, filtered air and the lighting were provided by machines situated in still further depths. Secretive, unsuspected, and sinister, we spent our working hours in artificial light and air—a make-believe existence akin to that of cut flowers, which appear alive though they are dead.

Now that the staff had been replenished with new civilian local labor, we received several male additions—some delightful, like a retired English army colonel and a humorous admiral with infallibly good manners; some bizarre, like a former lion tamer, and a porter from Claridge's. Among the new women, the most likable was Queenie, an ex–chorus girl, greatly in demand for telling the future out of teacups. Our old crowd of four kept close together in the Zone of Interior and during the luncheon hour, but I rarely saw them at night, when they went out with their lovers, and I did not meet them at parties, because I had stopped mixing with our officers.

About two months after our settling in London, Sergeant Parsons stopped at my table. "I thought you'd like to know, ma'am," he began.

"Oh yes," I said listlessly. There was precious little I wanted to know in those days, and the stories concerning a little girl called Eve—"Isn't it strange? Eve, just like you"— had ceased altogether, because my behavior had remained exemplary.

He said, "The General counts on you to come to Paris with us when we move. You are one of our best, and we can't afford to lose people like you. But then, a girl wants to look out for herself, and nothing lasts forever."

I said, "I don't want anything to last forever, but you know I want to go to France, the same as Claudia and June and Betty."

"You are so stupid, you women," he remarked. "Don't you know that when a man is interested in you he'll always have ways and means to find you?"

"Charmed, I'm sure. Much obliged," I said.

"I happened to have a word with Admiral Parker, the old boy," said the Sergeant. "And he'd like to take you along to the British War Office. The English are getting ready to move out, too—the same as our people. And the job would be so much better. You'd have classy work and a much higher salary."

"Will they be going to France?" I asked.

"That I cannot say," said the Sergeant, "but it would be worth your while finding out—it won't be as bad as going to the dentist's, and it's all on the 'old boy' level, what with the Admiral. He has a very soft spot for you—why, I can't think. He wants to do you a favor, and you don't want to hurt him. You run along, and don't forget that a very nice girl wears shoes to match her purse."

I did go with the Admiral to St. James's Square, where I was given two examination papers, and I passed through three interviews unconcernedly, as I had no wish to be found acceptable. When I was dismissed with the phrase "We will let you know in due course," I was certain this meant the same as, "I'll give you a tinkle soon, one of these days." But the excursion was enjoyable nevertheless, because the Admiral took me afterward to Shepherd's, where I had never been before and of which I had heard so much from Claudia, June, and Betty. He drank my health with a charming Edwardian gaiety:

> Here's to you and here's to me,
> And here's to the girl with the well-shaped knee.
> Here's to the man with his hand on her garter.
> He hasn't got far yet, but he's a damn good starter.

Six weeks later, they did let me know. I was offered the rank of captain with the British Army of Occupation in

Germany, though the war was not yet over, and a salary that was three times as much as the one the Americans paid me.

"What a giggle," said Claudia. "Imagine Prescott-Clark as a captain. Will they salute you in the streets?"

"Don't be silly, Carter," I said. "They can whistle for me. I'm not going."

"Come along, you lasses," said June. "Let's have a bash at Queenie and the tea leaves," and we went in search of the chorus girl, who could be relied upon to assure each of us that we would be granted our "heart's desire."

"I'm mighty glad for you, ma'am," said Sergeant Parsons later.

"I'm not," I said. "I mean, it's very nice to know that somebody thinks I'm worth all that money, but I shan't take it, of course."

"I think you are very wrong," he said. "We none of us can see into the future."

"Queenie can," I said, "and I'm all set for France."

"You have turned them down already?" he asked.

"No. They've given me two months' grace to think about it, and I'll take my time over it. Let them think I'm brooding day and night. Claudia, June, and Betty all say that I'm quite right, too, we should stick together. We'll sit in Paris in the Ritz and swill champagne. And when the cork hits us in the eye we'll come to you and you'll pull it out."

Two days later, the Sergeant stopped at my desk again. "I thought you'd like to know, ma'am," he said, "that I heard from the Major—the Colonel, that is."

I felt I was turning pale. "Which one?" I asked. "There

are so many of them flitting about these days that I can't keep up with them."

"There is only one for you, ma'am," he said, "and I just had word he's been shipped to the Zone of Interior."

"They have sent him to the States?" I asked.

"They have."

"Why?" I asked. "Has he been wounded?"

"No," said the Sergeant. "He's gone crazy."

"It's not true," I said. "I've never seen a saner man in my life."

"People always say that at times like this," said the Sergeant, and he pressed his lips together carefully, making them still thinner than they were.

I watched him. It seemed to me he was shutting away some further knowledge which he was unwilling to impart. "It's not true," I repeated.

"Would you rather have him dead?" he asked pleasantly.

"Are you trying to tell me that he's dead?" I asked.

"I'm not, ma'am. It might be better if he were, perhaps, from your point of view. But it comes out just the same. You can write him off for dead, as far as you are concerned."

"How do you mean?" I asked.

"You are so stupid, you women," he said. "You want to throw everything over for the sake of a man, and you can't understand that a man likes to be comfortable, above all, and once he is home, in his own country and with his family and people he knows around him, he won't break out and destroy his setup."

I said, "You mean he's too lazy and he'll stay where he is?"

And I added, slowly and carefully, as though speaking in a foreign language, "As a matter of convenience?"

"Yes, ma'am, and you can't blame him," said the Sergeant.

I had to wait till the lunch hour to seek out Sergeant Kelly. He said, "Buttercup, have you heard the latest definition of a wolf? A wolf is a man who when he meets a sweater girl tries to pull the wool over her eyes."

I forced myself to laugh, and after thus having paid to gain his attention I made my inquiry.

"Yes, he's gone back to the States," said Kelly.

"And you believe this rot about his madness?" I asked.

"I don't," he said. "That's Parsons's idea. Some of the boys guess he's faked being screwball, now that the war is almost over, so he'd get back home in advance of the others and get himself a swell job."

"You are screwball yourself," I said. "He'd never— The very idea of it— You make me sick."

"I don't believe it myself, either," he said. "I don't know what to think. It kind of beats me."

"What do you think, then, if you don't know what to think?"

"I figure he ran into some kind of trouble," said Kelly, "and they didn't want to court-martial him, so they made him plead screwball to get fired. You don't know half of what's going on there."

I did not consult with Claudia and June and Betty, because to them I had remained no more than "Prescott-Clark, who got on with the Major like a house on fire." It was useless, I knew, to go to the General's; information of that kind would be withheld from anyone but the next of kin. I knew my only hope was Sergeant Parsons, and I decided to have another try at gleaning information from him.

The next day was my day off, and I spent it tediously, washing, ironing, and going to the hairdresser. On the following morning, as I was riding in the bus toward Oxford Street, I heard as we drove past Marble Arch a whisper going from seat to seat. It was a sibilant sound—"Selfridges, Selfridges." I got out at Selfridges and went round the side of the store. There was rubble lying across the street, and the house where the pub had been, on the corner, was demolished. Three windows of the store's food department were boarded up, with streamers stuck across the front bearing the by now familiar "Business As Usual" sign. I went through the narrow doorway and climbed down the stairs to the office. On the last landing there were many people assembled, civilians and military, all from our office. I got nearer and stepped behind the General, who was just calling in his high, peevish voice, "Parsons, where is Parsons? I want Sergeant Parsons." And I heard Kelly's voice, deferential, answering, "You can't have Sergeant Parsons, sir, because Sergeant Parsons is dead."

My sight and hearing grew blurred. I heard talk going on around me without taking it in, and I kept staring into our office, which was tidy and empty, bathed in the artificial daylight, and the only unusual sight in it was a bottle of Rose's lime juice, with its glossy label and gleaming cap, standing on one of the desks. I think it was Queenie's. Then I recalled that for the past two weeks there had been a large display of

Rose's lime juice in one of the windows of the food department of Selfridges. I still did not understand.

Sergeant Kelly came and said that we civilians would
have two days off and please to report to work on the third
morning at nine sharp, as usual. I left with Claudia and June,
and we went to the Danish coffee shop in Wigmore Street,
round the corner. Betty was not with us; it was her free
day. They told me the Sergeant had been killed the night
before by a V-2, together with about two hundred other
people, and that there had been such a crowd in the street
because the bomb fell at eleven o'clock, which was the closing time of the many pubs in the neighborhood.

"But he never touched drink," I said. "You know he
didn't."

"He didn't," said Claudia, weeping. Like many hard
drinkers, she was easily given to tears. "He stayed behind in
the office, straightening up after us. He often worked late
hours. And he got out in the street just at that moment."

"Why couldn't it have killed someone else instead?" said
June.

"What's going to become of us now?" I asked.

The Sergeant had not been crushed by falling masonry
or struck down by flying debris. The same invisible force
that had lifted a bottle of Rose's lime juice from the display
shelf in the window and placed it unbroken and upright on
Queenie's desk had caved in his chest. Later on, we knew
that this had been the last V-2 to fall on London.

FOR SOME DAYS, we could not eat or sleep, and we shivered with cold. We could not accept the Sergeant's death, as we accepted, later on, the death of Sergeant Danielevski, who was killed in battle, and the death of Sergeant Kelly, who, during a drunken celebration of V-E Day in London, walked out of a fourth-floor window.

Claudia, June, and Betty all went to America and got married to their lovers. Betty was unhappy and would not admit it, and she was spared from admitting it forever after when she became a widow suddenly, during her first year of marriage. June and her husband opened a private clinic near Chicago, and they ran it successfully.

I met Claudia three years after the end of the war, one day as I came out of the reading room of the British Museum at lunchtime. I saw her walking across the street. "I'm back for good, Prescott-Clark," she said. "I am going back to Bathdale. I'm here because of my lawyer—I'm getting a divorce."

We went to a pub on the corner. She had on a coat and skirt of soft thick camel's hair and carried a long coat of the same stuff over her arm. I was impressed to see that her shoes and handbag were of brown crocodile.

"You look rich in a nice way, Carter," I said. "Are you rich?"

"He is, Prescott-Clark," she said. "He turned out to be even richer than I thought he was. When I got to New York, he met the boat with a mink coat and an emerald ring. Then we went to Mexico. I'll tell you what's wrong with Mexico, Prescott-Clark."

"You tell me, Carter."

"It's got low air pressure," she said, "because it's so high up in the mountains. Too utterly awkward, because you take a drink and you fall flat on your face. You can't devote yourself to the booze there, Prescott-Clark."

I had on my old gray glen-plaid suit and a red-and-white cotton blouse, and I wore scarlet kid pumps and carried a scarlet handbag. "Rich or poor," I said, "we are still nice girls. A nice girl presses her skirt every night, and when she is a very nice girl she has matching shoes and purse. I thought you'd like to know, ma'am. You women are so stupid. Is that what's been bothering you? I used to know a little girl named Claudia—strange, isn't it? Claudia, just like you."

"Stop it, Prescott-Clark," she said, "or I'll weep and ruin my makeup."

"So be it, Carter," I said, "but tell me why you're back."

"He bored me, Prescott-Clark," she said. "I admit he was good in bed, but you can't be in bed all the time."

"It's a pity one can't be, though," I said. "But anyway, you had your fill. So what the hell are you talking about?"

Irresistibly

It must have been bewildering for the guests entering the main hall that evening to be faced by an innkeeper leaning against the lintel of the wide-open glazed double doors leading into the brilliantly lighted reception rooms. Tall, portly, florid, heavy-jowled, in shirtsleeves, and wearing a green baize waistcoat with tarnished metal buttons, and black trousers glistening with grease stains, he might have been the owner of a tavern in the main square of a small market town. The sight of him seemed to conjure up homely smells of stale beer, stale gravy, sweat, and drains. With one hand resting on the bronze rosette of the doorknob while he waved a red checked napkin with the other as if intent on chasing off flies, he greeted the arriving couples one by one and offered remarks like "Lucky you turned up today. This is our day for apple strudel. And there's dumplings, too, with white cab-

bage stewed in wine—red wine, not vinegar, never fear."
Ignoring the shrieks and howls of laughter from the latest
guests, he pointed his thumb in a coarse gesture behind him
and turned to the next group, now growling, "There's some
sausages left over from yesterday. You'd better look sharp,
they won't last forever. Speak to the missus, in the kitchen—
that's where she belongs."

He was Mr. Haussman, the governor of the Union Bank
of Prague, having a lark while hosting the last of the Haussman receptions in that winter of 1932. The Haussmans
were Viennese. They had arrived in Prague about ten years
before, and the magnitude of his banking post could be
guessed, even by a little girl (as I had been then), by the fact
that the substantial "villa" on the spacious, sloping grounds
of the Weinberge, in our city's prime residential quarter, had
been built for them by the bank before their arrival.

The Viennese like to say that we in Prague are always
offended, and it is true. Always inclined to feel inferior and
provincial when confronted with anyone from the capital
city of what once was our empire, we tend to bristle and to
say things like "Don't forget that we had the first paved
streets in central Europe while you Viennese were still slush-
ing ankle-deep in the mud." Or, in a more jovial mood,
"Count Bobby meets Count Rudy, on the Graben, in Prague.
He says, 'Where've you been all this time? Been ill, or what?'
Rudy says, 'No, I've been to Vienna. Funeral. Buried my
mother-in-law.' Count Bobby, 'Ah, Vienna, the city of our
dreams!' "

My mother soon became Mrs. Haussman's best friend, to everyone else's bewilderment. She explained this by stating that Mrs. Haussman, unlike the other Viennese, was not uppity and never gave herself airs. And while this was quite true enough, the Haussmans began living on an unexpectedly grand scale, and it soon became the general opinion that it was just this quality of Mrs. Haussman's that was such a shortcoming. Because Mrs. Haussman was wrong. Not outrageously, deliberately wrong—like, say, Countess Sternborn, who had enjoyed, even in old age, behaving like a brat, never letting one forget that she had once been a chorus girl, and thus felt free, in the drawing room, to take out some of her artificial teeth and, passing them round, to ask the guests to admire how well they were made—but wrong in lesser and more deadly ways. My grandmother knew that Mrs. Haussman was wrong, even before she met her.

It was Karasek, the chef, who brought the tidings. Karasek worked for Lippert's, the largest and finest delicatessen on our most elegant avenue, the Graben, and he could always be prevailed upon to supply choice dishes for important at-homes and dinner parties. "She comes and says, 'Mind, you let me have the boiled beef, too, when you've done with it,'" he told my grandmother. "I say, 'How so, madam? The beef will be thrown away.' 'Not for me, it won't,' she says. I say, 'But, madam, for a double-strength consommé such as you want, the beef is boiled for twelve hours—the meanest cuts, shins and shanks—and it ends up like gray rags. None of my ladies ever—' She says, 'There's always a first time. We cut it up and dress it with onion and oil and vinegar, and it makes a supper dish for the children and the governess.' "

Conversation is made up of talk, but not all talk is conversation. Finding out that Mrs. Haussman had no conversation took us in Prague less than ten minutes. Even this might have been shrugged off, considering her husband's standing, but not after the first Haussman tea party my grandmother was invited to—which she soon declared would be her last. The two dining rooms in the Haussman villa— the "everyday" one and the "good" one—were on the second floor. As soon as the table was cleared that afternoon, Mrs. Haussman went out to the landing and yelled to a manservant—thus betraying that she was not accustomed to a large house, where one rings for the staff. The manservant, in any case, shortly appeared, bearing a long jute sack, which he opened, throwing the contents—remnants of silk, tweed, and cotton—onto the parquet floor. The scandalized ladies were invited to help sort these out, kneeling and squatting, and choose the most suitable for making up into a quilt. While the ladies, still speechless, went on exchanging glances, she explained that eiderdowns were expensive, while a quilt, by contrast, could be filled with rubbishy fluff and would do splendidly for the governess's bedroom.

This, too, was resented by the guests. Whereas it had been considered only amusingly scandalous when the Countess Sternborn had once lifted her skirt at the bridge table, undone her garter, and used the tongue-shaped rubber part for erasing an error on the scoring pad, thus showing off her famous legs, it was unforgivable that Mrs. H. should expect her guests to work for their tea by making such demands upon them, in her obsessive thriftiness.

THE PAINTER Miroslav Dalibor was, as my mother said, "not madly entertaining," but, on the other hand, "one knew what stable he came from." Being unmarried, he was also an asset for parties. I had last seen him two years earlier, when I was fifteen, but finding him now at the Haussman villa was a happy surprise. The villa's reception rooms were on the ground floor, and the moment I entered the first drawing room I could see him in the last, the third one, as the rooms were enfiladed. He was standing in a niche formed where a wall met a bay window, half hidden by the folds of the crimson velvet curtains. This was not astonishing. In whatever drawing room Dalibor happened to be, he would always place himself in a corner and as far away from the main entrance as possible. There he would remain, never milling around, never joining a group.

Various opinions were given about this behavior. There were those who said that Dalibor always felt at a disadvantage because he earned his living by doing the portraits of the wealthy and sometimes even of the famous. Yet at the same time, because it was vital for him to strike up acquaintances, it was considered that he might be taking up the stance perversely, as though to deny all that.

Others said that this was nonsense and plunged into further long, delicious conversations about his history and his money. There was no question of his living from hand to mouth: there was still a regular income he could draw on, from the Dalibor estates in the Burgenland. No, he was just plain snooty. True, one uncle of his had been the minister of foreign affairs in the old days. But Dalibor *père* had been nothing but a privy councillor (two a penny in old Austria) and had labored in some obscure ministry, too—railways or possibly pensions, I ask you. No, he was just standoffish. Was he doing us a favor coming to Prague once in a blue moon this way? He was Viennese—need one say more?

"Dalibor," I said, coming to a halt in front of him. "I am irresistibly drawn to you."

"So I see," he said. "I can't very well return the compliment, though, can I? Seeing that I'm standing here, nailed to the spot. Sufficient to say that I watched you wending your way through the throng. Will that satisfy you?"

"It will," I said, although I was aware of being less than pleased with my dress—pink net, strewn with embroidered forget-me-nots—which was a last year's bridesmaid gown. But since I was not yet eighteen, I had no claim to anything like a regular evening gown, and also I knew that my presence at this reception had been permitted as a special favor to me. I was grateful to Dalibor for speaking to me in the manner he had, for he was aware of a diffidence I felt not only because of my age and my dress but also because I felt tainted as compared to my schoolmates, who all had fathers at home, whereas I was the only child of a mother who had been twice divorced before the age of thirty—the first time from my father—yet who was socially acceptable everywhere, living sumptuously as she did in her mother's (my grandmother's) house in Florence Street.

Dalibor was in his late thirties—"a lovely age for a man," as my mother would have said. But he had none of the seductive glow that was hinted at by this remark. He was of medium height, and looked shorter than he actually was, owing to his build, which was sturdy, broad-shouldered, wide-chested. His pale blond hair was wavy, but rolled into curls around the temples and at the nape of the neck, where it had been left to grow longer than was usual. The low, very wide, and bumpy forehead and the small, deep-set eyes gave him an air of brooding obstinacy.

"And why do you find me irresistible?" he asked. "This is so sudden."

"Because— There must be about one hundred people here? Roughly?"

"Oh yes, easily. Certainly no less. But do go on."

"And you are the only one among them who is dressed," I said. "Not just dressed for dinner, but in the grand manner."

"Oh yes," he said. "I put on white tie so as not to be taken for a waiter. In self-defense. Because waiters in tails put on black tie, you know. Just so as not to be taken for gents."

"True. But don't be beastly. Do come on. Tell me, where are you off to after this? You only came here to make *acte de présence,* to kill time, didn't you?"

He lowered his eyelids and bent his head, feigning humility, pretending to be found out. Then, straightening up, he declaimed with sarcastic solemnity, "I'm going high up.

To the very heights. To the highest hill. To what you might truly call the Acropolis of Prague."

"To the castle?" I said. "The President? But you've done him already, once."

"No. But you are getting warm."

"To the Czernin Palace? That's Foreign Affairs, isn't it?"

"You are getting colder."

"The Sternberg Palace, the art gallery?"

"You are getting pretty hot."

I said, "The Archbishop's Palace!"

Once more he went through his mime of humility.

"Golly. Devastating! The Cardinal Archbishop? Golly."

He said, "You are repeating yourself."

"That's because I'm so devastatingly impressed. 'Thrilled' isn't the word."

"Oh, do stop your society gushing. You're trying to sound like your mother. Enough time once you get to her age. Behave, or I'll never again give you a sip of whiskey from my glass behind your mother's back. As I did two years ago. That was a do with one hundred, too, wasn't it?"

"Yes," I said. "Though we've never done such a crowd since. But do tell me, what's he like, the Cardinal? I've only seen him once or twice. That smile, sheer heaven. When he looks at you, you feel all has been forgiven."

He said, "That smile. Carefully studied in front of the mirror. To me, he means just work. But in private he can be quite . . . Do you know what happened to me the very first time I was presented to him? To start with, there were some people milling around, secretaries and creatures. Then, as they leave—once we are left alone, with the doors closed—I fall on one knee and want to kiss the ring. He says, 'Cut it out, brother.' "

He watched me laughing, remaining grave himself.

"But the priceless thing happened at another time, at a party at the Austrian embassy. Along comes—I shan't tell you who, because gentlemen don't tell. Sufficient to say a cabinet minister. Staggering and weaving, in his usual state of—sufficient to say. He comes up to another guest and utters, 'You gorgeous creature in red, come and dance with me, I inshist.' Yes, he did say 'inshist.' And the gorgeous creature in red says, 'I don't think it'd be a good idea. Because for one thing I'm a man, and, for another, I'm the Cardinal Archbishop of Prague.' "

Then, after pretending to be astonished by my laughter, he said, glancing over my shoulder, "There goes our gracious hostess. Always true to her motto—dressed simply but with bad taste."

And when I just nodded, he went on, "And yet, if she were a grande dame it wouldn't matter. She could drape herself in her kitchen curtains and get away with it. And she hasn't even got a walk, have you noticed? She doesn't walk, she flits like a weasel."

"You say that because you haven't been asked to do her."

He said, "No, it isn't sour grapes. I haven't been asked to do her, that's true. But even if I'd been asked, I would have refused. How could I draw her? She hasn't got a face."

I said, "What on earth?"

"Haven't you noticed? Each time she gets herself a new

lover she takes on a new personality. The image her lover wants her to have."

I said, "And you can tell all this when you only come here once a year, or not even once in *two* years, and stay only a few weeks? And you can't hear all our gossip, either, because you are not really in our crowd."

"I needn't listen to gossip," he said. "I look. And I see. Most people look but they don't see."

We fell silent. Then, glancing above my head, he said, "I believe their governess is looking for you. She's trying to catch my eye and signaling that I should tell you."

I said, "Drat that governess. I know what she wants. I'll have to go now. The Haussmans' driver will take me home. I was allowed to come, but only for an hour or so, because the Haussman boys are downstairs, too, and they're all around my age, take a year, drop a year—Franz, Rudy, and Ricky. It's idiotic, that governess—I mean, that they've got her at all. Ricky, the eldest, is eighteen, in his last year at school."

He said, "Quite. Sufficient to say that they change the governess each year, and that she is always no more than twenty, and tall and blond and hefty, no matter whether she is English or French or German. Because our gracious host likes them that way. And he likes change, too."

I said, "Golly. That's devastating. And I've known them all these years. And it's never occurred to me."

Without replying, he lowered his eyelids and bent his head.

IT SHOULD NOT BE said that our family was alien to
the world of art. Professor Wieland, Dean of the Academy
of Painting and Sculpture in Prague, had supplied us with
all the pictures we owned. There was a life-size portrait of
my mother at the age of four, costumed for a children's fancy-
dress party in the brittle blue-silver-yellow brocaded attire
of an infanta of Spain, done in the manner of Velázquez.
There was my uncle Frederick as a six-year-old, in the guise
of a boy of the Styrian Alps—in chamois shorts and a green-
trimmed loden coat, resting on a spade, with a basket filled
with flaming blue gentian flowers at his feet—all painted in
the smoothly glossy, idyllic Biedermeier manner. The professor did admit that, in accordance with the genre, there
should have been a small black-and-white dog in there instead of the gentians, but that he had not felt up to it. There
was also a head-and-shoulders of my grandmother, as a
young woman of twenty-eight, wearing a feather boa, which
was stippled in the Divisionist manner of Segantini. And
there were four large, equal-sized flower pieces, which the
professor had brought to bloom in the shadowy, mushy, vel-
vety style of Odilon Redon.

We are always dissatisfied when confronted with the portrait of someone we know. This is inevitable, because we
have not known that person as the painter has. But since I
had not known my mother, or Uncle Frederick, or my grandmother, at the ages of four, six, and twenty-eight, respec-
tively, I held no grudge against their portraits and was truly
fond of them. The only hint of resentment I felt was in my
grandmother's case, not because of her lush, fleshy beauty in

the portrait—she now had a marmoreal distinction—but because in the picture she had an expression I had never seen on her. In the portrait the short, voluptuous lips were half parted, revealing a glimmer of teeth, while her eyes were half veiled and hooded, under strangely heavy lids. All this lent her an unfamiliar, unfathomable, haughty, triumphantly satisfied air that I found perplexing and troubling.

Late one afternoon, a few days after the Haussman reception, Professor Wieland came to call, explaining that, finding himself in our neighborhood, he had wanted to drop in and lay his admiration at my grandmother's feet. She was not in, as it happened, yet he could not refuse to join my mother in the drawing room for a short while.

Emma, our parlor maid, was sent to fetch me. "You'd better go in, Miss Edith," she told me. "Give a helping hand to madam your mother. Finds him a bit of heavy going. You get along and show a pretty snout. Madam your mother's got to tugging at her pearls already—that's always a bad sign."

Despite my mother's dislike of having to listen to disquisitions on theories of art, it could not be denied that Professor Wieland was an ornament in any drawing room. Tall and narrow-boned, he was a much sought dinner guest who had kept his elegant leanness even now, in his seventies. With his gold-rimmed pince-nez and short white pointed beard, he bore a striking likeness to the distinguished figure of our President Masaryk—a mold often encountered among academicians of his generation. Always formally dressed and never gesticulating, he could be relied upon to listen with a grave yet tolerant urbanity and to fill embarrassing blanks in the flow of conversation with meticulously sexless anecdotes about celebrities in the arts. I cherished this one: Brahms, asked to dinner by a rich admirer, has his glass filled as the host murmurs, "This is the Brahms among my wines." Brahms takes a sip, considers, and says, "Let's have up the Beethoven, shall we?"

As soon as I had joined my mother and the Professor, I burst out with the news that Dalibor was going to do the Cardinal Archbishop. It was inevitable that Dalibor should then be discussed. The tone, I knew, would be acid, because Dalibor was an almost nationally known celebrity, whereas the Professor's name had never reached anyone outside Prague society. From the beginning, Dalibor had made his name with his flattering portrait drawings—heads and hands in red chalk, on pike gray paper, which gave even uncouth clients the conviction that they belonged to the elect. His spectacular rise to widespread fame had been achieved by his portrait of President Masaryk, which, in reproduction, was displayed, year in and year out, in the windows of most of the select shops on the seventh of March, which was the President's birthday.

"The trouble with Dalibor," the Professor said now, "is that he is supposed to be a draftsman. But he doesn't draw, he embroiders." He saw our bewildered glances and explained. "The great masters—say, Raphael, or, if you want to get contemporary, Braque or Picasso—when they draw, it's done in one single, thin, clear line. And with this, miraculously, they get depth, volume, texture, expression, all in one clean sweep. Dalibor labors. He *knits*—one plain, one purl—and then does crochet work on the edges, and the victim's head comes out of the murk like the marrow dumpling floating up in the noodle soup."

My mother nodded with what she no doubt hoped was a thoughtful air and tugged at her string of pearls.

"Yet one could forgive him his doodling if he were a nicer person himself," the Professor went on. "Only the great can afford to be nasty. But no, Dalibor plays the game with the cards held close to his chest, and if you try to get near him he can get quite nasty. Doubly naughty. Because he does it all so wickedly that you don't realize he is jeering at you."

"What's the good of jeering at someone if they don't know it?" my mother said.

"That's where his wickedness comes in. He gets a thrill out of being offensive without letting the other one know, and at the same time he takes good care that all the other people present should see he's jeering. Don't you see?"

"I don't see," said my mother.

"I've been with Dalibor at a dinner party," said the Professor, "when the host was trying to draw him out about van Gogh. Granted, one does not much like to have to sing for one's supper. Dalibor said, 'Do you mean van Gogh the Flemish sixteenth-century still-life painter of fowl and game?' Then, looking wide-eyed up and down the table during the sudden silence, he said, 'Well, how was I to know which one you meant?'

"But that's nothing. I'll tell you a truly outrageous performance of his. We are at an at-home, at the Baron Borodyn's, and we are standing in this corner, Dalibor and I, and up comes this woman, rush rush rush, gush gush gush, and we are trapped. She starts on Dalibor: how she's always wanted to ask him did he have this wonderful gift from the cradle or did he hit on it later in life? Dalibor says, 'Later in life, and by the merest chance.' He tells her it happened when he was seven years old, and sitting on a rock shelf in the Carpathian Mountains, minding his father's goats, and, with a hazel rod, drawing idly in the soil at his feet. Along comes this stranger, stops behind him, looks at his tracings, and says, 'You are a God-gifted artist. And I, Picasso, shall see to it that you get the tuition you so richly deserve.' "

"This sounds perfectly crazy," my mother said.

"Not perfectly crazy, dear madam. Just perfectly naughty. Because what Dalibor was dishing up was, of course, the old chestnut about how Giotto was discovered by Cimabue, but brought up to date."

"How very interesting," said my mother, her voice bleached with boredom. Then, in a tone of renewed vigor: "Who was she? The gushing woman, I mean. Anyone one knows?"

"Zavadil."

"Which of the Zavadils—the ones who are in distilling, or the ones who are in spinning and weaving? Did she have an enormous bosom right down to her knees?"

"Exactly. Architecturally speaking, the balcony came right down to the columns of the edifice."

"That's the one," said my mother. "Handkerchiefs and tablecloths. They have their factories up north. In Hohenelbe."

"As far as I'm concerned you can leave Hohenelbe out of it," the Professor said. "The bosom was quite enough."

After a silence he went on. "The trouble with Dalibor is he has no love."

"How do you mean?" said my mother. "He never pays court to a woman, that's true. He's never been known to be keen on anyone. But then, for all you know, he may have someone tucked away in Vienna. Doing it on the cheap— milliner's apprentice, that kind of creature. Called Mitzi. They're always called Mitzi."

"I wasn't referring to that," he said. "Not that kind of love. I meant that he can't be bothered, Mitzi or otherwise."

"Selfish, you mean?"

"No," said the Professor. "That's not what I meant, either. Because if he were egotistical he'd be in love with himself, and that wouldn't be so bad, would it? The trouble with Dalibor is that he doesn't even love himself. If you ask me, that's fatal."

"This is getting too high for me," my mother said. "And too deep." Then, giving me an angry glance, she said, "Edith, do stop lounging. Sit up straight." Whenever she was feeling at a disadvantage, my mother would turn on me in this fashion, but I did not resent it on this occasion. I had found the Professor's conversation rewarding, even if it made me share my mother's bewilderment about Dalibor. My mother never understood. I did, but later.

⁂

I RAN INTO Dalibor the very next day, on a bright, wind-still, frosty afternoon on the Graben. He was standing in front of Lippert's, contemplating one of their display windows with brooding stubbornness. He seemed completely unaware of his surroundings. I knew that the chef Karasek, who was probably now in his kitchen at the rear of Lippert's devoting himself to the care of someone's double-strength consommé, was a Sunday painter, and that my grandmother had once prevailed upon Professor Wieland to look at Karasek's pictures, and that the Professor had declared that the chef had "a true gift for the rhythm of pattern making," evolved from his habitual "painting" with aspic and mayonnaise. This had been kind of the Professor. It occurred to me now that Dalibor would never have been willing to be party to such a charade.

Dalibor, on this day, was not wearing the opulent, beaver-lined, Astrakhan-collared coat one might have expected but a dark blue topcoat with a narrow velvet collar: sleek, modest, sober. It went perfectly with his habit of standing apart from the crowd, here on the Graben or in a corner at parties.

"Dalibor," I said. "I was just thinking of you."

"Irresistibly?"

I said, "Irresistibly."

"This is so sudden."

"It isn't. Because only yesterday we were discussing you. I couldn't resist telling Professor Wieland that you were doing the Cardinal Archbishop. Because I wanted to see him turn green with envy."

"And did he?"

"Oh, quite."

"Grass green or bile green?"

"Bile green."

"It's odd how impressed you are," he said. "To me it's just work. One head, one hand. If it's both hands, I charge more." And when I looked at him doubtingly, he added, "But now I'm going to do something really worthwhile. Out of the ordinary. May I walk along with you? Because it's getting cold standing about?"

We started toward the Gunpowder Tower, and he said, "I'll explain. A brother. A brother and a sister. In their sixties. He two years older than she is. Living in the sticks in Moravia—small castle, fields growing mainly cucumbers, the mean, nobbly ones, for pickling. Now, when he was ten and she was eight, they had their portraits painted, half-bust—he holding a lemon, she holding an orange. Now, fifty years later, they want to be done again, half-bust: he holding a lemon, she holding an orange. I'll do them in oils, trying to hit them off in the same style as before. That's what I call 'rewarding.' "

I did not reply.

He said, "You have even stopped looking at me. The story makes you feel shivery, doesn't it?"

"Rather, but I don't know why," I said.

"I'll tell you why. Because you've guessed that, needless to say, neither of them ever got married. Never moved away from their place. Didn't want to."

"Ghastly," I said. "It makes you think."

"You are wrong. Portrait painters never think. They paint."

I gave him a glance and looked away.

He said, "It reminds me of something else. Something the same, though different. Quite aboveboard this time, no incest. Listen. Friends of mine in Paris, they have this picture. Small thing, like this and like this," and he sketched the size with the fingers of both hands spread wide. "Eighteenth-century, pure Louis Quinze. A harbor scene, sort of Neapolitan fanciful. Men fumbling about with boats and nets, sliver of sea, rocks, that kind of stuff. Bright sun, hot-looking aerial perspective, the figures bending or stretching, all stock-in-trade but very slick.

"Next to this picture, another picture. Same size, same place, same harbor, same figures doing their stuff. But sea in turmoil, sky stormy, gloom and menace. Now, how do you like that?"

"Wonderful," I said. "Who did it?"

"No one you've ever heard of. St. Croix de Marseille, a follower of Joseph Vernet, who was the best seascape painter in France at that time. The odd thing is, these friends of mine, they had the sunny picture for ages. And picked up the stormy one, oh, about ten years after the other. At an auction."

I said, "I suppose you go a lot to Paris."

"I don't. I don't like Paris. And I don't like the French. This *politesse française* gets on my nerves. Even when they are excessively nasty, they are excessively polite. These friends of mine aren't French, by the way. They're from the Burgenland, the same as I—half Bohemian, half Hungarian, half Austrian, the same as I. I'd never go to Paris if it weren't for them."

We had by now reached Joseph's Square. Halting in front of the military barracks, and taking off his hat as a sign that he now intended to depart, Dalibor added, "The French are such formal people. It's a wonder they ever manage to make children." I looked away, embarrassed, and when I saw the soldiers standing guard in the sentry boxes flanking the portal of the building, I felt still more flustered, although I had told myself that they could not possibly have heard us. I left him without saying good-bye.

MRS. HAUSSMAN, although never outrageously, absurdly, extravagantly wrong, like, say, Countess Sternborn, had been found unacceptable to our inner circle because of her lack of dignity. And yet by the end of March that year, just two months after the reception that I had attended, she was startlingly and horribly given a sudden dignity: a face that no longer frowned or pouted, a walk that became ponderous and no longer flitting, and a voice that no longer screeched through the villa but had changed to a barely audible murmur. Her husband had died.

Who of us has not been marked, not once but many times, by a blue bruise? And watched this colorful reminder of a knock or fall change from its first blackish violet blue to purple, then to a brownish rust color, then to a faded green suffused with yellow, until the yellow, melting into cream, makes us at last forget the injury? Doctors call it "hematoma." How could it be, then, that Mr. Haussman, governor of the Union Bank, should have died of a hematoma, at the age of fifty-one? Standing in the corridor of the express train that was to take him from Prague to Vienna, for a conference, he had been thrown against the ashtray jutting out beneath a windowsill as the train was rounding a curve, and suffered a bruised thigh. He died a few days later, after a blood clot, traveling from the bruise, clogged his heart.

No less bizarre and unexpected was the news, at exactly the same time as Mr. Haussman's end, of the death of Dalibor, aged, the papers stated, thirty-eight. All the obituaries carried the same unlikely story. Dalibor had died in Paris, killed in the Champs-Elysées by a falling tree, during a storm, at five o'clock in the afternoon. All I could think of was our talk while walking down the Graben on that sunny, frosty afternoon, when he had made me feel ill at ease, first with the orange-and-lemon story, and then with his remarks expressing his dislike of the French.

It was to be expected that, in discussing the almost simultaneous deaths of Haussman and Dalibor, everyone would speak of "tragic and inexorable fate," and go so far as to link the two victims in that phrase. And yet a bare two months later, after the Haussman family had vacated the villa on the Weinberge, voices were heard saying that in Mr. Haussman's case, at least, fate had not been tragic but benign—a remark connected with the news that Director Glauber, who had been Mr. Haussman's right-hand man at the bank, had been committed to prison for serious fiscal improprieties, and had hanged himself there.

When, on an afternoon in early April, Professor Wieland again called on us, he did succeed in laying his admiration at my grandmother's feet, adding, "At your tiny feet, madam," and being rewarded with one of my grandmother's rare smiles. Emma, without being bidden, carried in a tray with the apricot brandy to which he was partial, and he told her that she had guessed his "keenest hidden desires"—praise she received impassively, although she was perhaps not feeling unmoved.

My mother was in her room, in her millefleurs peignoir, filing her nails, when I came in to tell her that Professor Wieland was in the drawing room.

"I've already told Emma that I'm not at home," she said. "I've still got half an hour before I have to go out—it's a late-afternoon do—but Mama can carry on without me. God knows, I've always been for the highest things in life—haute-couture clothes and Hungarian counts and the rest—and I've got quite enough on my mind without sitting down with him and getting one of his lectures. That last time he was here, with all that talk about St. Peter's in Rome, that was enough to make you hit the ceiling."

"I liked it," I said. The Professor had explained how St. Peter's, as originally designed by Michelangelo, had been crippled by additions tacked on to the façade by a succession of lesser architects.

"And I can tell you this about St. Peter's," said my mother, "now that we are alone. When I went up there, two years ago, and was climbing those never-ending inside stairs up to the dome, the guide put his hands on my bosom from behind. He said he had to steady me. If he does that with me, at my age, where would he put his hands with a young girl? You ask the Professor. From me. When you go in. And remember I'm not at home."

As I returned to the drawing room the Professor was saying, "No, dear madam. Haussman did have a sad fate, granted. But with Dalibor it was destiny— No, please, let me finish. You've only read the papers and what the papers said was true and wasn't true."

I thought, True and not true, why can't he make up his mind? He really can make you hit the ceiling. My face must have betrayed me, for my grandmother gave me a reproving look.

"No, please," he repeated, and I realized that he couldn't leave Dalibor alone, even in death, because he could not forgive his having captured the Cardinal Archbishop.

He said, "It's come to me through a grapevine that starts with those friends of his in Paris. But the story doesn't start in Paris; it starts in Zurich. It starts with Dalibor, who wants to get a break from his hard work in Prague and so he goes to Zurich. In Zurich—he must have felt pretty low— he goes to a fortune-teller. I can understand this. I do not find it silly. That's where his naughtiness comes in. I mentioned it once before, to madam your daughter. And to Miss Edith here."

"Yes, you did," I said.

"As I was saying, he likes to flirt with the irrational. Or maybe he thinks of it as just an entertainment, his kind of entertainment. Pretending he takes the fortune-teller seriously, while he's jeering at her. But she turns the tables on him. She asks him point-blank how soon will he be going to Paris. He says he isn't going to Paris, hasn't been there for ages, and doesn't intend to go.

"She doesn't stop. 'But I *see* you going to Paris. You must go to Paris! The event of the greatest magnitude in your life is waiting for you in Paris.'

"Now, these friends of his from his own homeland, Burgenland or somewhere, are in Paris, and he thinks, Why not? I'll look them up. When he told them that he had decided to visit them because of this fortune-teller rigmarole, they didn't know what to make of it. They even suspected it was one of those stories of his he liked to make up. His friends said, afterward, that he wasn't his usual self. He was morose and restless. They put it down to overwork— artists are moody, that kind of thing.

"He couldn't stay at home, they said. Kept going out and about, wandering, not knowing where he wanted to go.

"On that day, about five in the afternoon, he is on the Champs-Elysées. The storm brews up. At that time, there were people all around him, hundreds of them, milling about. It hadn't started raining yet, but the wind came up all at once. The tree didn't crash—it couldn't. Such an enormous tree doesn't keel over in a flash.

"You could see it swaying and bending. You could hear it sighing, groaning, grinding. And Dalibor was standing quite far away from it. Everybody—but *everybody* who witnessed it, they were unanimous about it—said they all knew what was coming and ran away from it. There was plenty of time. No one else got so much as a scratch. And in the scramble, Dalibor walks up slowly to the tree, stands under it, and waits to be killed. Fulfilling his destiny."

"Irresistibly," I said.

They both turned their heads to me, astonished and reproachful. Astonished that I was there, reproachful because I had spoken. They had both forgotten my presence.

The Professor said slowly, "Yes, Miss Edith is right. Irresistibly."

He was not looking at me, though, but at my grandmother, and she was looking at him, each in a fashion that wholly excluded me. He said, "Destiny is what we make ourselves. Because our destiny is always irresistible to us." Her lips were half parted, and she bore that unfathomable expression of haughty, triumphant satisfaction that I recognized, at last, from her portrait.

The Dress Rehearsal

I was watching the group of nuns at the far end of the passage, and I noticed how oddly they resembled gentlemen in evening dress— a party company in white tie and tails. Then I saw one nun walking away from them, accompanied by a man. They stopped and faced each other. She raised the rosary swinging from her belt and swished it, laughing, against his sleeve. He kissed her hand, and she, still laughing, came toward me, turning her head and calling after him, "Be quiet now. I shan't listen to another word."

As she approached, I recognized my mother. I gazed at her with disgust and admiration—disgust because of her behaving in this worldly manner, so outrageously ill-fitting to her costume, and admiration because it suited her so well.

"You look wonderful, Mama," I said. "I'm staggered. I never thought you'd look so well in this getup."

"That's what I always tell you whenever there is a new fashion and you complain it will be unbecoming," she said. "It doesn't matter. An ugly woman remains ugly and a pretty woman remains pretty. Never be afraid of a change in fashions, Edith. Let it be a lesson to you for life."

"Yes, Mama," I said, "but why have you got your outfit on already and we haven't been promised ours till just before the dress rehearsal? It isn't fair."

"Naturally," said my mother. "Your smocks are easy to make, and they don't have to fit, either, because they're loose. That's not a problem. We've got priority because they can't direct us if we don't walk and move properly, and in modern clothes we are hopeless. I've got to be back now. I think they'll want us to walk onstage any minute. You haven't performed yet, have you?"

"We did the May song in a little room, round the piano," I said, "and they are very decent and don't mind us singing out of tune. Because we are supposed to be natural. Like real children. They are waiting for the maître de ballet now—the real one, not just a dogsbody assistant—to go over the dance round the Maypole with us."

"It's a ridiculous waste to get the maître de ballet to make you hop round the Maypole," said my mother. "If at least he'd teach you something of enduring value while he's at it, like the steps of the tango."

"We are supposed to be real children," I said.

"Well, so long, now," said my mother. "Go on being a real child. And when you have been, don't wait for me. I told Emma to be here at five to fetch you."

"Yes, Mama," I said, and I watched her going back to her group of nuns. Like her, they were society ladies of Prague who had agreed to take part in the gigantic crowd scenes of *The Miracle,* a fake medieval play under the direction of Max Reinhardt, which had been a sensational spectacle in Vienna, and which now, in this year of 1929, Reinhardt was taking for single-night performances to every capital city in Europe. *The Miracle* was eminently suited for international showing, because it enacted a legend with a scandalous content and a pious message, and because it was done in mime. The only spoken words were in the May song of my own group, and in the Latin prayers and litany during the church and convent scenes.

Reinhardt brought only his staff of assistants and his star actors with him to Prague, and enlisted, for unpaid crowd work, children from schools, undergraduates from universities, and members of the idle rich. For most of us, it was a unique adventure, but this was not the real reason my mother and her friends had consented to take part. What had drawn them was the brilliance that radiated from one of the two female stars, who were supposed to, and really did, look so alike onstage that one could not tell which was which. One was the American actress Rosamond Pinchot; the other was the young Lady Diana Manners, the daughter of the Eighth Duke of Rutland. If Lady Diana was willing to display herself before the world, the fashionable women of Prague were delighted to give support.

After leaving my mother, I walked to the end of the passage, past the last few entrance doors to the boxes, rounded a curve, and began to ascend one of the twin stairs that led to the dress circle, the first-floor boxes, and the bar and smoking rooms. We had been told to assemble in the ante-room opening onto the bar. Before this, I intended to lean over the red plush ledge of the first row in the dress circle and watch the proceedings on the stage. I found it frighten-ing to sit downstairs, listening at close quarters to the yelled orders and the furious answers that continually passed from the stalls to the wings. I was halfway up the stairs when some-one came skipping past me. As he passed, I saw it was a young man. He suddenly turned and barred my way, leaning against the balustrade.

"I have been wanting to speak to you," he said. "I saw you yesterday. I watched you for half an hour, by the piano, doing the May song."

"I didn't see you," I said.

He was dressed in flannels and a dark-red pullover. Over the arm that rested on the top rail was draped a green fur-bordered cape, and in his other hand he carried a blue-plumed hat. Clutched to his side, within the crook of his elbow, was some kind of silvery weapon, probably a sabre. He looked to be in his twenties, but he was not boyish. There was no softness in his countenance, no hesitance, none of the wide-eyed look that goes with youth. He had dark wavy hair and deep-set eyes, which were too small for his lean, strong-chinned face. He looked at me intently, seriously, searchingly. I could not imagine him smiling.

"I didn't see you," I repeated.

"I know you didn't," he said. "I was standing behind the open door."

"They are very decent here about the singing," I said. "At school, in music lesson, they never let me sing with the others, because I can't sing in tune. Here they don't mind. I do mind, myself, though. I can hear myself doing it wrong, and I know when it's flat, and yet I can't get it out right."

He said, "This happens often in life. In all kinds of circumstances."

"What do you do?" I asked.

"I study medicine," he said. "I'm in my last year."

"I didn't mean it that way," I said. "I meant what do you do in the play?"

"I'm in the tavern scene," he said. "I am one of the roistering fellows who chuck the wenches through the air and catch them as they come down. We've been picked for our strong arms and steady hands. It's nerve-racking, and on top of it we've got to look abandoned with joy. We rub our palms with chalk before we go on. It's slippery work, making the girls go from hand to hand. They are Corps de Ballet, though, thank God. They are used to sorrow."

"I've never watched it," I said. "I can't ever stay as long as I'd like, because Emma always comes to fetch me."

"How old are you?" he asked. "Twelve?"

"Yes," I said.

"Hold this for me," he said. "And this here," and he handed me the hat and the weapon, and flung the cape over one shoulder. I watched him lighting a cigarette. We both remained silent. His conversation seemed to have run out, and I reflected that he would not be "an ornament in any-one's drawing room," as my mother always said. He had spoken the last words in the tone of a matter-of-fact order, and had not even said, "will you, please?" Now he lounged against the balustrade with one foot on a lower step than the other, and in this half-crouching position he still barred my way.

"You are enchanting," he said at last. "You are utterly lovely and enchanting. I could not stop myself looking at you yesterday, all that time."

I looked at him, aghast. There was nothing lovely about me, either in face or in figure. Moreover, if he had been watching my group in search of enchantment and loveliness, he would have surely remarked two of my classmates, both conspicuously good-looking and seeming older than their years, who never failed to be praised by a chorus of mothers and governesses when we were fetched from school. Then it occurred to me that there was one part of me that my mother and Emma always said was fine and graceful, and this was what they called the *"décolleté"*—that composition of throat, neck, arms, and shoulders revealed when one wore evening dress. But this was for later on, they told me, when I would be going to balls. It was like having a savings account in the bank, and he could not have guessed it in any case, since I was clad in a long-sleeved dress of brown-and-blue tartan plaid with a close-fitting white collar.

"You've got it all wrong," I said.

"No," he said. "But of course you yourself don't know how ravishing you are."

I shook my head, and glancing over his shoulder, I could see a few girls of my group running up the other stairs. "I must go now," I said.

"Go," he said, but he did not move for a while and kept looking at me, with his long, full lips slightly parted, as though he still intended to speak. Then he straightened himself with an abrupt movement, took the hat and sabre from me, and stepped aside. I had forgotten that I had been holding them.

I saw him at the next rehearsal and talked to him, and at every rehearsal after. I never looked for him, and I never met him walking toward me, but he always caught up with me, coming from behind and then turning and barring my way. My feeling that he was not accustomed to drawing rooms became a conviction. He was too silent, too grave, and too straightforward. In drawing rooms, one had to converse unceasingly, speaking in bantering, joking fashion, and one had to laugh often, even when nothing witty was being said. One behaved obliquely, as though standing a few paces apart from oneself, observing oneself speak and the impression one made on others.

He told me at every one of our meetings that I was enchanting, but he did not seem much interested in my circumstances, and he did not ask about Emma, either. This annoyed me, because Emma was pretty remarkable, and on our third meeting I gave him the information on my own. I said, "I must go now. Emma will be waiting for me down-stairs in the foyer, and she'll be huffy if I let her go hanging about. It's not really her job—she's not my governess, she's our parlor maid, but you'd never think so if you saw her on her day off, in a tailor-made and a black fox fur. I haven't got a governess anymore. I haven't had one for the last six years, though most of the girls in my class still have one. We can't afford it now. My mother hasn't got a lady's maid anymore, either. We've only got a cook and a scullery maid and an in-between maid and Emma, and to make up for the lady's maid the hairdresser comes every day at noon, and the seam-stress every fortnight for a few days, but it isn't the same thing, of course. Before this, we had much more money, and the last governess I had was English, and she'd been with the Prince Windischgraetz before she came to us—the one who was the nephew of the Emperor Franz Josef. And do you know what was the Prince Windischgraetz's favorite dish?" I paused, and said triumphantly, "boiled beef with bread dumplings and tomato sauce. Shattering, isn't it?" I watched him closely, waiting for his astonishment.

He did not show it. He said, "It's you who are shattering. Shatteringly enchanting." He stepped aside, and I walked away without saying good-bye.

THE REHEARSALS for the crowd scenes went on for three weeks, with one of the young assistant directors stand-ing in for whatever single role was required. I watched him celebrating a Mass, and I was much impressed with his acting. While he uttered the litany of the *mater dolorosa,* he seemed to be struggling, wheedling, and bargaining with the Holy Virgin. My mother, too, was full of admiration. "What a superb talent!" she said that night while we were at dinner. "And what a pity he isn't an actor. Nobody could possibly do any better. When the famous Reimers arrives, from the Burgtheater, from Vienna, to take over, he'll be a letdown, you'll see." The famous Emerich Reimers, a cadaverous and magnetic figure who had won an immense following for his performances in the plays of Goethe, Schiller, Schnitzler, and Shakespeare, arrived two days before the full dress rehearsal, and I sat in the stalls, watching him. He went onstage as an elderly, haggard, careworn mediocrity, rattling off his prayers in the most businesslike fashion, tired, irritable, impatient to be done. He was the kind of priest we all knew. He was the only possible priest.

During dinner that night, my mother said with a sigh, "Did you see Reimers? Weren't you shattered? And do you remember what I said before? I take it back now, utterly. When you see someone like him, it makes you realize that famous actors aren't famous for nothing."

"Yes, Mama," I said. "I was shattered, too. Golly."

"There you are," said my mother, and then changing from noble melancholy to brisk animation, she added, "It really boils down to what I always say: You see a dress in the *Jardin des Modes* and you think it's most satisfactory, and then you come across a model dressed in Lanvin or another of the great leading lights of this world and only then do you realize. Say what you will, people like Lanvin don't ask ridiculous prices. They give something others can't give. Let it be a lesson for life to you, Edith."

"Yes, Mama," I said.

"You needn't look so worried about it," said my mother. "At twelve years old, you are not expected to face the burden of these problems. You wait till you get to my age."

"Yes, Mama," I said.

"And apropos problems," said my mother. "I've asked Dr. Hofmann, the lawyer, for dinner tomorrow, and I hope you will be on your best behavior. Don't sit there again looking like a sheep when it thunders. Be friendly and sunny. If you must look like a sheep, look like a sunny sheep. Even if you think he's ghastly. Do it for my sake."

"Yes, Mama," I said.

My mother's exhortation to be "friendly and sunny" toward a male guest was nothing new to me. Nor was "Do it for my sake." It had been like that ever since I could remember. The first instance of this trouble had taken place during my first school holidays, in the summer when I was six years old, while we were staying at an elegant lakeside resort in Carinthia. I had no governess then, and my mother had brought Emma along with us. She and Emma were the same age, and Emma had entered my mother's service as a parlor maid soon after I was born. I was proud walking about with Emma, who was much more decorative than any governess. She looked neat and glossy, as though carved out of wood and freshly varnished, with her massive, gold-blond plaits twisted into a heavy switch, and she carried her tall, narrow-boned figure in an exceedingly upright manner peculiar to her. She was resplendent in a dark-blue rose-sprigged dirndl costume with white cambric sleeves and scarlet satin apron, which my mother had had made for her so as to avoid the awkwardness of making her wear a maid's uniform or having her dress like a poor imitation of a lady. One morning, while we were in the bathing establishment built on wooden struts over and into the lake, where I went to have my daily lesson with the swimming teacher, Emma and I made the acquaintance of a man who was lounging near us on a towel spread over the rough-hewn planks that made up the floor. He was in his late forties and had the ungainly, plump-fleshed body of a person who has been weak and skinny in his youth. Though he was wearing only his bathing suit, he seemed fussily overdressed. He had an unfashionable mustache, a gold-rimmed pince-nez, dense and dark freckles on his shoulders, and a gold watchband, through which he had drawn a handkerchief whose colored border matched the color of his bathing suit. It was not Emma he wanted to engage in conversation; it was me. He wanted to know how old I was, how long I was going to stay. As he went on, my manner grew more and more con- temptuous, while his became progressively more humble and more admiring. Banal as his questions were, they were delivered with a disturbing, beseeching pressure, to which I was unaccustomed.

When Emma folded up her crochet-work, remarking that it was time for us to leave, he implored me to give him my hand.

"I wouldn't dream of it," I said haughtily, adopting one of my mother's phrases and her tone of voice.

"Just to please me," he said.

"I don't want to please you," I said.

"You are so beautiful and yet so cruel," he said sadly, and looked delighted. "When will you be less cruel? Will you bestow a kind glance on me tomorrow?"

"I don't know," I said.

"Then there is still hope for me, isn't there? I may go on hoping?"

My mother would not have tolerated my amazing rudeness, but Emma stood by in silence, contemplating her furled crochet lace with an ironic smile. When we left him, passing between the railings that bridged the way to the shore, Emma said, "You are a proper scream, Miss Edith. You make me laugh, you do," and she gave her short, affected laugh, which held no merriment.

"I'd have curtsied," I said, "and I would have given him my hand, as I do with everybody else, but he put me off."

"Clear," said Emma, "seeing he asked you for it special, as a favor, and a wonder he didn't go on his knees to you. And he such a gentleman, too—quite the perfect gent, wearing a gray pearl stuck in his tie, discreet-like, and in the winter pale-gray spats over his boots."

"How do you know?" I asked. "You've seen him before?"

"That I have not, Miss Edith," said Emma, "but that's what he goes in for, mark my word. When he gets to his office—seeing the likes of him always have offices—he stops at the door, and there's his doctor's diploma on the wall, under glass—notary or suchlike, I shouldn't wonder— and he moves it a tiny bit to one side, steps back, looks, goes at it again and tips it the other way, ever so slightly. 'Where's everybody's eyes?' he says. 'Can't you see the blessed thing was crooked? And if I hadn't put it straight it would have stayed hung crooked for the next hundred years. What's the matter with all you people? And how will you do without me, if I go off and die?' And they stand round him, making sad and sweet snouts, saying, 'Heaven forbid, sir,' and he ups and says, 'If you won't tell me, I will. You'd dance with joy.' And out and slams the door. That's the kind of awkward customer he is, as full of quirks as a dog is full of fleas."

"Really, Emma!" I cried. "You have been cheating. You've known him all along and you've been gossiping with his servant."

"That I haven't, Miss Edith. Just been reading what was written all over him, for all the world to see."

We saw my strange admirer every day after that, but neither of us mentioned anything about him to my mother. We did not see much of her during this time, and at dinner I had to sit with Emma at a separate table in the dining room of our hotel. Yet on the fourth or fifth day, as we were going down the stairs for the midday meal, Emma said, "It's no use, Miss Edith. We've got to come across with it to madam your mother, seeing the gentleman has given you two presents already and has entertained us at tea in the Schlosshotel, fit for an archduchess, and it's a marvel anyhow someone hasn't yet gone and shot her mouth to madam your mother. Better for us, open and sincere-like. I wouldn't enjoy madam your mother coming down on me like a ton of bricks, though she's gone in for slimming lately."

"She will be very pleased," I said.

"Or very to the contrary," said Emma. "Main thing, Miss Edith, you keep that rosebud mouth of yours silent like the grave and let me do the explaining."

My mother was neither pleased nor displeased. She glanced thoughtfully at the calling card that Emma had handed her, together with the gifts. "Utterly and perfectly ridiculous," she remarked.

I was furious with disappointment. Not only had the gifts seemed quite lovely to me but they were doubly lovely because they could have been given to a grown-up person. They were not toys.

I was greatly relieved when my mother added, "Much too valuable. This set of antique peasant buttons in gold filigree. And the Venetian necklace. Most embarrassing. I only hope you thanked him nicely, Edith."

"Gracious, madam," said Emma, sweeping me with a quick look of pretended outrage. "As though anybody in their senses wouldn't say thank you a hundred times over for this kind of presents."

I was breathless with admiration at the smoothness with which Emma had misled my mother without telling a lie. I had accepted the presents haughtily, without a word of gratitude.

"I don't know if we can keep them," said my mother. "Lock them away, Emma, for the time being."

"To be sure, madam, and always at your service," said Emma.

On the following day, my mother said, "I've made inquiries about Edith's friend. She may keep the stuff. I see no harm in it."

During the next few days, my mother repeatedly expressed the hope that I was making myself thoroughly pleasant to my well-wisher, and asked what we were talking about. I did not reply. I pouted and tossed my head. I could not tell her that most of our exchanges consisted of his begging for foolish favors, such as "Will you smile at me once, just once? How can you be so cruel? You know you are the queen of my heart," to which I listened delightedly and with a pretense of contempt. But as time went on, my mother's interest became more outspoken. "Hasn't your friend ever said he would like to meet me?" she would ask.

I shook my head. This time I did not have to dissemble. "I think you should invite him here, to tea," she persisted. "It is not right to accept his many kindnesses without giving anything in return."

"I won't," I said.

"You are being ridiculous," said my mother. "Besides, I've never seen such ingratitude."

"I don't want to," I said.

"Even so," said my mother, "do it for me. Do it for my sake."

"I don't think you'd like him, Mama," I said. "He's got too many freckles."

"He has good points apart from the freckles," said my

mother, "and Emma tells me you are very standoffish with him. I want you to be nice to him, so that when he comes here he is in a good mood."

"I won't," I said.

"But don't you understand?" cried my mother. "He's a most important and influential person. He's a *Börsenrat*—a councillor from the stock exchange in Vienna. It'd be a marvelous connection for me."

I knew all about the stock exchange. It was the page in the daily paper that looked to be composed of dead ants. Men could study it openly, in public, but there was something shameful about women being interested in it, which was why my mother used to read it furtively, in the seclusion of her bedroom. I was not interested in the stock exchange, and I was not going to surrender the only man I had enslaved to my mother, who was never without one or two admirers.

"You are perfectly maddening," my mother said. "All I want is to get a few tips. Or just one tip. One good one would be enough. I should have thought you'd be more helpful."

"I won't," I said.

"Get out of my sight," said my mother. "Take her away, Emma, and don't let her speak to me for the next twenty-five years."

AS I GREW OLDER, my unwillingness to be friendly toward men for my mother's sake kept recurring, in different circumstances, and though it exasperated her, it never again

roused her to violent anger. Never again was I the source of
attraction. It was always a case of me against one of my
mother's admirers. These men, when confronted with my
presence, tried to ingratiate themselves with me, and invari-
ably I resented their efforts. I knew they did not care for
me, and it hurt me to realize that whatever gifts and atten-
tions they offered were not meant for me but were obliquely
aimed at her. I hated their clumsiness, their way of flattering
my mother at my expense. Did they think it conceivable that
I would be put in a good mood by being told, "You must be
very proud to have such a charming mother. Of course, you
do take after her, but you'll never be a patch on her. There's
nobody like her in the whole world"? Or, "I never thought
you were mother and daughter. I thought you were sisters.
Astonishing, isn't it? It must be glorious for you to have such
a young mother"?

With some, my long-sustained, sullen stares produced a
laming of their conversational powers, which forced them
to utter the same phrases at each of our meetings. When I
was nine, we stayed in Montreux in the summer, and there
was a Mr. MacDonald who stayed at the same hotel as we
did. Every morning as I passed him in the lobby, on my way
to the garden, he said, "Which are you going to be today—a
good girl or a naughty girl?"

"A naughty girl," I replied wearily.

"Oh, I'm so disappointed to hear it. Will you be a good
girl tomorrow?"

"I can't tell yet," I said.

"Oh. And, by the way, how is your mother this morning?" he would ask.

I kept silent and gave him a disdainful look. I was convinced that he was my mother's lover and that he had spent at least part of the night with her, and I felt this question to be too idle to deserve an answer.

By this time I had become infallible in my discernment. During receptions at home, when I was required to go into the drawing rooms for half an hour, to curtsy and to answer the questions any guest wished to ask, I could pick out the lover of the moment from among fifty men, all strangers, merely by the way he behaved toward me. There was always the same forced jollity and embarrassment, broken by gleams of a fatuous pride, and a mixture of unwarranted familiarity and possessiveness. Some of them went in for a bold and hearty approach. They raised me on their shoulders or took me by the waist and swung me about, or lifted me to their faces and tried to kiss me. Then I wriggled, kicked, and scratched, as I had seen cats behave when I lifted them onto my lap and wanted to stroke them. Once, I knocked Mr. Ponsonby's glasses off his face and regretted they did not break. Another time, I smashed Mr. Bertram's fountain pen. They pretended to be amused, but I could see my mother biting her lips and tugging at her string of pearls. She said I was as bristly as a wire brush and did not know the meaning of friendliness, and it was a mystery. Why couldn't I be sunny and full of fun, like other children?

Tussles of this kind were no more than a passing irritation, but there was one occasion that I found deeply disturbing. One year, when I was about ten, a Hungarian baron became a frequent guest in our home. To my protestations of "What, the Hungarian again?" my mother would reply, "Such a blessing for parties! A good name, unattached, and an ornament in any drawing room." The baron's ornamental value escaped me. He was of middling height, thin, pale and fair, with a flat triangular face that showed no emotions, and the motif of the triangle was repeated in his eyebrows, which were pointed and strawy, like the gables of a tiny thatched cottage.

Though reticent about his activities in Prague, he was outspoken about other matters. According to him, the use of napkin rings was a vulgar habit; one should have fresh napkins for every meal. He refused the customary strip of lemon rind when taking a glass of vermouth, because he said that servants never washed lemons, only wiped them clean, and it was a fruit that passed through many dirty hands. The baron did not like me any better than the others before him, but he grasped my feelings at once. Accordingly, he did not hide his complete indifference toward me. In his presence, I was quiet and obedient. My mother was bewildered. "I can't make you out, Edith," she said. "Whenever someone goes out of his way to be nice to you, you turn nasty. And here, with the baron, who loathes children, you are a model of perfection."

My quiet dislike for the baron was shared by Emma. Just as he never brought me a present, he gave her no tips. Yet he was exceedingly exacting. He would ring for her to bring him the ashtray from the sofa table when he was leaning at the window seat. "He's bitter because he's hard up," said Emma, "but that's not why he's stingy. If he was rich, he'd be just as mean. It's like a built-in cupboard—you can't move it."

It was the baron's exactingness that made Emma commit several small acts of wanton malice toward him, which she performed with the cold-bloodedness that only highly trained servants can achieve. Once, she laid out his topcoat on the cane-backed settee in the inner hall in such a way as to display conspicuously a tear in the lining. She also knew of his fastidiousness in regard to contagious diseases, and thus she brought about the incident that I found impossible to forget.

That night, when the baron called to accompany my mother to the opera, I was in bed. I had been laid up for two days with a feverish cold and cough. Emma, opening the door, told him that my mother was still getting dressed, and added, as though it were a message from my mother, "And if you'd be so good, sir, as to look in on Miss Edith and say good night to her? Seeing she is always so disappointed when madam her mother goes out and she has to dine on her own. As a treat and a consolation, as it were."

I was astonished to see the baron entering my room. "Golly," I said, "I've never seen you in tails before. Mama is going to wear a new yellow velours chiffon with ospreys, and she had awful trouble getting them just in the right shade."

Emma remained in the door while the baron advanced and drew up a chair to my bed and sat down. Only then did she approach and gather up a half-filled glass of water with a spoon in it and a bottle with syrup from my bedside table. "That's more presentable-like," she murmured. Then she turned to the baron. "And if you'd be so good as to bear in mind, sir, not to stop too many minutes, seeing that Miss Edith's got a bit of a temperature and is still due for her medicine and must settle down for the night."

"What's the matter with Edith?" asked the baron, half rising from his seat and then sitting down again. This was the only sign he gave of his anger at being trapped.

"Just a cold in the chest, sir, and nothing to worry about," said Emma in a perfidiously soothing voice. "There's a lot of it about now, it being infectious, but no real harm in it, though the doctor says one's got to watch it, considering that scarlet fever and suchlike can start the same way."

"The longer I stay in Prague, the more I am impressed," said the baron. "It's got everything, even scarlet fever."

"As you say, sir, and always at your service." And Emma left the room.

The baron sighed and pulled up the creases of his trouser legs.

"It's nothing, really. It's practically gone," I said. "Emma just likes to drivel because it sounds important, and I had thirty-seven eight yesterday, but this afternoon only thirty-seven."

"You don't look feverish at all to me," he said. "I am sure you are all right. Let me see." He laid his hand on my throat. He had flat, veined hands with protruding finger joints. "Yes, you feel quite cool," he said. "Cooler than my hand. Just as I thought."

He kept his hand on my throat, looking not at me but in front of me, at the counterpane of white dotted muslin threaded on the borders with sky-blue ribbon. It matched the bedspread and the pane curtains. The furniture of my room was composed of Biedermeier pieces, leftovers from my great-grandparents' household—all odds and ends, not matching in wood or color. To impose some unity, my mother had had the seats upholstered in sky-blue linen the previous year, and repeated this hue with the ribbon trimmings, and I remembered one occasion when the baron had remarked that one did not tie up Biedermeier like a chocolate box.

Now, as I saw his fixed gaze, I expected another burst of derisive criticism, but he remained silent. His cool hand slowly enfolded my chin, and lingered there as though uncertain of the path to pursue. Then it moved on, tracing the outline of my ear with leisured insistence, and traveled to the nape of my neck and farther down, fluttering over my upper spine, and returned at last to the neck, rounding it and stroking it with an insistent pressure, as though wanting to mold it to its own wish. It was breathtakingly pleasurable. I had never been touched like this before, and I could not have guessed that there was voluptuousness in a man's bony-fingered hand. At the same time, I knew that the hand on my flesh was languid with experience, had done this many times before, was absentminded, was barely conscious of what it was doing—did it because it did not know what else to do, and was certainly not realizing it was doing it to me. If the hand was conscious of anything at all, it was probably dreaming it was touching my mother or some other full-grown woman.

The pain of this thought made me gasp for air and forced me to take a deep breath. This set off the grinding of the cough mill in my chest, and there was nothing to halt it. I had to sit up, choke, grope for my handkerchief, and the hand withdrew.

"What's on tonight?" I asked between coughs. "*The Magic Flute?*"

He raised a pointed eyebrow and gave a one-sided smile; it was an impressive mannerism of his, probably born of his habit of wearing a monocle. "Yes," he said. "Who cares? More flute than magic, as far as I'm concerned. Still. Well, anyway, as I was saying— What was I saying? Never mind. I'd better be off now. So long. Speedy recovery."

The memory of this bedside scene remained with me for years as an insidious snare, a mousetrap tied up with blue ribbon like a chocolate box, always ready to catch me with its painful grip whenever I saw a man paying court to my mother.

THE DRESS REHEARSAL for *The Miracle* was to start in the early afternoon, and we had been warned that it might continue till the small hours of the night. It was not just a dress rehearsal, but what the Viennese staff called the *Generalprobe*—a full, ultimate rehearsal and review before the public performance the following evening. We had been told to be prepared for storms of bad temper, and we had heard the saying that a dress rehearsal without hitches and without rows promised a disastrous first night. To my amazement, scene after scene flowed smoothly, entwining with stage sets and lighting effects and accompanied by peaceful dealings behind stage. It was like seeing a finished Persian rug which up till then one had seen being knotted only from the reverse side.

The only upset I witnessed was not a quarrel itself but its aftermath. It happened when my group had been assembled, before walking onstage for the dance round the Maypole. A deputy stage manager was standing in front of us, ready to lead us into the wings. Just as he beckoned to us to follow him, he was obstructed by several stagehands carrying props, who shouted some warning I could not make out, and then a lad came running, telling him to make a detour. An assistant director appeared from behind, urging us to get going, and thus we were led, by a roundabout way, through a door and into what seemed a passage, then out through another door opposite, and from there to the wings. But this passage was in reality a long, narrow room, and on a divan close to one wall crouched Lady Diana Manners, who was naked. I knew it was she, because her double, Rosamond Pinchot, was to be in our scene. Lady Diana was encircling one knee with her arms, with her head flung back; her face washed with tears, she was screaming with sobs. Near the wall facing her, close to a table, stood two stage dressers, holding between them a cloak of brocade that I recognized as the one worn by the Holy Virgin in the church scene. They were looking at it with the tense and reproachful coun-

tenance peculiar to women when they search for a rent
or stain in a piece of cloth. Suspended above the naked actress was a single dim electric light, which lit her hazily and
to advantage, suffusing her pale coral-pink body with am-
ber shadows. This, together with her extravagant pose of
abandoned grief, made her look like a mythological figure
painted by Correggio—an Ariadne deserted on Naxos, or a
Europa after the rape by the bull. In contrast, the two fat,
short, elderly women, absorbed in their prosy and thrifty
task, tightly and shabbily clothed in black and with every
wrinkle and every graying wisp of hair sharply limned in the
glare of a powerful lamp on a nearby table, while the rest
of the room was in a brownish gloom, formed one of those
domestic interiors painted by the Dutch masters in the sev-
enteenth century.

We were startled and embarrassed, wanting to stare and
yet averting our eyes. Some of us started to curtsy, to apologize for our intrusion. Neither the stage manager nor the
assistant director seemed to find anything unusual in the
situation. They clapped their hands at us and called "Tut,
tut" and "Come, come, come!" impatiently and foolishly,
like townsmen attempting to shoo along a flock of geese.
Lady Diana and the dressers did not give us so much as a
glance. The one continued weeping and screaming, the others went on examining their brocade.

In the interval of the dress rehearsal, we children were
still wandering about in our medieval smocks, with wreaths
of artificial field flowers in our hair, because we had to
wait our turn to use one of the communal changing rooms. I

was with two girls from my group, and we were in search of ices. Our mothers never allowed us to eat the cheap water ices sold on street corners and in popular establishments. The only place considered fit for us was Berger's, in the Vodičková, whose sorbets surpassed those at Rumpelmayer's in Paris and at Demel's in Vienna. We went into the bar on the first floor, where refreshments and a coffee urn were set out on a trestle table in front of the counter. While we were counting our money and worrying whether the woman behind the table might know who we were and refuse to serve us, a medieval roisterer appeared in the archway, with his fur-trimmed cape draped over one shoulder, revealing one yellow-slashed blue sleeve. He was carrying his blue-plumed beret in his hand.

"Come here," he said, in a low voice.

I went up to him.

"You are ravishing and enchanting," he said. "I've been all over the place looking for you." He drew his free hand over his forehead. "This is our last time," he said. "Have you thought of it? Next week, I'll start my internship in obstetrics, on call day and night, and after that it will be my finals, one oral after another."

I did not understand him. I only grasped that we would not be meeting anymore. "How very interesting," I said, in the way my mother did when she did not know what one was talking about.

"After this," he continued, "I'll have to go for my military, and you will be behind your bastion of"—and he set the beret on his head, splayed out his left hand, and counted off on its fingers with the forefinger of the right—"cook, scullery maid, in-between maid, parlor maid, the hairdresser every day, and the seamstress once every fortnight. I've remembered it right, haven't I?"

"Yes," I said.

"Edith, she's only got coffee and vanilla!" called one of the girls. "Are you still in on it? And there's no whipped cream."

"Come with me," he said, and, embracing my shoulders, he turned me round, stepped behind me, and took me into the anteroom that opened onto the galleried landing. "Here," he said, stopping in a corner. Still standing behind me, with his arms round my shoulders, he lowered himself to the floor and sat down cross-legged, pulling me into his lap. "My sweet," he said. "At last."

I saw people passing on the landing beyond. Two figures were bending over the ledge and looking down onto the stalls, from which rose the murmur of voices and the sounds of footsteps, shouts, claps, and bangs. The enervating fragrance peculiar to the theater—the smell of dusty plush, mildewed velvet, stale scent, stale sweat, and heated iron from the radiators behind latticed brass grills—made me languid to the point of weakness. I could not have risen even if I had wanted to.

I knew he was going to kiss me, but the struggling, kicking, scratching cat inside me, the animal that could fight free and run away, had deserted me. Inside me, in its place, there was a plant, and plants cannot run away. They want to open the bud they have grown and unfold it into a flower, and they are at the mercy of the weather and have to submit to every mood of the sky above them. I was sure he was going to kiss me, to kiss my lips and the inside of my lips, as I had heard this was what lovers do. And I waited for it.

What he did was not what I had expected; it was much less and yet much worse. He raised his hand to my head and slowly took off the wreath of field flowers, patiently disentangling the wire where it had caught my hair. With the same slowness, unhesitatingly and inexorably, his fingers went underneath the heavy strand of hair that always covered one side of my forehead, almost touching the eyebrow, and slid it aside, uncovering a bare part of me that no one ever saw. With the same deliberate slowness his mouth moved in where his fingers had been, and stayed there, insistently but with an ebbing and flowing of its pressure that swayed my whole body and made me lean against him with increasing closeness, until I felt I was melting into his arms. A shudder moved his mouth and went through me, and then his lips closed and stayed in calmness for a long time.

When he lifted his face, the coolness of my forehead remained for a while, from the moisture of his lips, and a lightness, from the absence of their pressure. I watched the green fur-bordered cape on his shoulder rising and falling.

"It is enough now—more than enough," he said. "You are sweet beyond my dreams."

"I can see you breathing," I said.

"Evenly?" he asked.

"Yes, of course," I said. "Why shouldn't you? You haven't been running."

"We must go now," he said. "No, let me do it. I must cover what I have uncovered. What belongs to me." And he made the strand of hair fall in a wave over its accustomed place. He lifted the wreath from the floor, laid it on his palm, and offered it to me.

"Thank God you remembered it," I said. "I'd quite for-gotten I had it. Golly."

"Be careful with it," he said. "Keep it for the first night. But don't put it on anymore now. Not today. The dress rehearsal is over."

Equality Cake

*I*n the kitchen of my grandmother's castle in Bohemia there were two implements for the removal of cherry stones. They were wire loops mounted on stems of white unpolished wood, and every time the cook got ready to prepare the cherries for equality cake, she took them both out of a nest of drawers and laid them on the table. Then, with the superb calmness of the habitual evildoer, she pulled a hairpin from the coil of hair that crowned her head like an outsize snail shell carved of ebony and used it for digging the stones out of the fruit. When this task was done, she wiped the pin across the front of her apron, restored it to its place, and returned the cherry stoners where they belonged, as their deceitful presence was no longer needed. I never remarked on this ritual, but because I was a constant visitor in the kitchen it was inevitable that, for me, equality cake stood for deceit. It was a bland, smooth, unpretentious cake, of blond appearance, closely paved with fruit, and when it came out of the oven the gentle swell of the pastry nailed down by the cherries made it look like a button-tufted sheet. I was a child in those days, in the early nineteen twenties, and to me equality cake was an eatable calendar, which marked the progress and passage of every summer I spent in the castle. On my arrival, in June, it was set with the early, sour, pale-fleshed amarelle cherries, which could not be eaten raw. Then came the sweet red cherries, then halved greengages, then quartered apricots, then the late, piquant black *griotte* cherries, and then, in the beginning of autumn, it ended with small violet-blue plums. By the time I was eleven years old, the benefits of advanced education lent a new character to my feelings about equality cake. I inclined to the belief that it derived its name from the French Revolution and the slogan *"Liberté, égalité, fraternité,"* and I tried to convince the cook that Robespierre had eaten it every day, washing it down with sips of his afternoon coffee. The cook was contemptuous of this conceit, though I had taken great pains to furnish her with historical explanations.

"I'm surprised at you, Miss Edith," she said one afternoon. "Everybody knows it's called equality cake because you weigh the eggs and then put in the same weight of flour, butter, and sugar. All equal. Simple."

"That's true, of course," I said, "but don't you see it's symbolic? *Égalité*—that's butter, sugar, flour. *Fraternité*—that's the eggs. Because with the eggs instead of weights you don't have to worry about decagrams, the way you do here in Bohemia, and if you were home with Mama and me in South Kensington you wouldn't have to bother with ounces, either. The eggs make it across frontiers, and that's the idea of universal brotherhood."

"Equality cake always was and always will be," said the cook. "Being an easy cake to make, and easy to eat, seeing it doesn't squash and crumble, and coming in handy, considering it stays moist for days on end. It's older than your French Revolution, the way I see it."

"But don't you see, equality cake is so truly and utterly equal it must have a special meaning? You always bake it in trays—never in the round—and then you cut it up in squares. And a square has equal sides and equal angles."

"And where does the liberty come in, if you please?" said the cook.

"I don't know, exactly," I said, "but I'll think about it. It's got to be somewhere, too. I'll tell you when I know."

"You do that, Miss Edith," she said.

This remark, coming from anyone else, could have been of an ironical nature, but with the cook it was not. She was incapable of irony or sarcasm, and she was also insensitive to them. That day, I watched her as she wiped the table with fierce large sweeps, as though needing to unfurl her energy after the finicky task of stoning cherries. She was perhaps not the perfect partner for discussing the higher meaning of equality cake, but she was willing to give her serious interest to anything I might say, and thus spared me the indifference

I would have met with elsewhere in the castle. Emma, who was my mother's London maid, and whom we brought with us to Bohemia on our summer visits, would have cut me off with, "You make me laugh, Miss Edith. You make me laugh, you do," adding one of her false, affected laughs. Uncle Frederick would have said, "You fascinate me," thus achieving the same ironical effect. My mother would have said, "If you didn't think up such utter nonsense, you might occasionally give your mind to washing your neck and cleaning your nails." And my grandmother would have dismissed me with, "Difficult to say," and made me fetch her patience cards "while you're on your feet."

I often imagined that the French Revolution would be delightful to the cook, considering the rebellious cast of her own nature. Unlike Emma, who could not see a filled salt-cellar without smoothing its surface with a spoon and imprinting on it with the end of its stem a pattern of overlapping crescent-shaped ridges, the cook was not governed by a desire for pleasing neatness. When it came to decorating, she liked a violent clash of colors—"making things a bit lively," as she called it—and thus she would give a dusting of fiercely red paprika to the jade-green cucumber salad, ignoring my mother's repeated protests that she was setting our mouths on fire. She also revolted against the decencies of thrift and privilege, by stealing the expensive bottled spa water that my grandmother drank for her gout and using it for the poaching of asparagus, saying, "A noble vegetable must be treated noble. This is a castle and not a poorhouse."

Or she would chuck a whole brick of butter into the sluggish flames of the kitchen range, muttering, "Burn up, will you?" I concluded that it was people like the cook who made revolutions, and that Robespierre had looked exactly like her, with the same imperious presence.

And yet one afternoon when I told the cook Marie Antoinette's remark, "If they have no bread, let them eat cake," and explained how it had brought on the French Revolution, she was not impressed. "For that sort of daftness, Miss Edith," she said, "you don't have to go all the way to France. You could have found it right here next door, in Sestajovice, with the old Countess Sternborn, if you'd known her."

"Oh, that," I said. Countess Sternborn, the mother of the present Count Sternborn, whose estates bordered on those belonging to my grandmother, had on one occasion been approached by a beggar. "Lady, I haven't eaten a bite these last three days," he said, to which the Countess replied, "That's very wrong of you, you know. One must force oneself to eat."

"Old Countess Sternborn didn't start a revolution," said the cook, "and I can't see how this Marie Antoinette did."

"That's because there was no Robespierre to listen to the old woman Sternborn," I said. "With Marie Antoinette, he was on the spot and heard it all."

"Maybe," said the cook. "But mark you, Miss Edith, your Marie Antoinette wasn't so singular, seeing we've got that same kind of talk right here, too, so who's to say your Robespierre was singular? For all you know, there's one just like him just round the corner, getting good and ready to get going."

For a while, I was speechless with fright. Then I said, "But he wouldn't come here to us. He would go to Sesta-jovice and cut off Count Sternborn's head, because Count Sternborn is nobility, and we aren't."

"You don't want to be so sure, Miss Edith," said the cook. "Count Sternborn's got the manor house—what's he got, all in all? Ten, twelve rooms—a handful, you might say—and once you're inside it, it's like a dumpling sitting on a plate. One look round and you've seen it all. But here you got the park, that takes two hours' fast walking to do one round of it, and you've got fifty rooms, with the painted rooms as no one else's got—the Austrian Room and the Saints' Room— and even the Garden Room is done with parrots, and who-ever did it did it because he was tired, seeing it's only got three walls, and the fourth wall missing where it should be."

"It's got to be open on one side," I said. "That's what makes it a *sala terrena,* and it isn't parrots, it's crested cocka-toos."

"Never mind," said the cook. "And Robespierre wouldn't mind, either, because you wouldn't be alive, not by the time he'd got that far."

"I wouldn't be here, because you don't have revolutions during the holidays," I said. "We'd be in London, Mama and me, and Uncle Frederick isn't here in the winter, either, and with Grandmama it wouldn't matter, because with her he wouldn't dare. Nobody dares anything with Grandmama.

You can't even be cheeky to her, and if Marie Antoinette had been like Grandmama, nothing would have happened to her, either."

"Maybe," said the cook.

FOR THE NEXT FEW DAYS, I was harrowed by the cook's remarks, wishing I could dismiss them as nonsense and fearing I could not. On the one hand, the cook was lacking in historical perspective. For instance, during our talk regarding Marie Antoinette, the cook had said, "Ah, our Lord the Emperor, he never did have any luck with his family," and when I told her that the Emperor Franz Josef belonged to the nineteenth century, whereas Marie Antoinette belonged to the eighteenth, the cook remarked, "Now you got me all muddled. You've mixed me up like a Christmas loaf." On the other hand, the cook was a person of sound judgment; she could lay a hundred eggs on the table and pick out the rotten ones, speedily and infallibly, without holding them up against the flame of a candle.

For me, the recent breakup of 1918, which had made Bohemia part of the republic of Czechoslovakia, was not in the nature of revolution, because my grandmother remained in the castle, the same as before, still presiding over her cast of elderly prima donnas. Kocour, the night watchman, and Prochazka, the coachman, were both in their seventies; Kucera, the head gardener, was eighty; the cook, who was in her sixties, was the youngest leaf of this fading but stalwart four-leaf clover. The other servants—the undergardeners, the stable lads, the housemaids, kitchen maids, and scullery maids—were ever changing, but only because part of their role was to be young. They were like the chorus and corps de ballet of an opera house, constantly being replenished without anyone's noting the difference.

One afternoon, the newly significant sight of a freshly baked equality cake decided me to seek reassurance. We were sitting round the table in the Garden Room, enclosed on three sides by the walls painted with fluttering cockatoos; the arched, pillared opening on the fourth side gave onto the flagged terrace. Behind its balustrade lay the rose parterre, the blooms enmeshed in the scrollwork of low-trimmed box. Beyond the lawn, at the far end of the chestnut avenue, the park stretched as far as the eye could see, full green and fading to blue in the distance. Emma had finished her coffee-dispatch service at the sideboard, where she poured out while the two other maids carried the cups to the table and offered the sugar from the box with the tarnished silver lid and the broken hinge.

"What would happen if there were a revolution?" I said. "Like the French Revolution, with Robespierre, I mean."

Uncle Frederick said, "He'd guillotine every maid who can't carry a cup of coffee without slopping it over. Isn't that so, Emma? Do you hear?"

"To be sure, sir, and always at your service," Emma said. With one hand, she was now offering a platter of poppyseed roulade to my grandmother, while holding the dish with the equality cake in the other, at shoulder height. Yet she was able to turn her head in the direction of the two maids leaning sloppily against the sideboard and to sweep them with a nasty glance.

"But he wouldn't guillotine Frederick," said my mother. "He'd keep him in the prison down in the park, and make him sing the 'Marseillaise,' ha, ha."

"And what would happen to the Austrian Room?" I asked.

The Austrian Room, with its panoramic frescoes supposedly inspired by the Salzburg Mountains, was my heart's delight. I had never got used to it, which meant that I never stopped loving it. It grieved me that no one else in the castle shared my devotion. The maids looked at it simply as a room with crazy wallpaper, accustomed as they were to the dull, unspectacular, and exceedingly fertile plains in our part of Bohemia. The cook venerated it, but without favoritism, just as she venerated the Saints' Room and the Garden Room—mainly because the Sternborns had nothing like it in Sestajovice. My grandmother looked upon it as "a pleasant accident," because it had only been discovered some years after my great-grandfather had bought the castle, when workmen were called in to repair a wall. My mother professed to be fond of it "because it's rococo, and rococo is always nice, it never goes out of fashion," using almost the same words and the same tone of voice as when she was being polite about someone's coat. And Uncle Frederick, who was an art dealer, had once dismissed it, saying, "With that sort of stuff you couldn't tempt a dog to come out from behind the stove, do you understand? What am I to do with it—scrape it off and peddle it round?"

"What would happen to the Austrian Room?" I repeated.

"They'd stable horses in it," said Uncle Frederick. "A self-respecting revolutionary horse won't feed unless it's housed in a frescoed hall."

"But how could they put horses in the Austrian Room," I asked, "when the Austrian Room is on the second floor?"

"You are being ridiculous," said my mother. "They'd burn the place down, of course. So there wouldn't be a second floor to worry about."

"And what would happen to the park?" I asked.

"They'd break the wall down and chop off every tree and trample it into the ground," said my mother. "And turn the cattle loose in it into the bargain, to make quite sure it's properly devastated."

"Do you really think so, Mama?" I asked. "If they came here and saw how beautiful it is— I mean, why should they?"

"Beautiful, ha, ha," said my mother. "Beautiful means nothing to them. What good is a castle to the canaille? And the park? They can't use it, and they can't live in it." Turning to my grandmother, she said, "Isn't that so, Mama? It's true, isn't it?"

"Difficult to say what would happen in such a case," said my grandmother.

There was no telling how much attention she paid to our talk, because during all that time she had been occupied with spooning up and swallowing the crinkled skin of the boiled milk in her coffee. She was fond of it, whereas the very sight of it made my mother shudder, and I had had interesting talks with the cook about this divergence in tastes. But at the moment this did not interest me, because I was gripped by anxiety. My grandmother's short, noncommittal utterance, although it was one of her habitual turns of phrase, scared me, whereas my mother's and Uncle Frederick's remarks had been too frivolous to be frightening. It scared me even more than the cook's conversation, because I understood the cook's violence-loving nature.

"But how could there be a revolution?" I asked now. "If you have to have canaille for a revolution, where would they come from? Do you have to make them come over from France?"

"You fascinate me," said Uncle Frederick.

"You are being ridiculous," said my mother. "Really, Edith, how can you talk such nonsense?"

"But Mama," I said, "you get your clothes from Paris, too."

"Not all of them," said my mother, her eyes sparkling with annoyance, "but naturally, some. Where else should I get them from? Show me the Patou, show me the Worth, in any other country in the world and I'd be only too glad—I'd be positively thankful, I assure you—but in the meantime—"

"Do you have to tell us, you extravagant goose?" said Uncle Frederick. "We all know your meantime. In the meantime, you could be in Timbuktu, and in the spring the cuckoo would sing, 'Patoo, patoo,' and the blackbird would chirp, 'Worth, worth.' "

"You are not being funny," said my mother. "Is it fair, I ask you, when . . ."

She was now changing from vexation to self-pity, and I knew that the entertainment value of the quarrel was over.

I thought how odd it was that even talk about revolution was bound to end in recriminations over my mother's dress-maker bills.

IN THE EARLY EVENING, about an hour before dinnertime, I sought out my grandmother in the Austrian Room. I knew she would be there, sitting over a game of patience. I wanted to speak to her alone, hoping to get her serious and considered opinion as to the possibility of a revolution. I found her sitting in a basket chair, whose green paint had worn off into lakes and islands, behind a wobbly bamboo table, which matched the other pieces in the room in age and shabbiness. She sat with her back to the window, close to my favorite wall panel—the one with the chamois on top of piled-up rocks, with distant crags veiled by a sil-vered, white-frothed waterfall. Unfortunately, my mother was standing behind my grandmother, looking at the cards laid out on the table.

As I came in, my grandmother was saying, "Three and four makes seven, and four would make eleven, but I haven't got a four."

My mother said, "Edith, if I had a neck like yours I wouldn't show myself till the hour of twilight. Get out of my sight."

I said, "Mama, I'm sorry about what I said about your clothes from Paris. I mean, I know you get some from Madame Rachelle's in Knightsbridge, too."

"Three and eight makes eleven," said my mother.

"Not so fast," said my grandmother.

"But what I wanted to know," I said, "is where does the canaille come from?"

"It doesn't have to come from anywhere," said my mother. "It's here right under your nose. It's all around us. What did you imagine?"

"Where? How do you mean?" I asked.

"You were right," said my grandmother. "Three and eight makes eleven."

"The village people, of course," said my mother. "Including the elite—I mean, the postmistress and the innkeeper. And the farmhands in the yard who perform with the cows and the pigs. And the peasants on the estate. And even the stationmaster in Celakovice, who salutes so smartly and makes such a fuss over us, and holds up the train for us when there's a lot of luggage." Turning to my grandmother, she added, "Isn't that true, Mama?"

"I'm afraid so," said my grandmother. "They'd all add up to a nice rabble, like five and six makes eleven. If you'd let them add up, that is."

"No," I said, "it couldn't be. They always greet you so nicely when we drive out with Prochazka. There's no one on the road ever who doesn't, and on special occasions they fall on their knees and kiss your hand."

"What do you imagine?" said my mother. "Do you think they love us? They'd string us up on the nearest tree if they had the chance."

"On which tree?" I asked. "On the linden tree in the gravel space?"

My mother did not speak.

"But why?" I asked.

"Because we're in the castle, living the way we do," said my mother.

"Why shouldn't we be in the castle if my great-grandfather bought it from those ladies Wagner?"

"You are talking utter nonsense," said my mother. "What would they care? They didn't care in Russia, when the Bolshies came, whose great-grandfather bought what from whom. How do you think I've got my manicure woman in London, who's a grand duchess? Not that I believe her, of course. But still. She's Russian and she had to run. So there you are."

"But do you really think the villagers here are canaille?" I said.

"Be reasonable, Edith," said my grandmother. "Just take an example. You know the wall round the park—why do you think it's there? And why do you think the glass splinters are stuck on top of the wall—for decoration? And do you know just how much it costs me to keep this wall in trim, year in, year out—twelve kilometers of it? And apart from that, there's Kocour with his gun and dog at night. Do you think that's all for nothing? If they had a chance, the people would break in and wreck the park and steal the timber and carry off the exotic trees, even now in full peacetime. No, I'll keep the three back—I'll put it by, and it will work out. So you can

imagine what they would do in a revolution, when everything is turned upside down and servants are masters and
masters are servants. But I can see no way out now, unless I
cheat with the nine and pay it back later."

"Don't, or you'll be sorry," said my mother.

I looked at both of them, speechless with astonishment
at the way they "mixed it up like a Christmas loaf"—life,
death, looting, dispossession, and a game of cards tangled in
between. I thought of the linden tree in the gravel space, and
how it really was the only tree near the castle, and how it was
braced with iron girders because it was two hundred years
old and charred black down one side, where lightning had
struck it. My heart shriveled at the thought of how indifferent they were to it all, how they could talk about the end of
everything without even a change of countenance or tone.

"And what then?" I asked. "Will Grandmama run away
and become a manicure woman?"

"You should, Edith," said my mother. "You'll start a new
fashion for black-rimmed fingernails, ha, ha."

"I'm stuck with the nine now. It's hopeless," said my
grandmother.

"And the castle?" I said. "Who'll have it?"

"The rabble, the mob, will have it," said my mother, "and
I wish them luck with it, what with no electricity and not a
single bath in the place, and only that one flushing lavatory
with a chain, because your great-grandfather said the servants needn't have one or there'd be no difference between
them and us."

"Too true," said Uncle Frederick, who had just come into the room. "That's what is meant by having a social conscience. He had a social conscience, do you understand?"

My mother said, "No, don't give up, Mama. It may yet come out all right."

"But in that case," I persisted, "as it's so uncomfortable, perhaps nobody would move into the castle, and the Austrian Room would be saved."

"The panes would break," said my grandmother, "and the doors would rot, and the snow and rain would wash off the Salzburg lakes, or whatever they are. If only I could have shifted the nine."

"That's not all of it," said my mother, "because the canaille would come in on Sundays, in loving couples, and write things on the walls."

"What would they write?" I asked.

Uncle Frederick said, "Fascinating and original thoughts. 'Vasek loves Mila,' and a heart with an arrow. 'All boys called Ferda are fools.' That's the true poetry welling up from the soul of the people, do you understand?"

"I've bungled it, and nothing can save me now," said my grandmother.

"Start another, Mama," said my mother.

"I'd rather wait till the lamps are brought in," said my grandmother. "My luck might turn with the light."

"I don't know about your luck," said my mother, "but I do know about the gnats and midges—they'll come in with the light, on the dot. They're the only things you can rely on to perform in this place. And when I tell Kucera to get

his men to clear out the lake, because it's so choked up
with dead leaves and duckweed you can't see a shred of
water in it, he goes and plays hide-and-seek in the hothouses
and sends impertinent messages. What do I care about his
creepy-crawly enormous Calville apples that he grows out-
size on that espalier only a foot above the ground, as ridiculous as a dachshund, and how nobody else can do it and
Sternborn in Sestajovice never had anything like it? And the
lake stays a mess, and we get midges from it, and Prochazka
sends us his flies across from the stables, because they are
filthy, too, as bad as the lake, but Prochazka isn't worried,
because he's an inverted camel and can drink for a fortnight
without doing a stroke of work. It's a scandal, Mama, and
you know it, and you sit year in, year out, between the im-
pertinence of the garden and the drunken stables and the
wasteful kitchen. I don't know how you can put up with it,
Mama. You must be a saint and a martyr."

My grandmother, disdaining, as usual, to reply, stacked
the cards and said, "It feels very close. Have a look, Edith, at
the sky. Does it look like thunder?"

I stepped to the nearest window and leaned out over the
sill, which was mottled like the bark of a plane tree, with the
dirty brown paint peeling off in patches. I craned my neck to
the right till I could see at least the farthest end of the terrace, where it curved round and where the balustrade gave
way to the ivy-clad crenellations, which were as fake as the
Gothic library wing itself. "Yes," I said, "it's black behind the
library. But over the park it's lovely and peculiar. Do look at
the sky, Mama."

My mother turned her head and said in a voice still weary from her grievances against the servants, "Yes, it's nice." Then she added, in a softer and more animated tone, "It's a good color. I once had a ball gown exactly that shade of green. You never knew it; that was before you were born. With diamanté straps. Frederick will recall it. Utterly and uniquely unusual. Nobody else had anything like it."

"Are you out of your mind?" said Uncle Frederick. "Do you think I can keep track of every blasted rag of yours? But it must have been utterly unique if you had it, because even then you were an utter and unique goose. But a younger goose, do you understand?"

"Do you always have to be offensive?" said my mother. "And do you always have to insult me with my age, when everybody else always thinks that Edith is my sister? Let me tell you, only the other afternoon, when—"

"Edith," said my grandmother, "run downstairs, will you, and tell them to shut all the windows before the rain?"

I left the room reluctantly, because this quarrel promised to be the most entertaining of the day.

II

IT WAS ALMOST four o'clock in the afternoon when I started out on a most familiar way, though this was the first time in my life I was traversing it on foot. It was wind-still and chilly, and it had been drizzling on and off all day. Ahead of me, the park showed only treetops, owing to a dip in the ground, presenting an impenetrable screen as far as the eye could see—a deep, drenched green, fading to a dull blue in the distance. As I reached the turn of the road, where Prochazka had always given the whip to the horses so as to achieve the drive in with an impressive rumble of wheels and clatter of hooves, the wall came into view, and just then the sun broke faintly out of the clouds and sparkled on the glass shards. I halted, choked by rising tears and shaken by a nervous laughter. The park wall, which I had known to be soiled, patched, pitted, and crumbling, was smooth and prosperous-looking, sleekly clothed in a coat of gray paint. I said to myself, Hurry up. It's no use dawdling. The afternoon coffee will be ready in the Garden Room. But there won't be equality cake—it's only the middle of May now, and the first cherries won't be ripe till June.

Skirting the wall, I reached the entrance of the drive. The gateposts were brilliantly whitewashed, but I refused to be dazzled by their surprising neatness; instead, I peered at them closely, searching in vain for a trace of the pedestals on which the stone poodles had used to sit—a pathetic pair, trying so desperately to look like lions. I might have known, I said to myself.

I turned into the drive, enclosed on one side by the stables and on the other by the garden wall, and picked my way through the soggy mud, between ruts and remnants of paving, barely glancing at the farmyard opening to my left. I followed the bend of the drive and stopped. Ahead of me, beyond the vast, rounded gravel space, stood the castle, its

matter-of-fact grandeur belying the absurdity of the fake
Gothic wing. With its lion-colored, rough-surfaced stones,
it had always looked more durable than neat, but now, to
my bewilderment, it had a new, smoothly delicious tidiness,
like an old print from which the smudges have been erased.
This, I saw, was because of the window frames, which were
painted a glossy white. I went across the gravel space, searching for the spot where the linden tree had been, but it had
vanished as completely as the poodles. I continued toward
the castle and found that the front door had vanished, too; it
had been transformed into twin pointed windows enclosed
in a pointed arch. But the door to the servants' entrance
stood ajar, and I went in.

I climbed the first flight of the servants' stairs and walked
along one branch of the passage, trying each of the six
doors there, knocking each time before attempting to enter.
They were all locked. I entered the other branch and tried
four more doors, including the last one, which shut off the
landing leading to the rooms overlooking the rose parterre
and the park. I knew that my last chance now to get into the
main part of the castle was to go up to the third floor and
descend from there by the iron snail—a harassingly steep
iron spiral staircase, which I had hated ever since I could
remember, and which still figured in my nightmares. Reluctantly, I started to climb the second flight, and came upon an
Irish setter stretched across the whole width of a step. He
didn't even bother to raise his head, and as I skipped over
him I began to wonder about the whereabouts of his master.

I halted and said over my shoulder, "Bark, will you? Bark and raise a noise."

He still didn't move, and I called, "Anybody there?"

I heard footsteps above me, and the closing of a door. Then silence. I called, "Anybody there?" There was the creaking of a door hinge, and further silence. I yelled, "Anybody there?" and then I saw a woman above me in the dark, shadowy passage, gripping the rail and bending over. I was choked with astonishment. What on earth is the cook doing up there, messing about in the spare rooms? I said to myself. And not properly dressed, either—slopping about in woollies and skirt and a tiny grubby apron? And since when has she had her hair waved? She does look a sight. Wait till I tell Grandmama.

"What do you want?" she said.

Startled by the indifference in her voice, I awoke from my hallucinatory state of still being Miss Edith. She was not the cook, she certainly could not be the cook; for one thing, she was about forty—much younger than I had ever known the cook to be. She was of a similar build, though, and as tall and heavy-boned. Her hair was dark, too, and the straight, thick Robespierre eyebrows were there, but tidier and more subdued-looking. She had the large-carved, gentle, sorrowing countenance of a Niobe, and lacked the cook's peppery intelligence.

"I'd like to see the castle," I said.

"Well, you can't," she said down the stairwell. "The curator's gone, and I haven't got the keys."

"But look here," I said. "I've come over here specially to see the castle."

"Then you must come another time, when the curator's here," she said. "Because he's gone and he's got the keys."

"When will he be back?" I asked.

"Not today anymore," she said. "Didn't you meet him on your way up from the village?"

"No," I said. "But when will he be in?"

"Can't say," she said. "Sometimes he's in and sometime's he's out."

"Charming," I said. "In that case, I suppose I'd better apply to him in writing, don't you think? And maybe he'll reply? That is, if he's in the mood?"

"You could try," she said.

She really is like the cook, I thought. Completely insensitive to sarcasm. Still craning up the stairs at her, I said, "I've come all the way from London to see the castle."

"Have you?" she said, without a sparkle of curiosity or a glimmer of doubt. "What am I to do? You could go and walk through the park. That's all right. You go and have a look at the park."

I knew I had lost, but forgot myself. It was like being slightly drunk, listening to myself talking, being perfectly aware of what I was saying, and yet being unable to stop myself saying it. "Blast you, woman," I said. "I've lived in this place on and off for years. My great-grandfather bought it, and my grandmother lived in it, and we managed without the blasted curator and his blasted keys!"

It was the worst possible thing I could have said. Everybody had told me, everybody had warned me, whatever I did, not to let on that my family had once owned the castle.

Now I watched her in dismay as she placed her hands on her hips.

"For heaven's sake," she said.

I'd better trot off, I thought. What if she calls the police? I've insulted her and the curator, and she and the curator are part of the people, and the people make up the People's Republic, which means I've insulted the state. I turned my back on her and descended the stairs; the dog was not there anymore.

"For heaven's sake, where are you off to?" I heard her calling.

I stopped and looked up.

"And why couldn't you say straightaway that you belong to the family?" she cried. "What do you imagine—how am I to recognize you, if you please, with all due respect, if I've been here only the last four years? Hold on, will you? I shan't keep you waiting. I'll only fetch the keys. I shan't be a minute."

She joined me on the stairs, clasping the keys to her waist. "You will excuse me, won't you?" she said. "I did hear a movement and someone calling, but I was cleaning upstairs, and I didn't expect— We don't want any of the people nosing around here. After all, it's a castle, isn't it? And there you were standing—I still don't know exactly who you are."

"I'm Edith," I said.

"Ah!" she cried, striking her forehead. "So you are little Edith. Miss Edith. The curator's got a photograph of madam your mother and your uncle Frederick when they were small, as lad and lassie in Austrian dress."

"I know the picture," I said. "I had it, too, and I've lost it. My mother holding a rake, God knows why, and Uncle Frederick with a spade, and edelweiss on his braces."

She nodded. "We've got a picture of the old gentry, too—your great-grandparents. But nothing of madam your grandmother. I've often wondered—"

"Don't ask me," I said. We were walking now toward the last door at the end of the passage. "What's happened to the stone poodles?" I asked.

"The poodles, yes. I never knew them, worse luck," she said. "They got smashed up before my time—willfully and nastily, you can bet. They say it was the Germans during the war, but if you ask me it was our own people. You don't know what they're like. They are proper fiends down in the village, and the farmyard persons are no better, either." She unlocked the door and stepped aside for me.

"My great-grandmother couldn't stand dogs," I said. "She used to point to the poodles and say, 'These are the only dogs I like.'"

"I must tell this to the curator," she said.

"I remember my great-grandmother, you know," I said. "I remember kissing her hand when I was four years old, and she was sitting on the bench that went round the linden tree—on the gravel space. She had disgusting hands, yellow and crinkled, and I loathed her. What's become of the tree? It was two hundred years old."

"I don't know again," she said. "That was before my time."

We were now on the main landing. She unlocked the second door and flung it open. "That's what you've come to see, isn't it?" she said. "The Austrian Room."

Standing at the threshold, I saw an expanse of clean but unpolished parquet floor and, beyond it, the three windows in their glossy white frames. My heart tightened. I thought, First the poodles and then the linden tree. And now what? I drew a deep breath and went inside. My deepest longing, my heart's desire, closed around me, enfolding me with its splendor. "Magnificent," I said.

"Yes, that's what it is. It's magnificent."

"It's overwhelming," I said. "But it wasn't like this. I didn't remember it like this. It was . . ." I paused, searching for words. The landscapes, especially the lakeside scenes, had a full shimmer, a melancholy and seductive depth, a surface serenity with an underlying hint of despair, which I had never known. "I can't understand it," I said. "It's so rich and so sad now. And it used to be more wishy-washy. Shallower and more gay. I suppose I used to be more wishy-washy myself, and more shallow and more gay."

"No fear," she said. "It's not you; it's the room. First they studied it and then they cleaned it."

"Who?"

"The professors from Prague," she said. "And they've written a book about it, too. About the painted rooms in the castle."

"Oh, God," I said.

"Didn't you know?" she asked. "They still keep coming out to study it. They are crazy about Navratil."

"Who is Navratil?"

"The finest painter in Bohemia, of that time," she said. "Didn't you know?"

"I never knew," I said.

"You were a little girl at the time," she said. "So you were not told."

"Nonsense," I said. "If I wasn't told, it wasn't for the lack of pestering. Nobody knew. And my grandmother, with her eternal 'Difficult to say. It's just a pleasant accident'—all because the two old maids, when they sold the castle, never told my great-grandfather. And the walls were plastered up, completely covered."

"That's right," she said, nodding her head. "The two Baronesses Wagner. And they had every blessed wall in this room plastered up because it irked them."

"What on earth?"

"Everything's been found out," she said. "They were leading a wild life, full of scandal, and never getting married, and traveling all the time, always on the move. First getting these paintings done to remind them of it, and then hiding them away to hide their past. Every panel is a real place, of course."

"Is it?" I said. "Nobody ever took it seriously."

"It's all been studied," she said. "Let me tell you. This is the Gmunden Lake, with the town of Gmunden behind it. This is the Dachstein."

I followed her, incredulous and bewildered, listening to this stranger, this pseudocook, who was taking me on a guided tour through the Austrian Room, and who knew the answers to questions that had haunted me for a lifetime.

"This here," she said, "is the Gastein waterfall."

"Oh, God, my favorite," I said. "With the chamois on top of the rocks."

"And these here," she continued, "are the two ladies Wagner, we think." She pointed at a couple of figures crouched on a mossy border at the foot of the cascade, white-robed and strikingly graceful, like ballerinas resting in the wings.

"But these are new," I said.

"That's right. They only came up two years ago. They had been painted out. And now, as I'm looking at you, I can see it could be you. Perhaps it is you. With madam your mother."

I thought, She really is like the cook. No sense of time—the only time she knows is when the cake is ready to be taken out of the oven. Then, growing serious at her reproachful stare, I said, "Please, go on."

"This here," she said, moving to the hilly meadows peopled with shepherds and shepherdesses, "is by the Wolfgang Lake, above St. Gilgen. Do you want a light on it? You've brought such dull, miserable weather with you."

"That's all right," I said. "It's so much bother bringing in the lamps."

"We've got electric light," she said.

"My grandmother could never afford it. But who is 'we,' anyway? Who's got the place now?"

"The place belongs to the workers, of course," she said,

"and it's being cared for by the Academy of Arts and Sciences. We've got nothing to do with the estate and the farm in the yard yonder. In the beginning, the farm people cast an eye on the castle, but heaven forbid! They would have used it as a pigsty. I mean it, because they've gone in for pigs now—one thousand pigs—and in the summer, when the wind turns! Just imagine what it would be like to get the farmhands swarming about in here. Beauty means nothing to them. They'd demolish the place. They are hellhounds, the folk round here; they are fiends and monsters. They'd burn and tear down everything they could lay hands on. Do you know what the park suffered since the gentry's days? What they've stolen and carried away in timber? You wouldn't know at first glance, of course, because the park is so immense, and thank heaven it's getting restored now—not that you won't weep over it when you see it, but we'll get it up to scratch again. We'll tackle the rose parterre first and get the fountain going—the boy with the goose and the boy on the dolphin, one above the other, and the water coming down."

"That's good news," I said, "as long as you don't ask me which boy goes on top of which. Because in my time the fountain was dry, and there was complete equality, because both boys were on the ground. They were in the garden, in one of the hothouses. But I suppose the curator will solve the problem."

She nodded. "He will. But it's got to be done slowly, because there's only so much money to go round. We had a lucky escape some time ago, when the gents from Prague wanted to turn the place into an old people's home. A convalescent home—I ask you! All because there's fifty rooms standing empty here, and that's not fair in a workers' republic. The curator says we've got the workers' revolution, and workers of the world unite—but not in the castle. We don't want a horde of old dodderers wiping their fingers on the walls of the Austrian Room. In the end, the academy people said it was much too damp and unhealthy here—it's true, isn't it? There's always the damp breathing in from the park—and sent them off to convalesce elsewhere, and I don't care how they rot, as long as it isn't here."

"Quite right, too," I said. "That's what's called a social conscience. My family was full of it, and I'm glad it's still about."

She looked at me with approval and nodded her head. Then her expression changed. "How did you use the Austrian Room?" she asked wistfully.

"For every day," I said. "As an ordinary drawing room."

"And it was luxuriously furnished?"

"Certainly not," I said. "It had the shabbiest junk you can think of—all simple but in bad taste, the overflow from my great-grandparents' town house. And in the bedrooms brass beds with broken knobs, and washstands with slop pails, and porcelain bowls and little pen trays that were used to hold toothbrushes."

She seemed crestfallen and gave me several probing looks, to make sure I was not making fun of her.

We went into the adjoining Saints' Room. "And how did you use this?" she asked eagerly.

"We didn't," I said. "It was too dingy and depressing. Only when we had visitors we weren't keen on, they got shoved in here to cool their heels." Observing her disappointed face, I added, "Of course, it wasn't like this. That painted ceiling was like potato soup, and you were lucky if you saw an odd arm or face sticking out."

I walked about contemplating the clean saints and angels on the ceiling, with memory and reality joining together like a completed jigsaw puzzle. For the first time, I saw that the greatest care, interest, and diversity had gone into the color and drapery of the garments; it was a celestial fashion show. "What a pity my mother never saw it like this," I said. "Who did it, do you know?"

"Navratil," she said. "Everything painted is by Navratil. He did it to show he could turn his hand to anything."

We went out onto the landing, where it formed an elbow. "Do you remember this?" she asked, leading me to the recess.

I was dumbfounded. It was like an inverted nightmare, where everything was better than it ought to be. The spiral stairs, which had been bleak, metal, mean, and ugly, were now entirely mahogany, of a superb dull finish. The spindle-turned railing was exquisitely fashioned, as though designed by Hepplewhite—a cabinetmaker's masterpiece.

"This used to be beastly cast iron," I said.

"Fancy," she said. "The curator says they were meant for certain purposes, for slipping away unseen and nobody any the wiser, if you get my meaning, so he had them done as they must have looked in the first place. And it's only fair, isn't it? If you have romantic stairs, you must treat them romantic."

"How right you are," I said, thinking she was more and more like the cook. I added, "This is a castle and not a poorhouse."

She nodded approvingly.

WE WENT THROUGH the Gothic wing and the library, where she said longingly, "You must have had wonderful books. I can just imagine."

I had to disappoint her once more. "We had no books at all," I said. "Only old account ledgers and seed catalogues and out-of-date timetables."

The afternoon was drifting away. "And now," said my guide, "we'll go down to the Garden Room and look at the parrots."

"They aren't parrots, they're crested cockatoos," I said.

"Never mind," she said. "We both mean the same thing. Do you know, I always think Navratil must have done the Garden Room at the very end, when he was good and tired, because it's only got three walls."

I started to laugh, but I fell silent when we arrived there, and I gazed with enchantment at this last and most frivolous of Navratil's creations.

"What did you use this room for?" she asked me. "For splendid feasts?"

"We had afternoon coffee in it," I said.

"And looked out on the rose parterre and the park? What a glorious sight it must have been."

"We never looked out on the rose parterre," I said. "We were too busy quarreling. Or complaining."

We stepped out on the terrace, descended the stairs, and went across the dismal grass plot into the park. "There's the opening of an underground passage at the end of the chestnut avenue," she said. "They are still working at it, digging it up. It's four kilometers long, and connects with the former Sternborn place, in Sestajovice."

"What on earth for?" I asked.

"They went in for that sort of thing in the old days," she said. "So that the gentry could run for it if trouble was brewing."

"A good idea," I said, giving her a sidelong glance.

"Naturally," she said. "We want everything the way it was in the old days."

"That's fine," I said. "It makes you feel the workers' revolution wasn't wasted, doesn't it?"

She nodded. "The curator says if the gentry hadn't built the castles the workers wouldn't be able to enjoy them now."

"What do you call this now?" I asked as we passed the walled-in well. "We used to call it the Jordan."

"We call it the Jordan, too," she said, "but we still haven't found out how deep it is, and where it goes to. Ah, this place is a marvel for mysteries. How you must have spent your days puzzling over them!"

"The only mystery we ever discussed was why the cook

had such black hair, considering she was older than my grandmother."

We were approaching a long line of trees; their boughs, to my astonishment, were reflected in a glistening sheet of water. "In my time," I said, "not even an elephant could have seen himself in the lake. It was so thick with filth it was like pea soup, and we couldn't get the gardeners to get down to it and clean it up. Your curator's obviously frightfully good with servants."

"There are no servants," she said. "They are employees of the state."

"Like those birds in the Garden Room," I said. "We both mean the same thing. And you've got the bridge repaired, too. In my time, it was broken, and nobody could get to the island."

"But what's the good of it?" she said. "There was this Chinese pavilion on the island. You knew it, didn't you?"

"Yes," I said.

"It's gone," she wailed. "And in Sestajovice, at the former Sternborns', there is a Chinese pavilion. They've still got theirs and we haven't. It isn't fair, is it? Why should they have it if we haven't?" She kept looking ahead of her, repeating, "It isn't fair, is it?" in an offended tone of voice.

As we made our way back to the castle, she asked with avidity for the names of the vanished exotic trees. Trying to console her, I said, "But look at the lilac. That's still the same, and it's coming out beautifully."

"Ah, that—that's nothing," she said crossly. "Anybody's got a lilac."

This made me remember Kucera and his fits of bragging, and, quoting him, I said, "It's not ordinary lilac, it's Persian, double-filled, and if somebody tells you he's got the same, anywhere up and down of Bohemia, then it's a lie, because what he's got is bushes, and ours is trees."

She grew cheerful at once. "Oh, really? I must tell this to the curator. He will be pleased."

We stopped at the foot of the ivied crenellations that circled the Gothic wing, where she showed me pieces of original lead piping which had been brought to light, and confronted me with the statues—the boy clutching the goose and the boy riding on the dolphin. I thought they did not make a happy pair, because the goose boy was as plain and discreet as the castle, while the other was as pretentious as the Gothic wing. My guide remarked, "The curator isn't sure about them yet. He thinks there must have been a little artificial waterfall at the end of the rose parterre and that's where the dolphin belongs. Do you have any idea?"

"No," I said, "but it's quite possible. Kucera, the head gardener, must have known and kept it quiet, because it would have interfered with his roses. That's the kind of man he was."

She gave me a probing, incredulous look. "He sounds like a Fascist to me," she said. "They've been stamped out now."

We reached the garden wall. "There's nothing there worth looking at," she said, "unless you want to see some smashed-up hothouses. But you don't want to leave without taking something alive away with you," and she stooped and picked three stalks of lilies of the valley.

"My mother's favorite flowers," I said. "Thank you."

We passed through a door and came out on the gravel space, where we were met by the setter. "You want to be careful of that dog," she said. "He's vicious. That's why we keep him."

"We've met before," I said. "On the servants' stairs—I mean the employees' stairs."

"And he let you pass?" she asked, stopping and looking at me full in the face.

"Of course," I said.

She struck her forehead. "Now I understand," she said. "He knows you belong. He knows you are the family." But this time I did not find her ridiculous. I had to suppress my rising tears.

We crossed the gravel space and halted by the drive. "I hope I'll catch the bus back to Prague," I said. "Do you know when it goes?"

"I don't," she said. "But if you miss it, come back and we'll put you up for the night. You don't think we'd turn you away, do you? Not that I'd like it to be known, because we haven't got any rooms to spare—not for anybody, and that's a fact. I've got two rooms and a kitchen off at that side, as you come in through the door, and it's cold and drafty in winter, you've no idea. But people always think—I don't know what they think. They think, Because it's a castle, and they don't know what it's like living in a castle. That's true, isn't it?"

"It is true," I said. "And good-bye and thank you."

"Good-bye," she said, hiding her hands under her apron.

Halfway down the drive, I turned and looked back, but it was stupid of me. I should have known that from there one could not see the castle anymore.

I walked back to the village, to the inn, where the inn-keeper told me that the bus would arrive in an hour's time. I asked for coffee and sat down on a bench close to the windows. There was a table of young men and a table of old men. They were all drinking beer, and the wireless was playing—a chorus singing Bohemian nursery songs that I knew by heart. The old men were discussing a tramway di-saster in Prague, and they cursed the government for being too stingy to keep the tracks in good repair. The young men talked about motorcycles, and then they went outdoors and stood about looking at each other's motorcycles. Then the innkeeper brought me a tumbler full of water to put my lilies of the valley in. But he did not ask me where I got them, or who I was, or what I was doing there.

A Coffeehouse Acquaintance

The man is always different in the beginning from anyone else one has ever known. By the time one has sorted him out as belonging to a certain type, the end is in sight, and he has become fit to be ranged on one of the shelves in memory's cupboard. But sometimes this is not possible. Despite a desperate search, the proper shelf cannot be found, and he cannot be stored away because one does not know what he is. One only knows what he was like.

On the first night of my arrival in Prague, I had dinner in the restaurant of the hotel where I was staying. On the second evening I would have liked to eat somewhere else, but when I saw that it was raining, I decided not to go out. The hotel was situated in a residential quarter, on a main road leading from a crossing at the nearby church along the ridge of a hill, running parallel to the course of the river below. It was a second-rate establishment of only sixty rooms, and part of a vast building which formed a whole block of the street, containing snack bars and beer cellars, a nightclub, banqueting halls, ballrooms for private hire, a wine tavern, a coffeehouse, and a restaurant.

At eight o'clock that evening the coffeehouse was half empty. The tables occupied were those close to the windows and walls, so that as I stopped by the swinging doors, the long room looked like one of those Brussels tapestries designed by several hands, where the richly wreathed surround has already been done but the center is still bare, waiting to be filled in. I walked down a path between the tables, toward the dining room, past a row of crescent-shaped blue-plush niches, each containing a group of guests. Only in the last one, nearest to the archway, there was a solitary man reading a newspaper. As I approached him, he said in a low voice and without raising his eyes from the paper, "Come here and sit down with me." It was murmured so casually that it sounded as though he were reading out loud a sentence to himself. As I moved past him, I heard his voice again: "Sit down." I entered the dining room, and only then, while pretending to look around to choose a seat to my liking, did I allow myself to glance at him. To my surprise, he was not looking in my direction, but was still bent over his paper.

I looked at him more fully and at leisure. He had large-waved, lion-colored hair which glinted like bronze in the light of the sconce above his head, and though he was not so

fair, he had the deep, evenly pink skin of white-blond people
who when exposed to the open air can neither freckle nor
tan. He had a long full face, a long tip-tilted nose, and long
straight lips, and he looked benevolent and dignified. Quite
apart from his hair, this also made me think of a lion, who
when at rest presents a deceptive picture of superb benevolence and harmlessness. At the end of the sleeve of his dark
brown lounge suit, I could see the cuff of his orange shirt,
and part of an orange sock between shoe and trouser leg,
and these seemed a bizarre contrast to his otherwise con-
ventional attire. But then his behavior too had been bizarre.

I sat down in a recessed bay from which I could not see
any of the blue-plush niches, nor be observed by anyone
occupying them. After I had ordered, I laid aside the novel I
had brought with me and began to reread the menu, which
I found astonishing. At the head of the impressively long
list of fare, there was the information that the dishes had
been chosen by Mr. Holub and approved by Mr. Dohnal,
the prices worked out by Mr. Drobny and checked by Mr.
Novak. Dishes marked with an asterisk were cooked in butter, nonmarked dishes in fat. The portions of meat served
amounted to one hundred and fifty grams, but in the case of
fowl, two hundred were provided. There is a Bohemian saying about a person one cannot make out: "I don't know
whether he comes at me with butter or with dripping," and
as I now recalled it, it occurred to me that this phrase must
have gone out of fashion.

About half an hour later, when I went back through the
coffeehouse, the man who had spoken to me was no longer

alone, but was listening to another man, who was standing in front of his table. He was not looking benevolent anymore either. He had his head tilted back and his eyes cast down, and he wore the expression of one hearing something he had been expecting but which he did not care to hear.

I went further down the room, past the glass doors, and sat down on a blue-plush bench close to a window and jutting into the room at a right angle, so that my book was turned to him. I ordered a black coffee and opened my book.

When a shadow fell over the page, I looked up. He was sitting down at my side. As I turned to him, speechless, he began to talk to me in a Slav tongue. I thought it was Russian, because I vaguely know the sound of it, just as I vaguely know what Polish sounds like. He was smiling all the time he talked, his teeth gleaming like freshly peeled almonds, and looking at me in a determined and cheerful way, as though convinced he would gain my approval. I waited till he stopped, then said in Czech, "I didn't get a word." He laughed and glanced at me as though unbelieving, then spoke again in the same tongue, still smiling and still more insistently. The sound of his voice, with the words rushing past, made me think of a horse in full canter. At the end of his speech he looked at me with such expectancy and encouragement that I started to laugh. "Sorry," I said. "I haven't got the faintest."

"Come on," he said, answering in Czech too. "Don't tell me you don't understand Russian."

"I don't—not a word."

"How is it possible?" he asked. "Then you really have no idea what I was telling you?"

I shook my head. During this exchange I had noticed that he was speaking Bohemian with the marked accent of the foreign Slav. Though he pronounced each word with ease, there was a shifting of emphasis, a derangement of rhythm, similar to the way Scottish people talk, who say "real*ize*" instead of "*re*alize."

"What was it you were telling me?" I asked.

"There is no need to repeat it," he said, "in any language. You know it anyway."

I did not reply.

"You needn't tell me anything," he added. "I know you are a lady; I know you did not come here to pick up a man." I continued silent. I half turned my head away from him, raised my eyes, and looked ahead of me to the narrow wall a few tables away. It was, I now saw, not paneled like the two long walls which held the windows and the niches, but set with an arc of pale green iridescent tiles, on which the reflected light shone in rainbow-colored streaks. In front, on a pedestal, stood a heroic-sized statue of a naked woman with mournfully bent head, as though she were inspecting the floor for cleanliness and not finding it to her liking. I was taken aback by the sight and turned toward him.

He was watching me. "You didn't know it was there, did you?" he said. "Disgusting, isn't it?"

"Amazing," I said. "Not exactly the decor one expects to find in a coffeehouse. But I wouldn't mind if it weren't so ugly. Still, I suppose there is something to be said for it. It is safe."

He said, "You mean a naked woman is a naked woman all the world over—is that it?"

"If you insist."

"I don't insist," he said, "and you are wrong. What if I chose to tell you that she represents Bohemia crushed under the Communist Russian yoke? It would make her highly objectionable, wouldn't it?"

I did not reply. Was he coming at me with butter, or with dripping?

"Or she could be Eve," he said. "In which case she would be acceptable. Because Adam and Eve were Russian— nothing to wear, only one apple tree between them, and being told they were in Paradise." He looked at me with an indulgently amused smile. I could not tell whether he was jeering at those in power or warning me not to do so. "Anyway," he continued, "I can tell that you haven't been around for quite some time."

My coffee was brought and he ordered a beer. "You should take Turkish coffee; it's much better," he said.

I said, "I had it yesterday and it was a dreadful fiasco. It has this crust on top, and when I poured, the crust dropped into the cup and the coffee splashed all over the place. And the beastly grounds floated about and nearly choked me."

"Let me show you," he said. "With me, everything goes smoothly. You can rely on me." And he gave the order as the waiter brought his beer. He took a sip and said, "The beer they give you here is Budweiser, and I come here only when I feel lazy, because farther up the street, at Soyka's, they have pilsner."

"I never heard of Soyka's," I said, "but then, we didn't live in these parts."

"I live near here," he said. "I have a flat only two hundred yards away. I'll write it down for you. Give me your notebook." Seeing my hesitation, he added, "Of course you have a diary. Every woman has a diary."

I blushed and reached into my handbag and gave him my little notebook. I was annoyed with myself for not having refused his request, and sensing his amusement at my confusion, I could not gather my wits.

He opened the notebook unhesitatingly at the month of April, turned to the date of the day, the twenty-seventh, took a gold fountain pen from his breast pocket, and wrote, in a hand so large that it covered all four lines reserved for each day, "Konstantin Blonik" and the name of the street and a number. The letters were so boldly written, with curls around the *K* and the *B,* that they made me think of an aria embellished with coloratura trills. "Now you've got me black on white," he said.

"I don't care one way or the other," I said, still looking at the open diary he had returned to me. But I did care. The very Russian, noble, large-limbed Konstantin was ill matched to the Blonik, of vaguely Slav origin, vulgar, undersized, like a mongrel. And it occurred to me that in his manner of speech, there was the same split. At first, when he had been speaking Russian, he had been aglow with a barely restrained fire. Ever since he had been Czech, he had been dull and sober.

"Now you are disappointed, aren't you?" he asked, watching me.

"Not disappointed," I said. "It's just . . . the Blonik doesn't sound Russian at all."

"I can't change my name just to please you," he said. "Would you rather have had me less truthful?" I shook my head. "And here is your Turkish coffee. Allow me." I watched as he seized the stem of the brass pot, tilted it slowly, held a spoon against the crust floating on top, and poured till the pot held nothing except the thick layer of grounds. "And now you have clear coffee and can stir to your heart's content."

As I took my first sip, he picked up my book. I had forgotten about it; I had not even realized that I had laid it on the table when he sat down. "Let me see what you're reading," he said.

"It's an English novel."

"I know hardly any English," he remarked. "Just what I learned at school. And the same with French. I speak Romanian and Hungarian fairly well, but that's nothing to be proud of, that's all in the day's work. Now let me see." He opened the book, looked at the flyleaf, shut it again, and said, "That's not an English-language edition. These paperbacks are not allowed to be sold."

"Aren't they? I didn't know," I said. "And I bought it in

London just now. I flew from London yesterday. I only arrived in Prague last night."

"Did you?" he said. "Let me have another look at it. It's called *The Pumpkin Eater*. 'Eater'—that's from 'eating'; 'eater' is a man who eats, that I do understand. And 'pumpkin'—"

I said hastily, "A pumpkin is a kind of large—"

He stopped me by raising his hand. I expected him to say something like, never mind, who cares? Instead he said impatiently, "You needn't explain. I know."

I was too startled to speak.

He laid the book down. *"Milostivá paní,"* he said, using the most respectful mode of address, which means "gracious lady," "I would like to continue this acquaintance in a way which is not possible sitting here and talking. But I cannot entertain you at my place tonight. I left it to friends, a man and his wife; they came from outside and were stranded. I'm like that; I can never say no to anybody. I moved to a room in the apartment of some people I happen to know. It isn't as comfortable as my own flat but it is decent enough. Now I suggest you go up to your room and fetch your coat while I get mine from the cloakroom here, and I'll wait for you downstairs."

"How do you know I'm staying here at the hotel?" I asked.

"Because you are not the kind of woman," he said, "who would dine alone and sit about alone, in ordinary circumstances. But tell me, why are you staying here? It is a bad hotel."

"I couldn't get in anywhere else," I said. "For six weeks the travel people in London kept me hanging about, dithering, and in the end they couldn't find anywhere decent for me. They said I'd better try my luck when I arrived here."

"I'd never stay in a hotel like this," he said. "When I travel I only stay in first-class places. I don't pay, of course; they pay for me. Now let us go."

When I came out of the lift he was nowhere in sight, but as I handed in my key at the reception desk, I saw him through the glass doors, standing in the street under the roof of the entrance, his back turned to me.

I went outside and stopped, still behind him, and observed him while I was slowly drawing on my gloves.

He was wearing a silky dark blue raincoat. The tall-crowned, wide-brimmed felt hat made him appear doubly outlandish, used as I was to menswear in London, and in contrast to the hatless men I had seen in Prague. He was leaning slightly forward over his furled umbrella, clasping the crook of the handle with both hands. As I watched, I saw that he was not gazing idly into space. The movements of his head betrayed that he was following the flow of the streetcars, automobiles, and passersby. This calmly alert stance had a balladesque quality, bringing to mind a shepherd on the crest of a hill, leaning on his staff and observing his flock, the distant valley below, and the sky above.

As I stepped soundlessly to his side, he said without turning his head, "It's only drizzling now, but I'll put the umbrella up for you. Let it earn its keep."

I laughed uneasily. I wondered whether he had sensed

that I had been watching him. I said, "You are taller and broader than I thought. If you are ever out of work, come to London and join the police."

"Why? How is that?" he asked.

I said, "Because for certain duties they need men of six foot two, and they want six-footers in any case. Nowadays they have such difficulty getting men of the right size that they even take shorter ones."

I expected him to laugh. To my surprise, he said gravely, "I'd be too old for them. I'm forty-two. Now shall we go?"

I returned to the hotel on the following morning shortly after eight. It was only an hour later, when I was bathed and half dressed and sitting over my second cup of milk and coffee, that I recovered from feeling dazed and drained, and started to frame questions. By then I already knew that even if I did see him again, I would not dare to ask the questions, let alone hope to receive answers.

There are people who, let us say, have a conspicuous jagged scar on their forehead, and even on first acquaintance one can ask them freely how they came by this disfigurement, and they will not be offended by this frank curiosity. With others, owing to invisible signals they radiate, one senses that one may never intrude on them with such a question. The Russian belonged to this group.

He had taken me up the main road, in the direction of the castle hill, and into a tree-shaded street branching off it that was lined with large houses dating from before the First World War. On the second floor of one of these, he had let himself in with his key into a dark hall and taken me to a room at the end of a long passage. He made not the slightest attempt, as is usual on such occasions, to impress on me the need for silence. It did not surprise me that the room was shabbily furnished with the white-lacquered pieces, cane chairs, and cretonnes belonging to the same period as the building, but only now, as I recalled it, did I remember that there were twin beds. Why, then, had he moved out of his flat for the sake of accommodating "a man and his wife who had come from outside," and why, if the room belonged to some people he "happened to know," was he so careless about making noise? When I reproved him once, for banging the door of the bathroom, he said, laughing, "I should worry." In the morning he had offered me the use of his kitchen and the bath without bothering to ascertain if they were free. And all the time there had been utter silence, none of the irrepressible sounds of a large lived-in flat whose occupants are getting ready to start the day. And yet he had made me get up early, at half past seven, saying that he had to go to work. There was no doubt about it: the whole apartment must have been empty.

He did not ask me whether he could see me again. We had walked briskly in the rain toward the hotel, and he left me at the entrance with a hurried good-bye, *milostivá paní*. As I visualized him now, hastening away in the direction of the crossroads by the church, it occurred to me that he had not been dressed in the lounge suit and raincoat of the night before, but in flannels, a woolen shirt, and a short gray zippered coat. Why, if he was occupying the room for one night only, had he brought with him a change of clothing?

That day the rain never stopped, and though I pretended to be vexed about it, I was secretly glad, as it gave me an excuse for staying in that night once more. I was halfway through my meal when I saw the Russian standing in the archway of the dining room, still dressed as he had been in the morning. He came to my table, lifted my hand, and kissed it. "I must apologize," he said, "I'm only just now back from work. I had dinner there. Finish your meal while I go home and change; I'll be with you by the time you are ready for your coffee. But wait for me, I'll pour it for you."

"Did you eat well?" he asked me twenty minutes later, as he sat down by my side at the same table we had been at the night before. By the time I finished dinner it had become vacant, and an elderly waitress had come up to me triumphantly and asked me to move, "so that the gentleman will not crick his neck trying to find you."

I said, "I got everything I wanted, but I don't know if I've got my memories wrong or if the present isn't really up to scratch."

He gave me an indulgently resigned laugh. "Now you are disappointed," he said, "just as you were about my name. You are a romantic. Besides, this isn't a first-class place."

"And besides," I said, "it's off-putting the way they write the menu. I don't want to know that Mr. Novotny has checked the prices, or that I'll be getting a hundred and fifty grams of rib beef, no more no less. It's like being in a clinic."

"Ah, that," he said. "You know, when I first went to Romania—I was in Romania for two years—and had my first meal there, I was dumbfounded. To start with, they brought the whole tureen for the soup, the way it's done in Paris, and when I ordered a steak, they gave me more than a quarter of a kilo. I couldn't believe it. All the time it was like that. I don't know how they do it; their economy is quite different. Altogether I liked it there. You sit in a place on top of a hill, with green trees all around you, and a band is playing. In the whole of Prague there is nothing like it. They have a gift for luxury, and the women—they are so elegant. They turn away their faces from the countries around them and they look to France. And believe me, Czech men are out of luck there—they despise the Czechs. And they are dainty and beautifully groomed, with eyes like black cherries— nothing like what you see here. These insipid blond Bohemian women—I can't stand blondes, by the way—with their pale, calculating little eyes, all sturdy cart horses, with large hooves and big fetlocks. Such good dependable comrades and helpmeets—it turns my stomach. Now you can guess why I like you so much, *per exclusionem*."

I smiled and averted my eyes. I said, "There are ravishingly pretty girls here, and you know it."

"So what if there are?" he said. "Even if they are acceptable in their looks, they stick in my gullet. You meet one, and even before you've had time to ask her if she likes her coffee black or white, out comes the hatchet, and she'll hack away at you—where you work, what kind of position you have, how much you earn. Revolting. You are a different breed. And of course, you are a foreigner."

"I am not," I said. "I was born and bred in Bohemia."

"That may be," he said, "but that doesn't mean you weren't born of foreign parents."

"I'm Bohemian through and through," I said. "My great-grandparents from both sides came from the south of Bohemia."

"And where did their parents come from?" he said. "But let's leave it at that. The main thing is that you are here now. Let me look forward every morning to the night and every night to the morning." I averted my eyes again, and as he passed me my filled cup he added, "At least by now I know how you like your coffee."

We went on talking. In his grammatically perfect Czech, he used literary, sometimes almost obsolete expressions, while I kept falling into the dialectical speech and schoolgirl slang of my childhood, such as, "That's on cement," when I meant that's certain, or, "All the frogs in my class," when I meant the girls, or, "I cough on it," when I meant contempt. Each time he shook his head reprovingly, saying, "The expressions you use." And when I laughed, he said, "I know you think I am a pedantic bore and a puritan. Well, yes, I am."

I said, "You can't be, really, or you wouldn't be here sitting with me now. You should be ashamed of yourself. You still don't even know my name. And it was disgraceful of me to go along with you last night. Like the lowest of the low."

"What a charming little fool you are," he said, "What do you know of the lowest of the low? Now come. I'll take you to my place."

The house he lived in was on the opposite side of the street, two minutes' walk away. Like most of the buildings in the street, it had been daringly modern in the time of my youth, with bands of tiles and marble on the façade and no moldings above the windows.

We took the lift up to the sixth floor. "It's only a *garçon-nière*," he said, "nothing much, but very comfortable, and the water is always scalding hot, and the heating is so efficient I have to open the windows even in the coldest weather." We entered a large square hall. "The geography is simple," he said. "The doors which aren't cupboards open here to the bath and here to the other place. There wasn't a kitchen; I carved it out of the shower closet. And now come in." We entered a modest-sized room. He went over to the radio by the French window and switched it on, saying, "Let it play to earn its keep. I'll turn it off if you don't like it."

Looking around, I thought it odd that the hall should have been of such impressively large dimensions, consider-ing the smallness of the flat—all the more so as his entrance door was the only one on that side of the landing. On enter-ing, I would have guessed it to be a four- or five-room flat, opening out from those doors which, according to him, were merely cupboards.

While he put away my coat I surveyed the room. It was lined with new-looking sideboards and paneled cabinets of dark red-flamed tropical wood with frosted glass insets, and contained a very wide divan, a desk, and glass-topped tables. The floor was covered with linoleum patterned to look like parquet. The room looked as though it had been furnished in the course of a five-minute visit to a store and, since there were no pictures or other ornaments, this time limit had run out before he had remembered to think of these.

Returning and seeing me pacing about, he smiled, pulled out drawers, and slid back panels and showed me cutlery, each piece in a nest of felt of its own, and tea and coffee and dinner sets for twelve, of a dim-flowered china of decent quality and discreet bad taste. The tableware and the room itself were the kind my charwoman in London and her husband would have longed to possess and would have bought on the installment plan. The china would never have been used and the room would have been called their front parlor.

He said, "And here is the roof terrace, if you want to come out and look for a moment. Not exactly an inspiring view even when it isn't raining—the part of golden Mother Prague of the hundred domes and spires which the tourists never see."

I followed him out to the spacious flagged terrace and looked at the distant factory chimneys of the industrial sector, which I knew bordered one side of the river, though I could not glimpse the water. "Then the terrace doesn't earn its keep?" I asked.

"It does," he said. "I air my bedding there when it's fine, the way it's got to be done. You can rely on me."

Closing the French window and drawing the curtains, he said, "The other day a friend came to see me. He's living it up in a luxury flat on the quaiside, with the old bridge and the castle hitting him right in the face every time he puts his nose outside his window, and he said, 'Come on and join the

Party and be one of us and you'll live the way I do. It's going to last another ten years, and then I'll commit suicide when it cracks.' At least he was sincere. But I'd rather stick to my shabby view. I will not join. I will not sit and nod my head and say yes and amen. Again and again they've come and begged me to join. They sent me to Marienbad too, once, to the ideological seminary. I took along some old newspaper cuttings and every time the lecturer imparted a new piece of official interpretation, I got them out and said, 'If you please, but last year or two years ago the official view was different; how is that feasible, with all due respect?' Till they told me they could do without me. In the Party, about two percent of the members are idealists and genuinely convinced. Mind you, I've nothing against the regime by and large, taking a generous view of it, but I won't be one of them. And the way they run their economy is a disgrace."

"I can't judge it. I don't know anything about it," I said.

"Where is the caviar?" he asked, facing me in full indignation. "I haven't seen any caviar for a year. That's just to give you an example you will understand."

"I haven't seen caviar for much longer," I said, and burst out laughing.

"You are a little fool," he said, "but that's as it should be, and a woman who is not a fool is not a woman. Now what would you like to drink? I can't do any serious drinking in the bars and other public places because they don't have the genuine stuff. What would you care for? White Label, Queen Ann, two vodkas—not Polish, heaven forbid—and Courvoisier." He slid aside a panel.

"Golly," I said, "that's from the Tusex shop, isn't it, where you pay with hard currency? That must have cost you a fortune."

"You could break my heart with your innocence," he said. "You are like Little Red Riding Hood who's come to visit the wolf. For one thing, nothing costs a fortune. You forget we are in a people's democracy. And besides, this is not Tusex stuff. They have decent liquor here, but not this. Now what may I give you?"

"Nothing," I said. "I'm very cheap that way. I only like a glass of red wine at night with my dinner, that's all."

He said, "In that case, if I guaranteed you your daily glass of red wine, would you stay with me?"

I laughed. He said, "Truer things have been spoken in jest." I did not reply. He said, "If you won't have a drink, I shan't have one either. I think we can both do with an early night. I won't go to work tomorrow, so we can sleep long. I'll only look in on them at midday for half an hour or so, to see what they have been brewing up in the laboratory."

On the following morning, as I sat up in bed, he said, "If you want to go to the bathroom, don't get up yet for a moment," and he rose, went out, and returned at once. "Here, put these on," he said. "I don't want you to catch cold. I don't know how I came to have them, but here they are," and he placed before me a pair of ladies' slippers. They were of the most common kind, gray felt with brown and black checks. When I met his eyes, he made a gesture of resigned helplessness.

He was still in bed when I came back to the room, fully

dressed and with my hair plaited and coiled at the nape of my neck. "I'll have breakfast in the hotel," I said, "just to make a good impression on them."

"You are a little fool," he said. "As though they didn't know you spent the night elsewhere. And will you really go through the business of taking your hair down and undressing and putting on your nightgown, just to impress the chambermaid with your virtue?"

"I will," I said, "even if you think it's screamingly funny."

"You are in a bad mood," he said.

"Am I?" I said.

"And I know why," he said. "It's because the slippers were not to your taste."

"That's true," I said, "and in more ways than one."

"Look here," he said, "I will get you a pair of slippers—anything you like—on one condition. You go back now and pack your trunk and move in with me. What's the good of staying there? You have no comfort, you haven't got a telephone in your room, and no private bath. And it costs you money. I'll give you a key and you can go and come as you please and I shall never question you. You will be free. But I'd be much happier if I had you here with me."

"It's very kind of you—," I said.

"But?"

"But I can't do it."

He leaned back against the pillows, watching me.

"I can't afford it," I said. "I've got a husband, and he knows I've put up at this hotel, and if he phoned or anything . . . I can't take the risk."

"Don't ever speak to me of your husband again," he said.

"He comes to the same thing as the slippers," I said.

He said, "You'll be sorry for that remark."

I did not speak.

He said, "If you won't leave the hotel, at least you needn't eat there. They cook with car grease and floor polish, for all one knows. I want you to come here tonight and have dinner with me. All cooked in butter—you can rely on me."

I smiled. I asked, "And what will I have to do to earn my keep?"

"*Milostivá paní*," he said, "you are not for use, you are for pleasure."

THAT EVENING, on entering his room, I went over to the bookcase. It was filled with many-volumed works on history and economics. On the ledge of the stand holding the television set, there was a stack of journals and a single book. I picked it up. It was entitled *Happiness in Married Love* and was written by a gynecologist. I said, "That's the only worthwhile book you've got, as far as I'm concerned. It looks heaven. Is it good?"

"That rubbish," he said. "How should I know? I haven't read it. I really don't know how it got here." He gave me the same helplessly resigned smile and gesture as he had that morning when producing the slippers.

"May I read it?" I asked.

"You may," he said. "I'll see about dinner and you sit with married love in the meantime."

"Don't you want me to help you?"

"I don't."

"Goody, goody," I said. "I hate to give the helping hand. I don't like to receive it, either, which means that my laziness is not really—"

"You needn't make any excuses," he said. "I'll tell you straight out that I never want you to touch anything in the kitchen. You could kill yourself if you tampered with it. I rigged it up myself—the hot plates and kettle and grill—in a most unorthodox manner, with high-frequency current which is forbidden in dwelling places, and I have to switch transformers and adaptors all the time because there is only one plug socket." He gave his indulgently resigned laugh and added, "That's the only practical advantage I got out of reading physics. Of course, I was lucky, I am of poor parents, so they sent me to the university. I was always a heavy gun, already at school, in mathematics and physics, but it's a disgrace, their legislation, as though the innocent children of rich bourgeois parents could help it that their parents had been rich. Now they've realized that some of them are brainy too, and they admit them for higher studies."

"You have a degree in physics?" I asked.

"Of a kind," he said. "But when the radio goes wrong or the television, I am no use, and I have to get it repaired, like everybody else."

He laid the table with two sheets of felt and a cloth. "You are laughing at me now, because I'm so pedantic. But it's got to be."

Half an hour later he carried in giblet soup, asparagus,

boiled chicken, and rice. He poured red wine. "The wine is good," he said. "When I tell you, you can rely on me. Wine I do understand. I was brought up in a wine shop."

"But the asparagus," I said, "you shouldn't have . . . It must be the first this year—it's the end of April."

"One must eat something," he said, "and there are no run-of-the-mill vegetables just now, not even ordinary greens for the soup. Mismanagement of transport and distribution. Where are the carrots and leeks and parsley root and parsnips? It's a disgrace."

"But what do the poor common people do?" I said.

He said, "You mean the people. There is a compote of apricots and cherries, homemade, out of the glass. Do you want it with the meat, or later?"

When we had coffee I said, "Now comes the painful and unavoidable question, the way Virgil put it, when he wrote about washing up, *'venit summa dies and ineluctabile tempus.'*"

"Don't worry about it," he said. "That will be seen to tomorrow."

I said, "Better get it over with now. I'm quite used to it from London, and shared misery is halved misery."

He said, "Maybe, but you forget we are in a workers' democracy. Someone will attend to it tomorrow. I'll only stack away the plates and dishes now, and you can't help there either, because the kitchen is too small for two. The best thing for you, altogether, is to keep away from the kitchen."

I said, "For ever and ever, amen."

He was not amused, but nodded gravely. I thought that his utter lack of humor and irony was probably typically

Russian, so different from the Czechs, who never fail to insert a bitingly disrespectful and sarcastic comment. It also occurred to me that I had never seen him burst into genuine openhearted laughter. Unlike most people, who have several kinds of laughter, he had only one kind, of the indulgently resigned sort, which was no more than a symbolic show of amusement. I wondered whether this lack of spontaneity was not due to his speaking in Czech, and I recalled the fire with which he had been aflame, in those first few minutes, when he had spoken to me in Russian.

There was yet another thing which made me wonder. On all those occasions when he had informed me that we were in a people's democracy, he had stated this in such a way that it was impossible to tell whether he jeered or approved. Was he coming at me with butter, or with dripping? But soon I ceased to wonder. He had crowned an excellent meal with excellent coffee, and I was filled with the drowsiness of well-being.

When I told him that I would be going to the theater on the following evening, he said, "Then you will get back to the hotel by ten, and I'll wait for you in the coffeehouse. But I want you to understand once and for all, I hate eating out and I hate eating alone, and I want you to eat here with me. I am limited in what I can do, but everything I do is first-rate, I promise you. And when the warm weather sets in at last, I'll make you some cold supper dishes. I'll make a brawn of pork and veal, and the aspic will be crystal clear—I pass it through muslin, you can rely on me—and with it I'll give you a sauce *tartare,* but a proper one. When it comes to *sauce tartare* I can look anyone straight in the face and needn't bow my head in shame."

"Is that the one with crushed egg and chives?" I asked.

"No, that's *rémoulade*," he said. "And now you are laughing at me again because I'm so pedantic. But I don't mind. Go on, laugh. Why have you suddenly turned serious?"

"Because I've just been thinking," I said. "When it turns really hot, I shan't be here anymore. I leave the first week in June."

"Don't leave," he said.

"I can't stay on," I said, "and you know why."

"I do know," he said. "We had this the other day. You can stay here with me and get a divorce in absentia. And your husband can whistle for you. As long as you are here with me, he can't get at you."

"You forget that I am British," I said.

He said, "You are British and you are wrong. A people's democracy is beyond the reach of the capitalist states."

"There is a British consul in Prague," I said. "What is he here for—to pick his nose?"

"The expressions you use," he said. "But yes, that's exactly what he is here for."

"How do you mean?"

"Because," he said, "you are here in the country of your birth. The British cannot protect their nationals if they happen to be in the country of their birth. If you were put in prison here, nobody from over there could interfere."

"I know," I said. "I was warned about that before I came out here. But I didn't think you knew."

"You are a little fool," he said. "It's no secret—it's printed on every British passport."

"I can't leave my husband," I said.

"Nonsense," he said, "you've left him already as it is."

"Don't be ridiculous," I said. "I only came out here for six weeks. And what's wrong with that? It's my hometown, and to him it's nothing—he would only be bored."

"You are exactly what I want," he said. "And you are not what your husband wants or he wouldn't have let you travel alone. Do you think I'd ever let you travel alone?"

I did not reply.

"You needn't decide," he said, "but I can take the decision out of your hands. Come to bed now."

I went to the theater the next evening, as I had intended to, and after that, several times more, and though his attitude toward art in general was one of respectful indifference, each time he tried to discourage me from seeing that particular performance. "You are going to the Viola tonight? Yes, avant-garde cabaret, I know. And avant-garde it certainly is, the avant-garde of expressionism, the way it was done in Berlin thirty years ago." Or, "Tonight it's opera, isn't it? Oh, yes, *The Bartered Bride*. I might have known. That's a phenomenon for you. They play it year in, year out, at least once a week, and every performance is sold out. You haven't seen it since before the war. You'll be thrilled to see the eighteen-year-old Marenka sung by a well-preserved post-climacteric lady. Altogether, when one goes to the Prague opera nowadays, one gets the impression that all young women born in Bohemia and Moravia in the last twenty-five

years were born mute. Of course, it may be better in Bratislava, for all I know. The Slovaks have more get-up-and-go, I
believe. Why don't you take a plane to Bratislava and have a
look at what's cooking in their culture pot?"

I said, "Oh, the Slovaks—I cough on them."

"I wish you wouldn't use these expressions," he said. "But
the way you said, 'Oh, the Slovaks,' with that hatred and
contempt—now at last I know that you are really and truly
from Bohemia."

"How do you mean?" I asked. "Of course I am really and
truly—I told you so, didn't I, the first evening I met you."

"So you did," he said pleasantly, "but I didn't believe you."

"You didn't?"

"I did not. I also didn't believe you when you told me you
had flown in from London the day before," he said, still with
the same pleasantness.

"You didn't believe that either?" I asked.

He said, "No, but I know now that it was true."

I said, "But if you had asked me, I could have shown you
my passport. It's written in my passport that I was born in
Prague."

"I wouldn't have wanted to see your passport," he said,
"even if you had offered to show me."

"Why on earth not?"

"What is a passport? A passport doesn't mean anything."

I felt deeply flustered. I said, "No, of course not. I hadn't
thought of it, but I suppose you are right."

He said, "You are a charming little fool, and the less
thinking and supposing you do, the better."

I felt my face turning hot under his glance. Though his voice had remained smoothly pleasant, his countenance had lost the benevolence of the lion at rest. Was he warning me not to try guessing why I should not enter the kitchen, or whether there were doors hidden behind the built-in wardrobes in the hall, or all the other questions which kept coming to mind? I forced myself to laugh, and said, "If I stay with you much longer, I'll stop thinking altogether and become a complete cow. I'm well on the way already, as it is, what with you giving me these marvelous meals and coffee—and the rest . . . I don't know how to explain it."

"You needn't explain," he said, in the tone of curt finality he had used that first evening about the pumpkin. "You have calmed down beautifully. If I may be zoological, when I first met you, you were restless and questing like a goat, and now you are serene like a ewe."

"Now you are talking like Khrushchev," I said. "Once he made a speech about foreign countries, and he said, 'This particular hen shouldn't be cackling just now.' "

"Oh, Khrushchev," he said. "I met him once and he shook hands with me. That was in Hungary when he came on a state visit. I happened to be a rather high . . . official at the time."

I noticed the hesitation and kept silent, adding it to the collection of facts about him which I had gathered. On the whole, ordinary conversation was not possible with him, because I could not ask him any questions. Mostly he expanded in monologues about the economy of the country and its mismanagement, and I soon stopped trying to follow his words and merely listened to the sound of his voice. He had a deliberate and decisive way of speaking, and owing to the shifts of his Russian accent, his full, hard baritone had a quality like the glitter of brocade. And yet I was not bored. I fell into a daze of well-being, of feeling secure and at peace, and I only roused myself from this languor when he said, "Now I'll see about the dinner," or, "Now I'll give you a last cigarette and then I'll take you to bed." This feeling of being bewitched in his company never left me, and it was underscored by the fact that we were sitting in a room on the top floor, as though in a lighthouse or in a shepherd's hut on top of a hill, each of us alien to the character of the room, each of us not belonging to the city beyond, and enjoying luxuries which were unobtainable to the common herd.

By then it was obvious to me that whatever his work, it was not an office job; he did not get up at the same hour every morning. Moreover, I could not picture him doing any kind of sedate work. I could never rid myself of my first impression, of seeing him as a balladesque shepherd figure observing his flock; this open-air look of his was due not only to his deep pink out-of-doors complexion but also to his powerful body, recalling that of a dockworker or woodcutter.

A few days later he again asked me to marry him. He said, "Husbands can be left and I am free. I'm divorced; I got my divorce two years ago. One day at breakfast I get this anonymous letter. I pass it over to my wife and I ask, 'Is this true?' 'It is true,' she says, 'and it's been true for the last two years.' So I took her to court. But she played her cards badly be-

188   EDITH TEMPLETON

cause the man left her three months later. She is doing very well, she has a job with the government; she is a Party member. And that's why, when it came to splitting up, I had to let her have the car and I only got the country cottage. I've still got the cottage, but I haven't been there for the last six months—it's no use to me. I'm going to sell it now and get a car again. So now you know how I stand. I'm free to marry you."

"I can't," I said. "I've got a child. And you haven't, have you?"

"No, thank God," he said. "I used to wish for one, but as it turned out, it's a blessing."

Yet only on the following day, when I told him I had taken lunch in the Brussels Pavilion in Belvedere Park, he said, "That was my daughter's favorite place. After every walk through the park, it was, 'Daddy, now we'll go to the pavilion and you will order a little plate with a little ham for me.' "

"Oh."

He said, "I didn't want to bring it up the other day; it's too painful to talk about her. And do you know, there happened to be a party there once, of Chinese children, and they crowded round my little girl and she looked at them so bewildered, with her big blue eyes, and then she fed them the ham. It was touching. I see her from time to time, of course. She's eight years old now and goes to second grade—primary. But I wasn't soft with her. If she didn't arrange her shoes and clothes properly at bedtime, there was nothing doing, I wouldn't say good night. She'll be spoiled now, and that's the worst for me, not the wife."

He continued to resent my going to the theater, but once he took me out himself. This was only, he stressed, because it was a Russian show, the Alexandrovniks, a famous group of military performers who were internationally known and had not come to Prague for ten years.

It was on this occasion that I came to add two further items to my collection, and I found them the most interesting I had received. One occurred when he explained to me the military ranks of the performers. The tenor who was singing was a major; and the conductor, "He is pretty high. He is a general, but not a full general. I have a brother who is a very big gun indeed. He is a general in the Russian army, and he was a full general already when he was twenty-eight. At that time he was the youngest general in the Russian army." He gave his indulgently resigned laugh and added, "I haven't seen him for ten years."

The other occasion happened during the interval, while we were standing in the foyer. A man passed by us and greeted him respectfully; he was obviously hesitating whether to stop or to walk on. Then, glancing at me, he bowed and went away. "Funny that I should run into him again," said the Russian. "I haven't seen him for years. Of course, I might have known he'd be here. He's on duty."

"How do you mean?" I asked. "He doesn't look like a journalist. Is he the theater doctor?"

"No, you little fool," he said. "Nowadays it isn't doctors who are on duty in a theater. He is secret police." And seeing my astonishment, he added, "That's normal and proper. They have to walk about among crowds listening to what people say. Then they hand in their report on the mood and the morale of the population."

"Good God."

"It's done all the world over," he said. "It's funny the way I met him. That must have been . . . ten years ago, in the summer. I was staying in Moravia in a resort, for a holiday, and this man kept getting into conversation with me and tagging about after me on all my walks. He was quite pleasant, but I just didn't want him. In the end he said to me, 'I do like you so much, you are such good company. Don't worry, you may talk to me quite freely, I am secret police.' He was quite sincere, of course. He longed to be friends."

"And were you?"

"No," he said, smiling, "of course not. The fool. Czech secret police. The Czech idea of security. You drive out into the country, into the sticks, and you get out and there is a little gnarled wrinkled nut of a woman, and you say to her, 'Little mother, I am looking for a certain special place, away from the village—a busy place, little mother, with soldiers running in and out like ants on an ant heap,' and she says, 'You mean the launching pad for the rocket.' "

During my whole stay, there were only four nights I did not spend with him, and this was because twice he went away, each time for two days. About the first journey he said nothing at all; about the second he said, "I had to go to Bratislava, and I thought, Shall I take the plane? I'm such an unlucky person, if I take the plane it will crash. So I took the train. And unlucky as I am, the heating in the train broke down and it was chilly during the whole ten hours. And on top of it I lost my fountain pen. I'd had it for six years, drat it. It's no use looking for it—it's gold, unfortunately."

"How did you lose it?"

"I didn't lose it," he said, "not exactly. I used it and put it down, and went out in a hurry because I wanted to speak to someone, and then I had to go off with him and couldn't go back anymore."

"That's awful."

He gave his indulgent laugh. "I'm unlucky altogether," he said, "because I want you and nobody but you, and you won't stay with me."

His "I'm unlucky altogether," though in utter contradiction to his usual "With me everything goes smoothly," did not astonish me. It was no more than the remark of a man who has every reason to be pleased with himself, and it served the same purpose as the tiny black beauty patch used by rococo ladies to enhance, by contrast, the fairness of their skin.

DURING MY STAY in Prague, I had been searching for my favorite cousin, Ferdinand. The last time I had heard from him, shortly after the war, he had still lived in the country, in my uncle's manor house, but when I finally found him, he was living in Prague, in a house on the Vinehrady, which was one of the family's former town houses, in a flat which belonged to Linda, his mother's erstwhile lady's maid.

I had visited him several times at Linda's flat, and been entertained at lunch there, but I had never been with him in

the evening because he worked as a night watchman in a picture gallery in the castle. Thus I had never had to tell the
Russian of his existence.

On the third day before my departure, Ferdinand asked
me to dinner; that night he was not on duty, and it was to be
our last meeting. When I told him, the Russian was coldly
angry. "It is just as well you are leaving," he said. "It is high
time. A few weeks more and I'd be so used to you I couldn't
be without you. If you are serious, this is your last chance to
get away."

I said, "You couldn't keep me against my will."

He said, "You are a little fool. You don't know what you
are talking about. Don't provoke me."

I burst out laughing. I said, "You mean, this particular hen
should not be cackling just now?"

Soon after dinner I said I wanted to leave, and Ferdinand,
as a matter of course, saw me home. It had stopped raining
and we walked all the way to the hotel. By then a new storm
was rising and the first heavy drops began to fall. "Come
upstairs and have a last drink with me," I said.

It was about ten o'clock. We took a seat on one of the
blue-plush benches facing the arch with the naked statue and
gave our orders to the headwaiter. When the elderly waitress
arrived, she murmured while setting down our glasses, "Begging your pardon, madam, but the gentleman over there
has been sitting alone there for the last hour and looking
very sad."

"Never mind," I said, "let him sit and look sad." And
glancing sideways I saw the Russian sitting five empty tables

away from ours, with his back turned to the door and not facing us directly. He was reading a newspaper.

"What's all this about?" asked my cousin indifferently.

"Oh, it's just . . . ," I began, still watching the Russian, and paused when I saw a stranger greet him and join him at his table. He was a conspicuous-looking man, not only because of his cornflower-blue suit but because of his striking appearance; he had thick white-blond hair and a handsome lean face, as though carved with a few strokes of a hatchet.

"It's only . . . ," I started again. "There is a man over there . . ." I halted with embarrassment. "I happen to know him. I sometimes meet him here and we talk."

"Good God," said my cousin, who had been following my glance. I was taken aback at the sound of his voice. It was very low and sounded as though he had gone pale with fright. "What is he?" he asked.

"He is a Russian."

"Good God," he said once more.

"What's so dreadful about him?" I asked. And then it occurred to me with great relief that it was probably the handsome striking white-blond stranger whom he had meant. I said gaily, "Which one of the two do you mean? If it's the cornflower, I've never seen him before."

"Oh, that one," said my cousin impatiently. "Who cares? It's the other one I mean, for heaven's sake. How long have you known him? How did you meet him?"

"I met him here in the coffeehouse," I said. "You know how it is. And if you are going to tell me that I am a married woman with a husband and a child, I am going to scream," and I forced myself to laugh.

I knew quite well that my cousin had not spoken with moral indignation, and that as a former cavalryman he treated amorous irregularities of any kind with careless amusement. I had made the remark as a desperate attempt to ignore the fear which so obviously had seized him.

"A coffeehouse acquaintance," he said slowly, as though pronouncing a monstrosity. "What does he do?"

"I don't know exactly; he never told me," I said. "It's something with a laboratory."

"It wouldn't matter even if he had told you," said my cousin, "because they always have a genuine job of work as a cover."

"How do you mean?"

"How dim can you be?" asked my cousin.

"How do you mean?"

"But don't you see," said my cousin, "the fellow is a typical secret intelligence man? He belongs to what we call the obscure force."

"And how dim can you get?" I replied heatedly. "He's got a degree in physics and he's worked in Hungary and in Romania. He sometimes travels because of his work, and he's divorced and has a daughter—"

"Stop it," he said. "Of course he's told you his story. They all have a story—they can't just say they've dropped from the sky. And the claptrap about divorce and daughter fills it in and makes it less fake."

"He isn't fake," I said. "He's highly educated, he's simply

dripping with Latin and Greek. You can't fake reeling off the prepositions governing the dative and the accusative, the way he did once to exasperate me, and then he recited the rules about the forms of the aorist till I felt like screaming. And he's not a Party member—he won't join. He's not even a Communist, so there."

"Not even a Communist," repeated my cousin. "Not even a . . . Of all the— Can't you see that's part of his story, to put you off your guard? And you really believe he is not a comrade, only because he said so?"

"You are being idiotic," I said. "The only comrades you know were your horses, and you've told me yourself how in the war you wouldn't eat horse meat because it would have meant eating your comrades. And there is nothing to put me off guard with him. Just to show you how wrong you are, he is the soul of discretion, and he's never ever asked me a single question about myself."

"Naturally," said my cousin. "That's because he's found out all he wants to know about you from his sources. Don't you see, even dumb as you are, that this again proves it? How long have you known him?"

"All the time I've been here," I said. "I met him on the second day I arrived."

"Good God," said my cousin, in a voice blanched with fear. "That clinches it. You get here, and straightaway they put him on to you."

"You're as daft as a brush," I said. "He talked to me because he liked me. What's so unusual about that? Let me tell you, when I got out of the number seven tramway the first evening, a man accosted me and wanted to go along with me. And when I had lunch at the Praha, a man followed me out to the cloakroom and tried to pick me up. And when I had coffee at Berger's, a man left as soon as he saw I was paying, and waited for me on the stairs and wanted to go off with me. They all were secret intelligence, of course."

He gave me a reproachful, exasperated look. "It sticks out a mile," he said. "But you haven't been through what we have been through here, so you can't know. I have learned how to pick out the plainclothesmen in public places. But this is worse, much worse. Of course he's highly educated, as you say—that I don't doubt. He's got to be; he's washed with all waters."

For a while we continued silent, and because I found my cousin ridiculously pitiful, I decided to stop protesting. I said reasonably, "If you were right, why waste him on me? I am nothing and nobody."

"You haven't got to the end yet," said my cousin. "You don't know what use he will find for you. Just before you leave he will put the pressure on."

"Make me earn my keep," I said, and burst out laughing.

"And to think," said my cousin, pointedly ignoring my merriment, "that I had to come here with you and that he has seen me."

"So what?" I said. "There are worse sights than you. You know how we used to tease you that you looked exactly like the Prince of Wales? Now you look like the Duke of Windsor."

"Look over there," said my cousin. "The oldish couple.

He's smoking. And the old girl has turned her chair away from the table. She's been like that all the time, they got here shortly after us."

"I didn't notice," I said.

"All the time she's been watching us," he insisted.

"She's looking at my dress," I said. "Everybody here notices my rags. To them they are simply heaven. It's pathetic. And you yourself—I don't know how you do it, but you still manage to live up to your former legend. You stick out a mile with your English tweeds."

"She isn't admiring us," he said. "Do you know what she is doing? She is too far away to overhear what we are saying, and yet she is listening to every word. She's lip-reading."

"You are crazy."

"I may seem crazy to you," he said. "I know full well that you think I'm suffering from ideas of persecution, but you haven't lived here since the war. And I'll tell you something more. When I get up to go now, I'll be followed by somebody and trailed all the way home. Because I'm suspect now, just by sitting with you, and being your cousin makes it worse."

"I give up," I said. I looked once more in the direction of the Russian. He was alone now; I had not noticed the other one leaving. "There you are," I said to Ferdinand. "The cornflower has faded away. Been sent off to relay a message. He'll climb to the top of the church tower wrapped in a scarlet cloak so that nobody will think him conspicuous, and signal with a torch straight to Moscow."

My cousin asked about the hour of my flight to London

in two days. "I shan't be able to see you tomorrow," he said, "because of my work. But I'll fetch you from the hotel the day after tomorrow and see you to the airport."

While he paid, the waitress gave me a tenderly reproachful glance. I hoped my cousin did not observe it; I reflected that if the elderly kindhearted woman had not been on duty that evening, the whole scene with my cousin would have been avoided and he would never have known of the Russian's existence. And yet, a few moments later I realized that the scene would have been unavoidable after all, because as we were leaving, the Russian rose from his seat. He caught up with us before we reached the door. "I kiss your hand, *milostivá paní*," he said. "Forgive me, I only wanted to inquire if you too are departing now?"

"This is my cousin Ferdinand—Mr. Blonik," I said.

The Russian barely gave him a look and bowed slightly.

"I'm only seeing my cousin out," I said.

"In that case," said the Russian, "may I hope you will return and give me the pleasure of your company for a while?"

"Of course," I said. "I'll be with you in a minute."

He inclined his head toward me, then toward my cousin, and turned away.

Ferdinand gave me a significant look and raised his chin. I glanced in the direction he wanted me to look. The Russian was not returning to his table; he went out ahead of us, through the swinging glass doors, past the cloakroom, where the attendant was knitting behind her counter, and then he was out of sight. If he had gone down the stairs we would have seen him, so he must have entered either the washroom or the telephone booth. "What do you say now?" asked Ferdinand. I did not reply. My cousin added, "Whatever he is or isn't, he certainly is Russian. That accent he can't get rid of or he would have done it. It's like a watermark on a banknote; it gives the show away every time."

After my cousin had received his coat—it was his old officer's trench coat—we dawdled in the lobby, talking, neither of us admitting that we were interested to see from which door the Russian would emerge. He did not appear. After a few minutes we descended the stairs and bid each other good-bye in the foyer of the hotel with a show of exaggerated heartiness.

When I returned to the coffeehouse, the Russian was at his table. He rose, smiling. "Let's go, shall we," he said, "unless you want another drink."

"I don't."

"That's splendid," he said.

"I'm sorry I kept you waiting so long," I said. "But after all those years, there is so much to talk about."

"Well, well."

"I'm awfully glad I did manage to find my cousin," I said. "At first I thought . . . I didn't have a clue."

"You don't look pleased, though," he said.

"Oh, that's because . . . ," I said, haltingly, and looked searchingly into his face.

"Because he made a remark about me," said the Russian. He closed his long lips tightly. His countenance had the same expression as on our first evening, when I had observed him listening to that man, as though expecting to be told something with which he was familiar but which he did not care to hear, anyway.

I took a deep breath. I was overwhelmed by a desire to see him flustered, shaken, just for once to shatter his sober self-possession, to see the sparks of the same fire he had shown when talking to me in his own tongue.

"He thinks you are secret intelligence," I said without taking my eyes off him.

To my furious disappointment he gave his resigned laughter. He said, "Is that all? I'm used to this. Before I was in the habit of coming here, I used to go to another coffeehouse, and I noticed that nobody ever would sit at a table next to mine if they could help it. In the end I asked the waiter, and he told me, 'They all think you are secret intelligence.' I don't know what it is about me, and being Russian doesn't help either, of course. Never mind. Let's go."

The next evening, when we met in the coffeehouse, I said, "I shan't come to your place tonight. My flight is at nine tomorrow, which means I must be at the airport at eight. I just couldn't manage it—I'd be too nervous."

"I understand."

We sat on till eleven. I said, "Now, I think, it must be good-bye."

"Yes, but not here," he said. "There is something more I want to tell you, and it had better be said outside. Walk down the street with me, no further than the church, and I'll walk you back to the hotel. I believe the rain has stopped just for once, mirabile dictu."

"Not mirabile at all," I said. "Now that I'm leaving, the good weather will set in."

"I'd rather have it rain and you stay on," he said.

It was mild outside; the sky was evenly clouded and it was still wet underfoot. I was walking down the street by the side of a man with whom I had spent most evenings and nights for six weeks, and of whom I knew the following: he was Russian and forty-two, brought up in a wine shop of poor parents, had worked previously in Romania and Hungary, had a degree in physics, was divorced two years ago, had a daughter of eight and a brother who was a general in the Russian army.

We were silent as we passed the length of the hotel building. Then he said, "You have been very good all along. You've never asked me a question about myself. Now, as you are leaving, I will tell you what I am. I am a physicist and I work for the army. I am a full colonel. They wanted to put me in uniform, but I managed to be spared that, at least. I cough on them, as you would express it, but I have no choice. I am on secret stuff, though I'd much rather be working on something else, and if I ever leave the army I shan't be allowed out of the country for five years. I don't want you to write to me; I shan't write either. If you ever want to come back to me, I'll be here for you—I'm strictly a one-woman man, that's my unfortunate nature. I'll always want you, you can rely on me."

We halted. "At least kiss me good-bye," I said. As soon as I had said it I knew it was a mistake. Like all good lovers, the

Russian had never wasted time on kisses. Besides, with his sober bearing he had always abstained completely from any show of affection in public.

He bent down rigidly and with ill grace, and I put my arms around his neck and touched my lips on his cheek. I said, "And I never even learned how to pour out Turkish coffee because you always did it for me."

We made our way back without speaking. A waitress came out of the snack bar flanking the hotel entrance, carrying a tray with a mayonnaise salad, and at that moment there came to us the music from the radio outside, playing the bars of the song which says, "You wait, I'll tell how you went after me, you wait, I'll tell what you wanted to get. In the garden a rose, under the window a kiss."

"Drat these folk tunes," the Russian said.

I RETURNED to Prague in 1968, three years after I had left, on a Friday in the first week of June. On the first night I was given a room in a good old hotel behind the gunpowder tower, in the center of the town. On the next day I was told that no accommodation of any kind could be found for me, not even in the second-rate hotel where I had stayed previously, and I was sent to a room in a private flat behind the national museum.

The owner's family was ill pleased at my moving in at such short notice; they had intended to leave in the afternoon for a weekend in the country. I assured them that I would be able to make my own breakfast, would turn off the gas, would double-lock the front door when going out, and would write down every call I made on the telephone. By then it was not necessary to continue with my enumeration of a lodger's virtues; they told me that they would bring me back some cherries and strawberries, and that in the meantime I could have the run of the flat.

On Sunday morning I could not wait any longer. I took the tray with my milk and coffee into the dining room, poured out a cup, set it on a chair by the telephone, and opened the directory.

I had never had occasion to call the Russian by telephone, and had never looked up his number. It was easy to find. There was only one Blonik in the book, and the address was still the same. The only thing which struck me as not being right was the first name. It was not Konstantin, but Antonin, which is the Czech form of Anthony. He's got two Christian names, I thought, and he doesn't want to use the Russian-sounding Konstantin.

While I dialed I conjured up a woman's voice answering, or his own, embarrassed and constricted, informing me that he was now married, saying brightly, "Of course I'll be very glad to see you," and adding in a murmur, "but my wife must never know of this."

The call was answered on the first ring. "Blonik here," said a man's voice. It was a baritone, and softer and weaker than the full hard voice that I recalled. Probably I had awakened him.

"It's Edith," I said. "I only arrived from London the day before yesterday. How are you?"

"Yey-yey. Edith from London, it sounds like a blooming fairy tale," said the voice, a voice without the glitter of brocade, and to my consternation it spoke in the slangy way and dialectically colored speech peculiar to the inhabitants of Prague.

"But aren't you Mr. Blonik?" I asked.

"Sure, but I don't know any Edith, let alone an Edith from London, as sure as the cat crawls through the hole and the dog jumps over the fence."

"But I don't understand," I said. "I used to know a Mr. Blonik in this very flat you are in now. He lived there."

"When was this?" he asked.

"Three years ago."

"That's not possible," he said. "Because I've been in this flat for the last ten years, and I'm sitting tight on it, with both cheeks of my behind, don't you worry, because this is a flat with all the comforts laid on, and there's some who would trade a flat of four or five rooms in an old house for a small place like this. You have it mixed up with someone else in this house."

"Your flat is on the sixth floor," I said, "that's the top floor, and as you get out of the lift, it's the only door on the left. There is a roof terrace, not beautiful, but good for hanging out the washing."

"Holy sacrament!" he said. "Forgive me for swearing, will you, but this is getting sacramentally complicated. Forgive me, Miss Edith from London, but what was the name of this friend of yours?"

"I told you," I said. "Blonik, Konstantin Blonik."

"Oh, Kon-stan-tin," he said, sounding relieved, rolling the name out in its full splendor. "Konstantin, the Russian."

"Yes, yes," I said eagerly.

"But he's not Blonik. What rubbish are you serving me up? He's Konstantin Biyelogradov."

"I never heard that name," I said.

"You must have," he said impatiently. "His brother is General Biyelogradov, and there is even a street in Prague named after him."

"Hold on," I said, "that's him. Of course. He told me his brother was a general in the Russian army."

"And you knew him three years ago?" he asked.

"That's right."

"And he lived in this flat?"

"He did."

"But how is it possible?" he asked. "Where was I at that sacramental time? Do you know, I can't remember." There was a pause. "I've known him for ten years," he went on. "You see, we got together because we were both getting a divorce at that time. Weeping cheek by cheek into our beer."

"Oh," I said. "He told me he was divorced, that's true, but only two years before I met him. I mean, that makes it five years ago, now."

"No, no, you got it wrong," he said.

"And he has a daughter," I added.

"That I can't say, he never mentioned her," he said. "Of course, we never did have much in common. I'm a plain man, I'm a printer, and he's a highly educated person."

"He certainly is."

"There's something, though, about his career that's clouded," he said. "He did study law, that I know, but I've always had the impression that he didn't work in a legal job, that he didn't get his degree."

"Law?"

"Yes, law."

"That's not at all what he told me," I said. "He was an academician, yes, certainly, but—"

"What did he tell you?" he asked in a tone of voice that was not merely keen with curiosity but had a sharp edge which I found menacing.

"He told me something entirely different," I said and paused.

He continued silent.

I added, "I shan't tell you, though. Because he told me in confidence and I don't want to break faith."

He said, "I understand that. That's very fine of you." I had imagined he would be disappointed, but to my surprise he sounded relieved. "Now look here," he said. "I see you are genuine, all right, and we must get you organized. I'll give you his address and phone number—I've got it, only I don't know where. This flat is so sacramentally small that you'd think it'd be easy to lay hands on anything. But no fear. Where are you staying? Give me your full everything and I'll ring you back as soon as I've found it."

I drank my second cup of milk and coffee. It was barely lukewarm; I must have had a longer talk with Mr. Blonik than I had realized. Despite my consternation, I was grateful for the man's existence. Here was the explanation of his

"*Married Love*? That rubbish? No, of course I haven't read it," and that vulgar pair of ladies' slippers.

I was still in the kitchen tidying up after my breakfast when the telephone rang.

"I got it for you," said Mr. Blonik's voice. He sounded matey and cozy. "Got a pencil? The flat is near where I live; he's had it for the last eighteen months, I should say. By the way, when was it that you met him three years ago? In what month, about?"

I said, "End of April till the first week of June, and raining all the time."

"That's right. Good girl. It never stopped pissing, and the entire summer was pissed-up too, as though we hadn't enough reason for being fed up just then, in sixty-five. You've come here in happier times now, and I don't mean just the weather."

"To me it's all the same," I said. "I don't understand politics, and the Malá Strana is just as marvelous as it was before, down to every baroque church and palace. But yes, there is an improvement. They have fixed up most of the baroque since I was here last. Only the Kracker frescoes in the St. Mikuláš are still being done over, but that's only in the side chapel."

"Never mind the blooming baroque," he said. "You can talk freely on the telephone nowadays, so you needn't be so heavy on culture with me. But tell me, you can't have had a very good time with Konstantin in that year, in those days."

"How do you mean?"

"Because . . . Well, he had a streak of pitch just then. I

don't know what he did before, mind you, and I don't know what he's doing now, but I do know that just at that time he was working as a chauffeur."

"No, never," I said. "He seemed very prosperous. And he went away twice on business during that time I was there, and it sounded important, I know, because he told me that he couldn't make up his mind whether to fly or take the train."

"He was a chauffeur," insisted Blonik.

I did not reply.

He said, "You know, it's funny. Now that I've talked to you I don't know myself anymore what to believe. I'm sacramentally bewildered. You've pulled the chair from under my arse."

"I should hate to do that," I said.

He said, "Yes, I believe you, you sound a very decent girl, Miss Edith from London. Now hold your breath and I'll dictate."

After he had rung off I began to wonder if all along I had not been speaking to the Russian after all. Alternatively, I reassured myself, recalling my cousin, "Whatever he is or isn't, he certainly is a Russian. It's like a watermark on a banknote; it gives the show away every time."

I was about to run my bath when the telephone rang once more.

"It's me again," said Blonik's voice. "Something came to my mind, seeing that you are from London, and big on culture. I'm a fan of American novels—Upton Sinclair and

Steinbeck. Now Steinbeck is alive, isn't he? I would like to write to him. Can you get me his address?"

"Easily," I said. "When I'm back in London, I can look up his publishers and you can write him care of them. Or better still, I'll get hold of the *American Writers Yearbook*."

"That's fine," he said. "But there is something else too. You won't be offended, will you? I'd very much like to meet you."

"With pleasure."

"It's not just cold-snouted curiosity," he said, "because, you see, there is something I want to ask you, and I can't say it over the phone."

"You can ask me whatever you wish."

"Yes, but not on the phone," he insisted. "Today is Sunday and I'm off work. Are you free this afternoon?"

"Yes."

"Could you meet me at four?"

"I'm free all day," I said, "and four will be fine. I'll meet you wherever you wish."

"Would the coffeehouse up my street suit you?" he asked. "The one in the hotel—you know, it's on the first floor?"

"Don't I know it!" I said. "I'll be there. But how shall I know you? What do you look like?"

With an embarrassed laugh he said, "What do I look like? It's a funny thing—you'll think it funny when I tell you—but I look rather like Konstantin."

I tried to steady my heart by taking a deep breath. "That makes it so much easier," I said, trying to sound matter-of-fact. "And I am small and have black hair. It's very long, and I wear it in plaits in a chignon, like my grandmother's cook used to wear it, and nobody nowadays wears it anymore. You could not have known my grandmother's cook, but I think it will give you the idea."

"The hand is in the glove," he said, "and I'll be there at four sharp."

I ran my bath but did not take it; I could not master myself. I rang up the Russian's number, which Blonik had given me, together with the address. There was no answer.

During the following hours I was tortured by doubts. Had Blonik let elapse ten minutes before ringing me up that third time because he had relayed to the Russian the information that I was in Prague, and had he received instructions from him to arrange a meeting with me? But the Russian was not in; he had not answered the call. Or had he been in and not answered, knowing full well that it would be me? Or had Blonik given me a wrong number so as to hinder me from getting in touch with the Russian himself? There was no telling, all the more so as the name Biyelogradov was not in the book.

And as to Blonik of the faulty memory, the plain man, the printer, he who could not recall having lent his flat to the Russian, nor where he had been himself during that time, did he come at me with butter, or with dripping? And what was the question he wanted to pose, the question that could not be safely uttered on the telephone, after having reassured me that the lines were no longer tapped?

I was in the coffeehouse at quarter to four. I chose a table in the center, facing the swinging glass doors. Before sitting down I turned around and looked behind me. Close to the mournful-looking naked statue were three tables where men were playing chess, all of them shabbily dressed and elderly. At the other tables there was not a single man on his own; there were only groups or couples. As I looked carefully at each, there was no one who looked in the least like the Russian, neither in build nor age nor coloring.

At a quarter past four it was clear to me that Blonik would not turn up. I told myself, "He can't turn up because he doesn't exist," and then, "Yes, he does; there are two of them, because of the accent and the voice."

To be sure that I had not been mistaken about his presence, I rose and viewed the guests once more. When I resumed my seat I saw in the shadowy lobby behind the glass doors the outline of a tall, powerful figure. A heartbeat later the Russian stood in the entrance. He was bareheaded and the lion-colored wavy hair was dulled with strands of gray. He was stouter than he had been; the face was fuller too, and the skin, though still pink, had lost its sun-ripe open-air glow. Perhaps owing to his portliness, he now looked more stately and openly commanding than before, the heaviness of his jowls recalling the portrait busts of baroque ruling princes.

He paused and our eyes met. Without showing any surprise, he came to my table. Still standing, he kissed my hand.

"Do sit down," I said.

"I'll put my coat in the cloakroom first, *milostivá paní*," he said. "I'll be with you in a minute."

As I listened to the full hard voice with the accent glittering through the words like brocade, I noticed how prosperous he looked in his tan lightweight loose-cut overcoat; then it occurred to me that he had entered wearing it, that he had not handed it in beforehand, that he must have been told I would be in the coffeehouse, that he had first wanted to make sure that I was there. He had clearly not walked in by chance, intending to spend an hour reading the paper.

"Will you have another coffee?" he asked when he sat down.

"Yes, thank you."

We faced each other in silence till he turned away under the pretext of looking for a waiter. Now I saw that what had appeared as baroque dignity from a distance was due to the dulling of age and the coarsening of high living.

"So you've appeared again," he said gravely.

"I arrived the day before yesterday."

"Well, well."

"Do you know why I'm here? In the coffeehouse, I mean?" I asked.

He gave me his indulgently resigned laughter. "Because you hoped to run into me by chance?"

"No," I said. "Because I was supposed to meet Mr. Blonik at four. But it looks as though he hasn't turned up."

He surveyed the room calmly, then said, "He certainly isn't here. I know him quite well, you can rely on me."

The sound of that familiar phrase made my tongue shrink; now, for the first time, I could savor the bitterness of its irony. Perhaps my distress showed on my face, or perhaps he

wanted to play for time, to delay the explanation he was certain I would demand. He turned around once more and said
in a show of annoyance, "The service is a disgrace. It's been
getting worse steadily, ever since you've been away."

"Is the old girl, the waitress, still here?" I asked. "The one
who liked me so much, remember, and who played *postillon
d'amour* that evening when I was here with my cousin?"

"She's serving in the wine tavern now," he said. "She's
under the weather. She's got trouble with her daughter because her daughter is in trouble. *Relata referro.*" He smiled
indulgently and with benevolence, still unperturbed, still the
lion at rest.

"But look here," he continued, "this is an awful table,
with the full draught from the door. Let's move away, shall
we? I can see a free table upstream over there."

We moved.

"Are you sure you want coffee?" he asked. "I'm off beer
now because I've been putting on too much weight. I only
drink wine."

"I don't feel like wine in the middle of the day," I said.
"I'll stick to coffee. In the meantime, don't you want to
know why I was going to meet Mr. Blonik?"

"Not particularly," he said. "You know I never asked you
a personal question."

"Of course not," I said. "You didn't have to; you knew
all the answers beforehand. Just as now you needn't be told
why I made a rendezvous with Mr. Blonik. Why did you lie
to me?"

He looked at me with perplexed astonishment.

I said, "Why did you tell me your name was Blonik?"

"Oh, that," he said, easily and indifferently. "That's because I happened to be in the middle of my divorce proceedings at the time. I couldn't afford any trouble and confusion."

"But you told me then that your divorce was through," I said.

Raising his chin lazily and glancing at me with half-closed eyes, he said, "Did I? It can't have been."

"How is your little girl?" I asked.

"She's fine," he said. "I've just been to see her." He paused. "She is eight," he added. "She's already in the second grade of primary."

I felt I was turning pale as my heart tightened with sadness and disgust. The evasively slipshod lying about his divorce had already sickened me because its very carelessness proved how indifferent he was to what I might think. Now the daughter whose loss had been too painful to talk about, the daughter with the big blue eyes who had shared her plateful of ham with a crowd of Chinese children, the daughter who had to arrange her shoes neatly before going to bed—that daughter was still eight years old.

"That's splendid," I said. "And is she doing well at school?"

"Fairly well," he replied. "Ah, here he is at last. What will you have? White or black or Turkish?"

"Turkish, please," I said. By then I understood; it was his outstandingly reliable memory which had betrayed him, the memory which held the exact ingredients of *sauce tartare* and *sauce rémoulade,* of all the prepositions in Latin governing the dative and the accusative, of the rules of the Greek aorist. That memory had been imprinted with the fact that in that certain role he was to play, he had a daughter of the age of eight, and he had automatically repeated the fact as he had memorized it.

"I've got a very decent flat now," he said, "not far away from here. Where are you staying? In this hotel again?"

"No, I had to take a room in a private flat. I wanted to get in here, and the Čedok woman telephoned in my presence, but they were full."

"That's not true," he said. "It's half empty. If you wish, I'll go downstairs and get you in. With me everything goes smoothly."

"No, thank you."

"In that case," he said, "why don't you go home now and pack up and move in with me? It's not grand, but it's much better than what I used to have."

"But you didn't have it," I said. "It was Blonik's all along."

"Not at all," he said, "it was mine. I took it over from Blonik. And that's why I didn't bother to change the name in the telephone book either."

"Sorry, I got it wrong," I said.

"Well, what about it?" he asked. "Come and live with me. I'll make you comfortable, you can rely on me."

"No, thank you," I said. "I am settled where I am."

"Think it over," he said. "I hope you change your mind."

By then his wine and my coffee had been set before us.

I fought against my emotions as I watched him while he seized the stem of the pot, slowly tilted it, held a spoon against the crust on the surface of the coffee, and poured without disturbing the grounds, just as in former days.

"And in case you care to change your mind," he said, "have you my address?"

"Yes," I said. "Blonik gave it to me."

"Show me."

I handed him the slip of paper I had taken from my handbag.

"That's wrong," he remarked. "What he's given you is my former address. I only moved to this place where I am now six months ago. Give me your notebook."

And again he opened it, unhesitatingly this time, to the month of June, turned to the date, and wrote in that large hand with curls around the capital letters, "Konstantin Biyelogradov," and a street and a number. "Here you are," he said. "Now you have me in black on white."

"It's a beautiful name," I said.

"It's my name," he said, "and I couldn't change it even if it displeased you. But I am glad you like it. May I offer you a cigarette, *milostivá paní*?"

Then he looked up and rose. A young couple were standing in front of our table. I had seen them approaching and taken no notice of them, thinking they had stopped just to look around for somewhere to sit. The coffeehouse had filled up completely by this time. "Hallo, Helen," he said, in a condescending voice I had not heard him use before, and, "Hallo, you there." He sat down again.

I looked at them closely. She was in her twenties, and her youth barely softened the sharpness of her features. Her dark shoulder-length hair was crimped and domed in the way favored by provincial beauties and factory girls. She wore a dark blue modest dress with an ill-fitting collar of machine-made lace. He was shorter than she, a dark-haired sickly youth with an alert air, in an imitation suede jacket and a checkered woolen shirt open at the neck. He looked like a garage mechanic who was saving up for a motorcycle, she like an assistant in a chemist's, or a technical-equipment store.

"May we sit down? There aren't any tables left," said the girl.

"By all means, Helenka," said the Russian, using the friendly diminutive of Helen. He made a lazy gesture toward a neighboring alcove. "Get yourselves some chairs."

With a resigned smile at me, he shifted his chair closer to mine. After they had joined our table, he made no attempt at introductions. He kept making random remarks to the girl, like, "Did you bring a coat with you, Helenka? It looks as though you'll need it. It's turned cloudy again."

After they had ordered ices, we were joined by yet another newcomer, a stranger to all of us, an obese young man who brought a chair over without asking our permission. He told us he had been to the cinema nearby, and was quickly served with a large helping of cold roast beef and *sauce tartare*.

"Excuse me for a minute, *milostivá paní*," said the Russian, "there is someone over there whom I would like to have a word with." He walked away in the direction of the naked statue.

I kept silent. The couple were spooning ice cream out of long-stemmed nickel cups and exchanging remarks whose sense I did not try to grasp. I looked down the room; the Russian had disappeared. "Excuse me, miss," I said, "but will you tell me the name of the gentleman who's just been with us? I know it's Konstantin something, but I get so confused with names, being a foreigner."

"Of course," she said with haughty indulgence, "he is Konstantin Goloviev."

"That's right, Goloviev," I said hastily, trying to control the nervous laughter which rose in my throat. "Goloviev. These Russian names are so confusing. But could you be so kind . . . could you tell me what he is? In the way of his profession, I mean."

"Oh," she said, and paused as though to gather breath before uttering an impressive statement, "he is the managing director of a large concern."

"Really?" I said. "But are you sure? How do you know?"

"How do I know?" she said, contemptuous of my disbelief and enjoying my ignorance. "Because I've worked for six months under him. I've left now, but he's still there."

"That's on cement?" I asked.

"That's on cement," she said. "He is the top."

We fell silent once more. The obese young man, who was eating his second ice topped with a whirl of whipped cream strewn with grated chocolate, had been following our conversation with undisguised interest.

"Where is he?" I asked a few minutes later. "I think he's been away now for half an hour." I addressed myself to the girl, Helenka, in particular, established as she was as an expert on the Russian. "Or do you think he's left altogether?"

Once more she became contemptuous of my ignorance. "He can't have left," she told me, "because there's still his wine on the table, and his lighter and his cigarettes."

"Yes, you are right, of course," I said, humbly and admiringly, though in my eyes a packet of cigarettes and a lighter were of too small value to serve as forfeits. I recalled how three years ago the Russian had complained of the loss of his gold fountain pen, and fell to wondering in what circumstances he had left it "lying about."

Seeing my doubting glance, Helenka tossed her head and told her young man, "Go and have a look round. You can see the lady is getting worried. Go and comb out the gents', perhaps he has been taken ill."

After the imitation-suede-jacketed youth had left, I rewarded Helenka by confiding, "You see, I haven't seen the Russian for some years, and I was struck by how he has aged."

"That's right," she said. "When you don't see people day by day, you notice it much more."

We were silent again, till the young man came back. "I looked all over the place," he said, "and he's not in the phone booth either. He must have left." He called the waiter and paid, and they went away.

I remained sitting with the obese young man who had been listening all the time with the Buddhalike air of wisdom peculiar to very fat people. Now he remarked, "You do meet odd persons when you are traveling, don't you?"

I nodded. By then he had finished a triangle of chocolate cake.

He was eating a cube of another kind of chocolate cake when the Russian returned. Seeing him approach the table made me aware again of how monumental he looked, like his own statue in a public square. "They have gone," I said, "Helenka and her swain."

The obese youth called the headwaiter, and we waited in silence till he left.

"The weather is turning bad again," said the Russian. "Eight degrees and it's the first week of June."

"Like three years ago," I said.

"Do you remember," he said, "how it kept raining all that spring, and how I said I'd rather have it rain on and on as long as you stayed?"

"I remember."

"But this year it will be different," he said. "It will turn very hot. You can rely on me."

"Will it?"

"I think so," he said. "You are a little fool. Don't you read the papers?"

"Not a lot," I said.

"It doesn't matter either way," he said, "because even if you did read the papers thoroughly, you'd get nothing out of them. And that's as it should be, because you are a woman. The trouble is, hardly anybody knows how to read the papers."

"How do you mean?"

"If a monkey looks into the mirror, what does he see?" he asked. "Only another monkey."

"Well, yes," I said, bewildered.

He was smiling, his teeth gleaming like freshly peeled almonds. Then he gave his resigned laugh. "It's no use sitting here any longer," he said. "The Sunday crowd is obnoxious. And the stuffy air. Shall we go?" He tightened his long straight lips, the way he had that night when expecting to hear that my cousin had said something about him.

Bending over my empty cup and stirring the inside with my spoon, I avoided his eyes.

"Shall we go?" he repeated.

"No."

"You are a little fool," he said.

"We won't go," I said. "I'll go. Good-bye."

On the following day it was less chilly, and the day after that there was a heat wave of thirty-four degrees, and the hot weather lasted during the whole of my month's stay in Prague. The Russian's forecast had been true. But it was only after the twenty-first of August that I began to think of his "You can rely on me" not with bitterness but with respect.

The Blue Hour

And don't flatter yourself, Louise," said Edmund, when I asked him to examine me, and to behave like a doctor, a "practical doctor," as he liked to call it. "He does this to every woman he meets."

"Surely not," I said. "Let's say, to every other woman. There must be some choice."

"How do you know?" said Edmund. During his twenty years in India, he had been a celebrated cardiologist, and though we'd now been married for twenty-five years, he had rarely treated me. Once, when I had what he thought might be a nettle rash, he had insisted on taking me to be looked at by one of these "real practitioners," saying that it was too much to ask of him to tell urticaria from scabies.

"I don't know," I said, and began to describe my sufferings: "I feel stabbed by every deep breath I take, pierced with every clearing of my throat, laughter impossible—not that I'd want to laugh—every movement like bending and stretching a torture"—while speaking, I kept my hand over the source of the pain, on my right side. I had waited until now, when Edmund was in pajamas and dressing gown and facing me across the long, low marble-topped sofa table on which he kept stacks of the *Lancet* and the *Herald Tribune,* to tell him what had happened that afternoon with Clarence, my cousin Sylvia's husband.

"He's contused my liver," I said. "What if I now get jaundice? The bile comes out of the liver, doesn't it—"

Edmund started to laugh. "Never mind your liver. I can diagnose you without getting out of my chair. He's cracked your rib. And there's nothing one can do about it. If you were one of my former patients, say, a maharajah or an estate owner—one must give the rich the idea they're getting their money's worth when they call me—I'd now have them run up so many X rays from so many angles that they'd need a lorry to cart them away." He went on, "Clarence is a fool and he is not quite normal. In my young days we had a name for it in psychiatry. We called it moral insanity. And the worst of it is, you've been unlucky in your bad luck. Because you got caught on the cartilage. Instead of on the bone. Bones heal fast because they've got what the cartilage hasn't got—well, never mind. But cartilage is the devil to heal."

I refrained from asking what cartilage had not got as opposed to bones. One did not query Edmund. I had learned my lesson early, during the first week of our honeymoon. In a small hotel, near Malaga, owned and run by an English couple for an entirely English clientele, Edmund had called room service and ordered a bottle of mineral water. It was brought by a waiter, a thin, pale, hollow-cheeked young man. It was obvious that before coming to our room, he had looked up our entry in the register and had seen Edmund's title, because, as soon as he put down his tray, he turned to Edmund and fastened upon him an insistently beseeching glance. "Doctor, sir."

"Yes," said Edmund, "what's troubling you?"

"It's pain," said the waiter, "here, over here." And he ran his hand down one side of his body.

"Quite so," said Edmund. "Hold on a minute, will you?" And he went to the bedside table and opened the jaws of the well-worn Gladstone bag which he took along on all his travels. After some rummaging he brought forth a flat white pill and placed it on the waiter's tray. "Take this, half an hour before going to bed. With a glass of water. Don't chew." And then, so as to cut short the waiter's profuse thanks, he raised his hand in the benevolent wave he had acquired during his travels abroad, with the King of Nepal. And though he had stopped all medical activity after the King's death, he still retained the mannerisms of a King's physician.

As soon as we were alone I said, "But Edmund, how could you? You've never seen him before. You didn't examine him. You did not ask him a question. You've no idea what he's got. What did you give him?"

"Just the first painkiller that came to my hand."

"But how could you, when you've no idea?"

He said, "No idea? He's got a tubercular kidney but he does not know it yet. And there's nothing I can do about it."

Now, watching me as I kept putting my hand to the right side of my waist, he said, "I'd say, four weeks to heal. There's nothing I can do about it. And it's no use telling Sylvia, either. You will recall that I—already, all those years ago, when I first met Clarence—I told you then that he was a fool and that he was bats in the belfry. What you are, you remain. Now, how long ago would that have been?"

"Let me think," I said. "I'm forty-five now, that makes Sylvia forty-eight. And when you first met her and Clarence, that was in Westbourne Terrace, they were living in London, and Julie, their first, was only two months old, and Sylvia was twenty-two when she got married, and lost no time getting Julie, so that makes—"

"Twenty-three years," said Edmund.

"Yes," I said. "And already then Sylvia was bitching and bellyaching that she'd rather live in the country but Clarence was still thinking he'd make it as a barrister and was sitting tight on his behind in the City waiting for his briefs. And when he didn't get on, she always said it was envy—Clarence Demolins, some of the bluest blood in England, *Des Moulins* from Normandy, come over with William the Conqueror, older than the Tudors, the Stuarts, the this and the that."

I recalled well what had happened during this long-ago visit of ours. We had stayed for twenty minutes—twenty minutes too long, according to Edmund. From the start the social climate had been, if not icy, at least cloudy, menacing rain. Sylvia was on her own when we arrived, while Clarence was expected to show up around six from the City. When Sylvia tried to pick Edmund's brain regarding a well-balanced diet, Edmund told her that he was all for it, meat and greens, say, chicken and green peas—say, one chicken, one pea.

Then it was about a drug Clarence's mother was taking against high blood pressure. "I've heard about it," said Edmund, "and I'm sure it must be very good because it is very expensive." He then added that one had to avoid being selfish, one had to act according to a humanitarian view, that is, that not only the chemist who sold it, but Pfizer, too, who manufactured it, could not be left to starve. It was at this point—while Sylvia continued staring at Edmund, who had been uttering all this nonsense with his customary grave courtesy—that we heard the screech of the front door. Sylvia gave a deep sigh, as though feeling relieved, and Clarence made his entrance. It was a theatrical entrance, like that of a knight in full armor. Why, I asked myself, had he not taken off his hat and coat in the hall? And why, having entered, did he remain planted on the threshold, thus forcing us, who were seated in front of the dismal gas fire, at odds with the decorous marble Victorian chimneypiece, which was a remnant of the former hearth, to turn around, playing the audience, while he was poised as on a stage?

After a murmured "So this is Edmund. How lovely. I've been longing to meet you," he went on in a stronger, declaiming voice, "I've had just such an encounter, such a scene, imagine it," and he paused impressively, offering himself to our view, as though still drenched in the dew of the law courts, with his bowler hat, black topcoat with narrow velvet collar, dark striped trousers, tightly rolled umbrella, and black briefcase.

"Imagine it. I get out of the tube here in Bayswater, and I'm on the top of the steps when I get accosted by a prostitute. 'Good evening to you, sir, and do you want a naughty girl?' So I stop and tell her, 'Do you know what you are doing? You are soliciting in a public place for immoral purposes. And though I'm only an ordinary citizen of the U.K., it would be within my rights now to seek out a police constable and have you arrested. And do you realize what would be the consequences for you? You'd be taken to jail, you'd be kept in jail for the night, you'd be brought in front of the magistrate in the morning, you'd be charged according to paragraph—,' " and he continued with a rigmarole of legal shop talk, declaiming numbers, letters, and sections of paragraphs, running on and on, gazing ahead of him and proudly smiling.

At the end of this performance he left the room walking backward, still facing us as though fearing to diminish the weight of his speech by turning to leave in the ordinary way. A short time later, he joined us, having shed his outdoor clothing, went to the drink trolley, and asked us in a matter-of-fact voice what we would care to have. Though he was neither short nor tall, the same height as Edmund, he seemed taller than Edmund. This was owing to his chunky, heavy-boned figure, as opposed to Edmund's narrow-boned slightness. (And this, inevitably too, was due to the fact that Edmund was almost a generation older.) He had a short,

blunt nose, a small full-lipped mouth, and round blue eyes set
flat in the face, with a blank stare, as though he never blinked,
and an evenly pink complexion, all of which combined to
make him, if not exactly handsome, nice-looking, rather like
a tailor's dummy—one who, owing to a malevolent fairy's
decree, had come to life and left the shopwindow where he
had been on display. The only odd quality about his looks was
his hair. Thick and covering his head in large waves, it seemed
chiseled out of pewter. He was prematurely gray.

As soon as we were out in the street, Edmund said, "This
man, apart from being a fool, is not normal. This is not
a normal reaction. The ordinary man, when he gets confronted in this way, takes no heed, feigns he hasn't seen or
heard, and just walks on. It depends on the mood you're in.
If you are in a really good mood, you might say something
friendly. 'I'll bear it in mind, when my ship comes home, just
now I couldn't afford a nice girl like you.' " He frowned. He
shook his head. "Sylvia's in for trouble, you can take my
word for it. He's now playing the young husband and father,
so happy, so proud, so everything as it should be. And all the
while so tempted, so taken by that tart, that he had to stop to
give her a lecture."

OUR CURRENT RUN-IN with Clarence had been brought
about by a telephone call three days before. Because Sylvia
and I always corresponded by letter, I had been gripped
by fear when I heard Clarence's voice on the phone, expecting bad news about her or one of their children. "Oh, but

I'm not in England," he told me. "I'm in Genoa. I'm quite near you, what with you in Bordighera. It's only two hours by train."

He then explained that there was a congress, sponsored by the Italian state, dealing with Garibaldi and the period of Garibaldi, and that he, as I knew, was a legal historian and had—too long to explain on the phone. He was going to give two lectures, one in English and one in Italian—the Italian he had written in English and it had been translated for him, of course, but he was to read it himself—anyway, there was a window in the wall of lectures and he was to have a whole day free. Could he come and spend the day with us? It would be the fifteenth of May, a Thursday. He would take the train which was due to arrive in Bordighera at two minutes past eleven, a civilized time, wasn't it? I agreed. I said I'd meet him at the station.

Clarence was sixty now. And when I saw him getting out of the train, even before he set foot on the platform, I saw that the most striking change in his appearance was his hair; still thick and smoothly waved, but now a chalk white, so startling that I suspected it was artificially bleached. When people grow older, their lids tend to droop over their eyes as though they've become wary of seeing more than what's needed. Yet Clarence's pale blue stare was as wide-eyed as before. The former even rosiness of his complexion was now broken up into a cobweb of red veins, and when he lowered his head there was the beginning of a double chin.

He was not dressed like a tourist but, as on that long-ago London afternoon in Westbourne Terrace, as though he'd just stepped out of a lawyer's chambers, in a dark-gray, pencil-striped suit, a three-piece, complete with waistcoat, and he was carrying a black attaché case and a tightly rolled umbrella. "But Clarence," I greeted him, "we are on the Riviera and this is the middle of May. It's more than warm now, it's getting hot." He replied, "Surely, you cannot expect me to go out for a whole day without an umbrella?"

"We needn't take a taxi," I said. "Walking fast, it's about three minutes. We haven't got a car anymore, Edmund isn't up to it."

"How is he? When you write to Sylvia, you never mention him."

"What is there to say? He never tells me what's really the matter with him. He isn't allowed to make up prescriptions here in Italy, because his English degree isn't valid, so he sends me to an Italian doctor just across the street from where we live, and whom he's never met, and this doctor sits down like a child at school taking dictation and copies out the recipes Edmund writes down, and never so much as dares to ask why and wherefore. We know very few people here, a handful of English and Germans, and the odd Italian general, retired, with a bee in his bonnet for painting, but people do talk, and it's a small place, and everybody knows Edmund for what he was, the greatest cardiologist, for twenty years, in the whole of India. And he does go out and about, nearly every day, on the seafront and to the coffeehouse, but at home it's mostly between the bed and the easy chair."

"But it must be dull, for Edmund," said Clarence, "after the kind of life he's led—"

"Well, for one thing, he wanted a place with no snow in winter, and then, he says, he's really always hated having patients, and if he could have afforded it, he'd have done nothing but research, and only the other day he got a request from the university in Leyden—they wanted a reprint of a letter he'd sent to the *Lancet*. Some of his former patients keep nagging him, they phone from London and York and Calcutta. Last week the Maharani of Kapurthala rang him up from London, on her way back to India, would he come out? She'd pay all his expenses. The Maharajah said he couldn't travel abroad because he couldn't afford a whole train for himself anymore and a retinue of thirty, and if he were, say, in a hotel in Europe, on his own, and wanted room service, who would pick up the telephone, even if he would give the order himself?"

Glancing at him sideways, I percieved that Clarence kept looking skyward, a behavior meant to indicate that he found the sky more worthy of interest than Edmund's India. Sylvia adopted this mannerism, too, when she wanted to express her dislike of a topic. I took the hint and changed the subject. "The street we're in now," I went on, "it cuts Bordighera exactly in half. It's called the Bond Street of Bordighera, and the house we live in is the last but one in the street. We're on the top floor, which is the second floor. All the buildings here must be kept low—it's urban planning—but even from this low floor, the view we get is splendid, always. In the winter, though, it's perversely lovely, because down below there are the oranges and lemons, ripe, glowing on the trees, and beyond, in the distance, two chains of mountains, bluish

with snowcaps. And that's not all. They say there are a hundred and fifty kinds of palm trees in Bordighera, but I've
never believed it. And that there is a corner, here, where the
bananas get truly ripe, not just half-baked, as they get in the
gardens all around here, and I don't believe that, either. And
Bordighera had the first tennis court in Italy and the first
manufactory in Italy—that's true, that still exists, they still
make tennis rackets. And now I've told you all the facts and
fictions about the place. And then there's a sort of legend, or
perhaps it's true. There's a hotel here—it's a ruin now, at
night it's full of tramps and drug addicts—but at the turn of
the century it was the cat's whiskers, the grandest on the
whole coast, better than anything even in Nice and Cannes,
and Queen Victoria booked a whole floor for three months
in the winter, but it was a washout because there was the
Boer War and she had to stick it out at home."

When I had left to meet Clarence, Edmund had still been
in his dressing gown of claret-colored silk with white dots.
Now, as we came in, I saw he had got dressed, which meant
that he was having what he called "one of his good days." In
his gray flannels, white shirt, and Prince of Wales check
jacket, casually elegant, he made Clarence look like a carica-
ture of the City gent.

He said, "Clarence, before you sit down, just turn around
and have a look at those statues on top of this bookcase.
They are not bronze. They are covered in gold. The larger
one is the Buddha, the smaller one is an incarnation of
the Buddha, a sort of saint. Tibetan. No museum in the
whole of Europe has anything like it. Only in America, in a

museum in Chicago. I bought them in Kathmandu, from the chief Lama, who dealt in antiques and owned and ran two brothels. When the King heard about it, he got angry, said he would pay for them himself, and the Lama had to return my money to me. The King gave the order the Lama should be paid from the royal purse, and of course the Lama never got his money."

"Why? The King cheated him?" asked Clarence.

"Of course not. It was a matter of the faithful, dependable underlings. When they are told to pay out, you can rely on them, they never do. The money is accounted for and then it just gets lost. On the way."

After lunch we went out to have coffee. When we returned Edmund said, "I'll now show you the picture of something you've never seen before and you'll never see after. I'll just find it, it's in the small safe in my bedroom."

I said, "And get the pictures of you with the King in Egypt. Imagine it, Clarence, first the President of Egypt, Colonel Neguib, received the King with his whole retinue, and then he picked out Edmund and said he wanted to receive Edmund all on his own, the next day. Edmund says he gave him a cup of coffee, and they talked for half an hour. But he never says what they talked about."

As soon as Edmund had left the room, Clarence, who had been sitting in the corner near the French window which gave onto the balcony, got up. He threw his head back, and with both arms outstretched, came running toward me, in an attitude as though of desperate longing. It was a pose that might have been assumed on the stage, but only in a costume play, and even then, only by a youth. The sight of this white-haired man of sixty, the raised arms in the pencil-striped sleeves, the flabby chin trembling, while he was on the run, was more than ludicrous. It was repugnant. As he came rushing at me in a straight line, to the sofa on which I was sitting, it was easy for me to get up and move out of his way to the French window. He bumped into the sofa I had vacated.

"Stop it, Clarence," I said. He now turned to the window, still with his pencil-striped arms raised. I left the window and sprinted into the dining room, which was separated from the drawing room by an archway with a sliding door that was, as usual, left open, as Edmund preferred to have one vast space instead of two small rooms.

I posted myself behind the dining table and gripped the edge of the lyre-shaped back of a chair. It was one of a set of six Biedermeier chairs, and I wondered whether I would be able to lift it and use it as a shield. "Stop it, Clarence," I repeated. "There's nothing doing, do you hear? It's out of the question." I added, "Think of Sylvia." Mentioning Sylvia did not produce the hoped-for effect, because now he made a dash for the archway. As he reached the dining table, I ran round the other side, got back into the drawing room, and from there into the passage leading to the bedroom. As I had expected, Edmund was there. Standing in front of a chest, bent over an open drawer.

"Edmund," I said, "will you please come back with me into the drawing room. And don't now, never again, leave me alone with him." He raised his head and gave me a quick glance. "Quite so," he said, picking up a folder.

"Come along, Clarence," said Edmund as he entered, "let's sit down at the dining table, where I can spread myself out. I've dug out some stuff to make your visit worthwhile. First of all, this here, this photograph, it's not amazing at first sight, is it? What do you see? A dagger. It's life-size, mind you. Never mind the blade, it's bronze, incised. Look at the handle; it is formed of one large single emerald. It belonged to the brother of a minor maharajah, both friends of mine, and he was desperately short of money. He wanted to sell it. I told him to send it to Cartier in Paris and let them handle it, they have worldwide connections, and I knew some people in the French embassy in New Delhi, I got one of them to take it along in the diplomatic bag, the usual way. And what do you think happened?"

"It got stolen," said Clarence.

"No," said Edmund, "Cartier saw it and they sent it back. The message was that they refused to deal with it. It was a unique piece, nothing like it in the whole world, as far as they knew, and so they could not, did not dare, put a price on it. How could they offer it and sell it, if he, the owner, would be within his right to claim they had cheated him and squandered it at a ridiculous price?"

Clarence had a return ticket to Genoa and was going to take the *rapido* at two minutes past eight. He was, he told us, exceedingly anxious about catching trains and would rather sit for half an hour at the station, in discomfort, in a dreary waiting room, and enjoy peace of mind, as long as he knew he would be on the train. Edmund went to the other extreme. I recalled one occasion when he, with the taxicab waiting at the door, had insisted on my preparing a dish of scrambled eggs.

Edmund liked a late dinner, after nine at night, because he never went to bed before one o'clock, and thus it was decided that I would get Clarence's dinner at seven, and he would eat on his own, after which there would be plenty of time for him to get to the station. I had, already in the morning, cooked the main dish, so as to avoid spending a long time in the kitchen later, during the day. It was several slices of osso buco braised on a julienne of carrots, leeks, swedes, and turnips, and it was useful because it spared me from fixing separate dishes like greens or a salad at the last minute.

"I don't suppose," said Edmund, "that you'll want wine after your two whiskeys. It'll be beer, won't it, grain to grain?" and Clarence meekly agreed. I first served him two triangles of toast spread with a liver pâté and then I brought in the main dish and a bowl of rice. "This is scrumptious," said Clarence, starting to eat. I was annoyed but not surprised as I watched him having three helpings. I could see that there would not be enough left for our own dinner. I had been told by Sylvia that, on some occasions, when there was a large array of food on view, Clarence was able to consume an extraordinary amount. At a dinner party, when presented with a platter of grilled chickens, after the other guests had each taken a quarter, Clarence had helped himself to a whole chicken. Sylvia told me that, maybe due to this incident, they had never been asked there again. I said to Clarence, "I'm so glad you like it," wondering whether this greed, this drive to grab anything that happened to be on view, was not of a piece with his former shameless, insistent chasing of me during the afternoon. I then gave him deliberately only one single square of cream cheese and some crackers, and refrained from adding the stuffed olives, the anchovies, and the curls of butter that I had planned on.

Edmund said, "I can see you're suffering from travel fever, a disease for which there is no cure. I suggest you get going. Louise will take you to the station straightaway. As you see, I got back into my dressing gown after our far-flung expedition to the coffeehouse. Now I'll take it easy, I'll dress in stages, and I'll join you in good time to see you off, at the station."

Clarence picked up his attaché case and the umbrella from the chair in the hall where he had deposited them on his arrival. He gripped the case with his left hand and hooked the umbrella over his left arm. Then he moved toward the door. But instead of keeping on straight ahead, he turned right and opened the door of the in-built wall cupboard and made as though to step inside. Still with his head inside the cupboard, he muttered something.

"But Clarence," I cried, "that's not the front door. Keep straight ahead."

We got out on the landing. As there were only two flats on each floor and as the flat opposite ours was empty just now, the lift was still there, as we had left it when returning from the coffeehouse. I let Clarence get in first and while I closed the door behind us, saw him groping at the panel. I said, "No, let me." There were only three buttons to press, ground, first, and second floor. We were on the second floor; I pressed *T,* for *terra,* ground floor.

As soon as the lift started descending, Clarence made a lunge at me, a forward thrust of the upper part of his body, with pursed, pouting lips. I squeezed into a corner at the rear and turned my head away, so that he managed only to brush his mouth against my cheek. Then he straightened up, and just as I thought, Well, that's that, for God's sake, he reached out with his right arm, the one not burdened by case and umbrella, and encircled my waist. I felt a dull, crushing pain. I knew he had done me a grave injury. He said, "Ah," in a triumphant voice and withdrew his grip.

I kept saying to myself, Keep quiet, keep still, don't move, you are at the mercy of a madman, play dead till we get out. He'll want to get out, he wants to catch his train. You can't fight him, and if you tried, he'd crush the very breath out of your body.

The lift stopped, I pushed the door open, and he got out first. The pain, now piercing, was above my waist, on the right side of my body, where I guessed my liver was situated. I calculated that the journey in the lift from second to ground floor had not taken more than fifteen seconds—the only fifteen seconds during the day when I had not been able to get away from him—and I thought that even Edmund, with his knowledge that Clarence was "bats in the belfry" and his promise not to leave me alone with Clarence, had not been able to foresee the threat of my being imprisoned with him in this minute arc of time.

I let him precede me to the front door, and as we got out into the street he turned and said to me in a reproachful voice, "Last time, when you came to visit us, in Farnleigh, Sylvia was with us all the time, so that we couldn't do anything."

I kept silent. I was flooded with relief, knowing that now, as we were in the open, nothing could happen to me anymore. He fell into a brisk walk and began to talk, looking straight ahead, but it was not talk, it was a babble, high-voiced, rushing, and monotonous, over and over the same words pouring out of him, like the coursing waters of a brook. "Tell me where we can meet so that I can rape you." He was in a ghastly, euphoric state, so tightly spun into the web of his derangement that he would not have taken in anything I might have said. Not that I wanted to say anything. The very words he kept repeating proved that he was truly insane. Because how could rape, if it was to be rape, be committed by mutual appointment? He ceased the babbling as we neared the crossing with the traffic lights. Then we entered the short street leading to the station square, with the station building at the far end, blocking out the view of the sea behind it, like a gigantic wedding cake covered in pink sugar icing and decorated with swirls of whipped cream and placed in front of a blue satin sheet.

THERE IS NO railway station I have ever seen which looks less like a railway station than the one in Bordighera. Built at the turn of the century, it seems a country manor, bereft of the park it should be overlooking. The peach-pink wall at the

front might have been added at a later date, so as to be furnished with three glass doors, while a smaller first floor,
crowning it, graced by arched windows with white trim and
green shutters, could have held the bedrooms of the owners
and some guest rooms.

As we were crossing the vast square, Clarence said in
a normal tone of voice, "I couldn't care less about Bordighera, I couldn't care less about Edmund's stories. I only
came to see you."

We entered the main hall. The man behind the ticket
counter watched us, then gave me a puzzled, questioning
look. We got out onto the platform. I said, "There are only
two railway tracks. You arrived on the one opposite. This
here, where we are now, is the right one for you, now."

"Let's sit down," he said.

The platform was almost deserted, perhaps a dozen
passengers, mostly elderly women and a couple of youths,
probably students. As soon as we had sat down on the nearest bench, Clarence, after having placed his case and umbrella on his lap, put a hand on my knee and drew it upward
to my thigh, while turning his face to me and giving me a
lewd, arch, conspiratorial smile. It made me cringe. I saw a
deliberately naughty little boy, trying it on with a grown-up
woman, perhaps a governess, looking out of the face of an
elderly white-haired man. I forced myself to be calm. I said,
"Stop it, Clarence. Everybody around here knows us, me
and Edmund, even this man here," and I pointed to a porter
who was passing by, trundling a laden trolley. The glow of
his smile dimmed. He withdrew his hand while giving me a

reproachful look, the same as when he had said, "But Sylvia was with us all the time and we couldn't do anything."

I got up abruptly and as I did so was pierced by the pain. I slowly moved away, along the platform. Behind the low white fence beyond the second track there was the sea, faintly rippled under the cloudless sky. Soon, I knew, there would arise the amazing reversal of colors, when the sky would turn pink above the blue sea and then the sea would turn pink under the blue sky.

I stopped in front of one of the boards on stilts flanking the door to the waiting room, displaying the sheets with the timetables. It was for departures. I was going to study it, or at least feign to do so, till Edmund's arrival. I was determined not to come near Clarence again until then. He is not entirely crazy, I said to myself, because when I told him that I was known around here, the penny dropped. No, that's not true. He is crazy. Because even a murderer specializing in children never does it when people are around.

Now a bell started pealing, a few yards away from me, behind me, shrill and quavering. I knew that this was the signal that a train had just left the station in Ventimiglia and was on its way to Bordighera. And then I saw the dishy stationmaster come out of his glass-walled office, where the variously colored lights kept flashing like jewels spattered over the blackboards and where he reigned like the privileged guardian of a treasure cave.

The peak of his scarlet cap cast a shadow over his face— the lean face of a man in his late thirties, but the lithe figure in the tight-waisted uniform was that of a young man, and he held himself so erect as to make all those around him look slouched and lumpy. He stationed himself beneath the clock and put a hand on the lanyard above his breast pocket as though wanting to make sure that the whistle within was in its place.

He looked at me.

I went up to him.

I said, "How are you?"

"Whenever I see you I'm well," he said.

I said, "Surely, this can't be yet the fast train to Genoa, it's much too early, isn't it?"

He said, "I shall not contradict you. For two reasons. First, because you are right. It's the slow train to Savona. Second, because even if it were not true, it would be true. Whatever a lovely woman says is right."

He had a way, when pausing, of closing his long narrow lips and smiling with his eyes, which tore at my heart. I said, "How many times before, to how many women, have you given this very same answer?"

"And what if I have? It's true, and is a truth less of a truth because it's been said before?"

I knew we were engaging in sheer *marivaudage*. It was like a cat's cradle: the strings could be crossed, uncrossed, and recrossed, forming forever the same recurring pattern, for as long as required.

He now said, "It is true and I am sincere. When it is a case between a man and a woman there comes a point when the man cannot lie." He gave me a deep smiling look. "As you know." His lips twitched faintly. "Or don't you?"

I did not speak.

He said, "How many years is it since you don't know?"

I did not speak.

He said, "But that's not the worst of it, is it? Before that, you did not like it. It was forced. On your part. Now it's even worse. Because you get the bitterness from him. He's blaming you. It's all your fault, isn't it. It's *you* who flattened him out. It's the old, old story, forever new. You needn't tell me. *I'm* doing the talking now."

I said, "Have you been reading this, between arrivals and departures?" He said, "I lead a double life. At night I do the rounds and I listen behind doors."

I said, "I do believe that you're doing the rounds at night. But I do not believe that you are behind doors, listening. Wasting your time."

He said, "What? Me? Having a woman in my bed at night? What do you take me for? I'm not a husband. One hundred and twenty seconds. The clock above me will tick it off in two minutes. Then roll off, turn your back, and drop off to sleep. And what does that make you feel like? It makes you feel like a prostitute. I only make love in the late afternoon. In the gloaming, when the light must melt away and the dark has come to rule. It does not last long. It is the blue hour."

I said, "Is that what they call it? How odd. Because the only scent I use is *l'heure bleue,* by Guerlain. The blue hour."

His lips twitched. "That friend of yours, that one you've come to see off. I saw you from my office. He's *anglicissimo,* isn't he?"—we were speaking Italian, and what he meant was, superlatively English. "He keeps looking our way."

"Let him," I said.

He said, "I'll tell you what's wrong with you ladies. It's that you cannot understand—you'll never be able to understand—that when you get married to a man you get a husband."

Now in the distance, though I could not tell how far away, there appeared, like a bumblebee, and faintly humming, crawling out of the chalice of a flower of which the petals were formed by the overlapping layers of mountain ridges and swathes and streaks of the sea, the "slow one to Savona."

The stationmaster raised two fingers to his cap, sketching a salute. A last smiling look, both sarcastic and tender. "Husbands," he said, and stepped to the edge of the platform.

I turned my back to the train as it was drawing in. I should have made sure that Clarence did not mistakenly board it. But the rage glowing within me turned all my decent feelings to cinder. Welcome to Savona, I thought, while taking up, once more, my feigned study of arrivals. Or departures. I could not tell. I said to myself, Let's have the truth. Just for once. When someone says, "To tell the truth," it's always something unpleasant. And don't ask for the pure and simple truth, because it doesn't exist. The stationmaster is a tripehound. Edmund is exceptionally distinguished. He was even a celebrity. And yet, I never, not even in the beginning, when he was head over heels about me—I was never drawn to him, there was no seduction. The stationmaster, whose name I don't even know, has in his little finger more than most men have in the whole of their body. It doesn't make sense, it can't be explained. It's not science, it's magic. As Edmund would say, there is nothing one can do about it.

It was sometime after the departure of the Savona train that I, giving a look to see whether Clarence was still on his bench, saw that Edmund had arrived. He was talking to Clarence, who was now on his feet. I went over to join them.

Edmund was saying, "You are in first class, aren't you? When the train comes in, you must walk ahead, where the locomotive is, because there are only two first-class coaches, and they are always right in front."

"How very knowledgeable you are, Edmund," said Clarence.

Edmund said, "That's because now, when we haven't got a car, one still wants to get about a bit. San Remo, Nice, Monte Carlo."

Clarence said, "Why don't you apply for a job as a stationmaster?"

"I'm afraid I would not be found acceptable," said Edmund. "For one thing, I'm over the age limit, whatever it might be, that's for sure." He did not notice the look Clarence gave me—reproachful, once more the willful little boy who wants to snatch and grab and has been foiled. No doubt he had observed that my conversation with the lithe man in the tight-waisted uniform had lasted much longer than the usual inquiry about trains.

On our way home we were silent except for one remark by Edmund. "It's not really fair on Clarence. He doesn't drink that much. Only two whiskeys before lunch and two before dinner. And yet he's already starting a drinker's nose."

NOW EDMUND CONCLUDED, reaching at last for the newspaper, "And it's no use either, telling Clarence what he's done to you. If you did, he'd either laugh or say you made it up and that you are a liar."

I said, "I can understand why he'd call me a liar. But why would he laugh?"

"It's the pride, the vanity—look what I've done, look how strong I am, and how cunning. It's, in miniature, the case of that Italian madman Luigi Luccheni, who killed the Empress Elizabeth of Austria as she was boarding the steamer in Geneva. He was very pleased with himself. He told the police that he wasn't an ordinary killer, he'd never have bothered to kill a washerwoman. No, he was special."

"But I still can't understand it. What went on in his mind, in the first place, when he tried it on, here, in the drawing room? What if I'd played along with him and fallen into his swinish arms? What with you down the corridor and not one hundred miles away, and liable to come in any moment? What then?"

Edmund said, "You must understand the drive taking over, drowning the reasoning faculty. And there is this element of vanity I've just mentioned, that he's special, he's protected. He'd snatch a kiss so fast that there'd be no risk."

I said, "But in the lift. What pleasure is there, I ask you, my cheek and my waist—it isn't like getting the thrill of really and truly laying a woman."

Edmund said, "The way I see it, he doesn't want that kind of satisfaction. I'd say it's a case of kleptomania, of stealing sex, but it isn't actual sex, it's only a symbolic gesture. You might say he had the satisfaction—in his mind—of raping you. And don't forget that he, as you told me, when he started driveling all along the way to the station, kept saying, 'Meet me so that I can rape you!' And for the real thing he's got Sylvia, hasn't he, and they've got three children who may be his—it's a clever child which knows its own father—and this grab-and-snatch he plays is a godsend to him, because it sustains his vanity and at the same time it makes him feel virtuous. Because—what's a kiss? It isn't adultery. But maybe what I'm telling you is wrong. Give me a nice coronary thrombosis and I'll tell you what's what. When it's a case of madness one should not try to seek a reason, a logical behavior, where there is none. That's what madness is. If it were reasonable it would not be madness." And before picking up the *Herald Tribune* he cautioned me once more not to tell Sylvia.

There was one more remark Edmund made regarding Clarence, and that was sometime later in the evening, when I told him that there was hardly anything left of the osso buco and asked him what kind of a stopgap dish he would like for dinner. "Mind you," he said, "there would have been one way of dealing with Clarence."

I said, "Do you mean I should have given him just one slice on a plate?"

"It's an idea, but it's not what I meant. I've been thinking that another woman in your place would have kneed him."

"What's that?" I asked.

"Raised a knee and hit him in the balls."

"I've never heard of it before," I said. "But if I had, of course, when he went for me here in the flat I could have managed it. But not in the lift. It would have been too much of a narrow squeeze, I'd say."

Edmund said, "Why not invite Clarence over once more and try it out? Theories aren't much use. If we hadn't done any experiments we'd still be believing in the phlogiston theory, wouldn't we?"

IN THE DAYS to come I did not speak to Edmund about Clarence, though my rage about him did not abate, especially as the recurring piercing pain, which stabbed me even when I turned lightly in bed, kept it aglow. I was convinced that Edmund was right that I should not tell Sylvia. And this not for her sake but for mine. Because I was sure that if I did, it would create an abyss of feeling between us.

Sylvia had always been what Maupassant called "a fanatical mother," and this admirable love, all-forgiving and all-accepting, she extended to Clarence as well. But I have never believed the wisdom of the phrase "What's sauce for the goose is sauce for the gander," for the obvious reason that, as the goose is different from the gander, the sauce cannot retain, when applied, the same flavor. I was certain that Clarence in his turn would not have been equally forgiving if confronted with any amorous waywardness on Sylvia's part.

Edmund had once told me, after reading about a case of passionate crime, that there were two patterns when a triangle was involved, made up of husband, wife, and the wife's lover. He said, "When the husband kills the lover, that's all right. That's where it stops. But when the husband kills the wife, he's got to kill himself afterward. Because he sees the wife as part of himself."

Two weeks after Clarence's visit, we went to the station to get a train to Monte Carlo, and there was another station-master posted under the clock on the platform. I also saw that the hanging flower baskets suspended from the narrow roof, formerly filled with petunias, were now filled with geraniums. My first thought was that the dishy stationmaster had been killed by a husband. Then I convinced myself that I was being idiotic and that the reason for the change was that he had been posted away, probably to a bigger, busier station. I did not inquire. I never found out.

It was in the late autumn of that year that I heard Edmund say for the last time, "There is nothing I can do about it."

It was one o'clock in the morning. Edmund was in the drawing room and I told him I was going to bed.

"I'll go to bed later," he said, "there may be some more news on the wireless."

"Well, good night," I said. "Oh, my God."

He said, "What is the 'Oh, my God' for?"

I said, "The state you're in. If nothing else, the look in your eyes. No, I don't mean the way you're looking at me. I mean the way your eyes appear—all clouded over."

He said, "There is nothing I can do about it."

On the following morning, as usual, I took the small radio into the kitchen, so as not to disturb him, and drank my coffee. Edmund would have his scrambled eggs, toast, butter, and coffee and cream much later, in the dining room. The news I heard from the English radio in Monte Carlo was that Indira Gandhi had been murdered. Edmund had known her. He had also known her sister, married to a lawyer in Bombay. And he had known her father. He had met Nehru at a lunch party in Kapurthala Palace and had been told by the Maharani that Nehru, upon leaving, had said to her, "The doctor has such an interesting face."

I knew that Edmund would be stunned by the news. I looked in on him. He was in bed, asleep I thought at first. Then I realized that he was unconscious. He never got to know the news. He died three days later.

AFTER EDMUND'S DEATH, on the fourth of November, and again before Christmas, Sylvia wrote and asked me to stay with them. "Clarence also keeps saying, 'Why don't you ask Louise?' He keeps telling me how he enjoyed that day he spent with you in Bordighera. He was fascinated by Edmund's stories, too."

I took this as a hint to me from Clarence, to keep my silence with Sylvia. But then I thought that I was seeing guile and guise where there was none. He was, as Edmund had said, morally insane. He probably imagined that, if I'd come to stay, he would be able to "do something" as he called it, and not be caught, or if he were he would have passed it off as a harmless prank.

In the beginning of the New Year, Sylvia sent me a letter telling me about Clarence's accident. It had happened on Boxing Day. Clarence had been pulled out of his car, unconscious, and even now could not recall what had happened to him. He had been on his way to a party in Brighton, to which they both had been asked, but Sylvia, who did not care for standing about in a crowded room with a drink in her hand, had decided to stay at home.

As it had happened in a narrow, bumpy, sandy country lane, enclosed on both sides by high tightly knit hedges, the police had been able to ascertain that no other car was involved when he veered off the lane and drove into the hedge. It had been his fault entirely.

The car was irretrievably damaged, and it was a miracle that he had survived. He had broken multiple ribs and a thighbone, but the doctors were sure he would soon be up and about with a stick and crutches.

But what was more amazing, Sylvia wrote, was Clarence's cheerfulness and high morale. He knew it had been God's will to save him. The car was a dead loss. God was not interested in cars. God was interested in Clarence and had not wanted him to die. It was truly a miracle, and was it not wonderful, wrote Sylvia.

I recalled that several years before, an old Englishwoman, one of our few acquaintances in Bordighera, told us how she'd had a quarrel with her neighbor. His cat had got into her garden and soiled and messed up one of her flower beds. On the next day the neighbor had been run over and killed by a car as he was crossing the road. "And when I heard about this," she concluded, "I thought, Dear me, I hadn't meant it as badly as all that."

Edmund had told me afterward, "She's a textbook case of paranoia. She sees herself as invested with magical powers. Her thoughts can kill."

I said, "But she's not a charwoman. She is an admiral's widow."

He said, "That's nothing to do with it. You might just as well say she can't get flu because she is an admiral's widow."

As this came to my mind, I thought that if I were the Admiral's widow I would say, measure for measure: having slyly broken one of my ribs when I was imprisoned in the lift, Clarence was now punished manifold. But I knew this was rubbish. And the fact that he was certain that his life was precious to God was only further confirmation of Edmund's diagnosis of those many years ago, in Westbourne Terrace, that Clarence was "bats in the belfry."

Edmund had been outstanding. Edmund had deserved his celebrity. It could not be denied. No one had ever denied it. Yet Edmund had not been admirable.

And there arises before me the vision of the lithe figure in the tight-waisted uniform. He raises two fingers to his scarlet cap, sketching a salute. His smile is tenderly sarcastic. "Husbands," he says. And then he steps to the edge of the platform.

Nymph & Faun

There is a kind of woman, rich and looking it, climacteric, widowed or divorced, who when faced with an empty afternoon panders to her gnawing malice and dissatisfaction by going on a fake expedition in the nearest well-to-do shopping district. There she will enter one or two opulent shops dealing in jewels or dresses. She will pretend to be searching for one particular item. She will be ingenious in telling the sales staff why a piece is "almost what I had in mind, but—," and leave, after half an hour or more. She will call this sport "turning their heads" or "giving them a runaround," adding, "There's no harm in it, is there? That's what they're here for, aren't they? After all?"

I have always despised women like that. I hate being teased or teasing. There was once a time when I did enter into this kind of game, though. And when I did, I was first curious, then touched, then hooked, then trapped, then dragged along, and finally brought to realize that my husband was really dead—that my marriage no longer existed and that he was not absent, as I had been feeling, but gone forever.

I must plead the excuse that in my case the game playing was not premeditated. I was drawn into it by chance, and I played it conversely, not pretending a wish to buy but a desire to sell. Outwardly I was well suited to play the game. I was rich, I was widowed, I was fifty-two, the sand in my hourglass running short, with ever-scantier bloodstains marking the passage of each month. I had been widowed after a marriage of some twenty years. But though the marriage had gone, I did not feel that it was finished. I still brushed and aired my husband's suits with more care than I gave to my own garments. I never sat at his desk, I never sat in his favorite chair, and in the winter, instead of using my eiderdown, I huddled in the heavy brown striped dressing gown of Turkish toweling which he had continually worn indoors during the last year of his life. And I never took a decision without asking for what I imagined might be his approval.

I had not, as people thought (considering that he was old enough to be my father), married him because he was rich. I did not know that he was rich when I met him. Nor did I know it during our marriage. I only found out after his death. What I did know, as soon as I met him, and what did not fail to fill me with admiration forever after, was his distinction.

I have the conceit that an admiral or a field marshal may be bottle-nosed, paunchy, or knock-kneed, but he must have such an air of command that he could walk stark naked out on deck, or stand that way facing a platoon, and still be obeyed and venerated for what he is. My husband, who was a physician, possessed this air of indubitable, unquestioned authority, no matter whether his slight body was draped in a bath towel or disguised by the discreet elegance of his Savile Row suits. This rare quality, as mysterious as it was impressive, seemed to me, who was not English, the acme of English distinction, and it shone through even in trite circumstances. Thus he could say to a servant, "I'll have to engage another maid to walk behind you and switch off the lights you have left on," and this would be received with a deferential smile. If I had made the same remark, using those very same words, the maid would have given notice.

There is this young woman in Hampstead, the story goes, who visits her doctor for a checkup. The doctor says, "And how are you feeling?" She says, "I feel well, really. Only, as you know, I am a widow. I have no love life." He says, "What do you want—you're in the same boat as all the married women in Hampstead." I learned the truth of the story, without regret, when my husband said to me after the first few years of our life together, "You bore me in bed. You are too passive. And you have no sense of humor." I didn't even ask him where the sense of humor came in.

How could I be hurt by his utterance, with Gordon ever present in my mind? Gordon had locked me up in his heart, had thrown the key away, and had walked off into suicide. He had broken with me suddenly, without my being prepared for it. He said, "It's got to finish. I shan't see you anymore."

I said, "You have another girl, have you?"

He said, "Yes, I have, and I'll be sick to death of her in six weeks' time. But that is not the point."

I said, "What's the point?"

He said, "Sexually I'd never tire of you—I could go on with you forever. But it's got to end."

I said, "Why?"

He said, "Because I'm afraid of what I might do to you. Look what I've done to you already. You are enslaved to me—you can't take a single step without me. I don't want to get rid of you, but I must." And then, forcing a jovial air, he added, "I've been eating you and drinking you and sleeping you. I have pleasured you. I have listened to your girlish babble—I, a highly qualified man. Have you anything to complain of?"

"No," I said.

Gordon was a psychiatrist, which made him a highly qualified listener. When I first met him, he had recently left the navy and taken rooms and surgery in Queen Anne Street off Harley Street. Gordon was not a soldier. He was a sailor. He was not meat. He was fish. And just as fish is to be eaten on Fridays and as Lenten fare, when meat is not allowed, in days of penitence, so Gordon meant for me torture, but torture leading to salvation. He also meant my being forced to disclose myself to him, being accepted, and being taken to his bosom. Shortly before the break Gordon said to me, "I'll hold you forever. Because I'll always find new ways of torturing you."

It is my own torture, I suppose, to continue to ask myself how it came to be that the two most important men in my life were both doctors. I cannot say why, except that I am certain that, rather than the pale similarity of their profession, it was the difference between Gordon (who was dead) and my living husband-to-be that urged me to make the marriage. Gordon was an obscure psychiatrist with a long term of service in the navy, while my husband was a cardiologist of international standing, with much research and many publications to his credit. By choosing him, by going eagerly into the marriage that way, was I not telling myself that I did not regret Gordon's suicide, that I had replaced all that, that I felt—had forced myself to feel—I had risen above a past of such sorrow?

WHEN THE TELEPHONE rang at half past three one afternoon last January I almost didn't answer it. Living, as I did, on the Italian Riviera, with Monte Carlo less than an hour's drive away, across the frontier, none of the people I was friendly with would be likely to call at this hour. They were expatriates, as I was, mostly retired and at leisure, who rested after lunch and were not disposed to be affable until later in the afternoon.

I took up the receiver, saying "Yes?" in a high, languid voice, ready to be annoyed. A man's voice said, "Mrs. Richardes?"

I did not know the voice. It was a full, hard baritone. I knew at once that here was an Englishman, ruling class, and no nonsense about it. I also knew he was precise and careful. He had not pronounced my name sloppily, as most people did, as "Richards," but had sounded the *d* and the *s*, giving the *e* between its full due.

I said, "Yes, speaking"—this time in a quite different voice.

He said, "I've got your letter in front of me. It was sent to me by our house in Paris."

I said, "Where are you?"

He said, "In Geneva."

I said, "But that costs so much."

He laughed faintly.

I recognized the laughter, indulgent, politely amused, which I had not heard for—what was it?—nearly thirty years. Sitting on the edge of my bed, I put an elbow on the bedside table, resting my forehead on my free hand. I closed my eyes in a foolish attempt to shut out my present surroundings and to be flooded by a wave of the past.

A few heartbeats later he said, "I see here in your letter you say that your Odiot tea set is 1808. How do you know? Who told you that?"

I said, "Nobody told me, personally—no expert, that is. My husband told me."

He said, "Your husband was wrong. Because with Odiot you can never tell the year, not like with other hallmarkings. Your Odiot can just as well be 1815, for all you know."

"I see," I said, humbly.

We were talking about silver. Odiot is the greatest silversmith in France. They started making silverware for Louis XIV, continued for Louis XV, and then for each succeeding reigning monarch, including Napoleon. They are still the most celebrated manufacturers of their kind in France.

He said, "Is it white silver, or vermeil?"

And, pleased at having understood him, I said, "White silver." By now I not only had recognized his laughter but also knew exactly what he looked like. Besotted as I was by the sound of the smilingly indulgent voice, I found my reasoning perfectly logical. And following this same benighted line, I also knew that anything I were to tell him would be received with interest and without judgment; it would be the same as it had been with Gordon. If I had said that I had just been strangling my father with my mother's guts, he would have accepted the news with a mildly cheerful "Ah, yes."

"Those candlesticks, that pair," he said. "Nearly twenty pounds' weight between them—you are sure of that, are you?"

I said, "Oh, quite. That's written down in an inventory I dug out. For the customs. That's when my husband sent them to Chiasso. I never set eyes on them—only photographs my husband took before the candlesticks were packed up for storage. Figures of a man and a woman. Ghastly ugly. Called 'Nymph and Faun.' Mind you, I know that beauty doesn't enter into it, when it's a case of rare silver. But I have a horrible feeling that they are not Renaissance at all. My

husband thought they were Renaissance, by wishful thinking, but he never got an opinion on them. What if they are
Victorian, of the most terrible period?"

He said, again with his caressingly indulgent laugh, "Don't
worry. Even if they are Victorian, there is a market for them.
A very decent market."

"Just as well," I said. "As long as they are sold. It's not
the— I don't care. I'm not starving. It's just that I'm sick and
tired of hanging on to something I've never even seen, and
paying money for it year in, year out."

He said, "And it's stored in Chiasso, in customs-free
deposit, is it?"

"Yes, it's been there for thirty years—that's to say for
thirty-two years, really, but in the letter I wanted to give a
round figure."

He said, "Ah, yes."

"They are stored in a crate," I went on. "I saw it once. I
was in Lugano at that time, and I went to Rosecrans, in Chiasso. I just walked to Rosecrans from the station, and then
we walked round to the free-bond office with one of the
Rosecrans employees. That was in '72. Now we are in '90:
how long ago is that?"

"Eighteen years," he said pleasantly.

I said, "You must be mad. No person in their right mind
could tell this straight off."

"Go on," he said, laughing faintly.

I said, "The crate was brought out and put on the scales.
The weight was right, sixty kilos, and the crate looked right,

too—not interfered with, you know. And then it was shoved away again."

"How big is the crate?" he said.

I said, "When it's stood up it's about like me. I'm just five foot. And it's insured for fifty thousand francs, against fire and theft and whatever."

"Ah, yes," he said. "And the payments have been going on for thirty-two years now?"

"Yes, my husband said it must never be sold, ever, because it might be very valuable," I said. "He had this thing that the longer you keep something, the more valuable it gets. And to Rosecrans I pay twenty-five francs a year for their *Mühewaltung*—do you know what that means?"

He said, "Indeed I do—it means that Rosecrans have the administration of it. Am I right?"

I felt gratified at this expertise of his, just as I had felt gratified before, when I mentioned the name of Rosecrans, the big international moving-and-storage firm, and he knew who was meant. He seemed to know, as well, that the Rosecrans office was in Chiasso, at the southern tip of Switzerland.

"But I have a problem," I went on.

He said, "Ah, yes, do tell me."

"The silver is in my husband's name. And my husband is dead, but they don't know it. What if they get sticky? What if they refuse to let go of it? You see, we've got a trust in Liechtenstein, of which I am the sole whatever-you-call-it. But what if my husband forgot to get the silver included in the trust? I have several last will and testaments—one made out in Lisbon, by an English lawyer there, and another one done in London, when my husband just happened to be there. They're all valid, with two witnesses, and they're all the same, leaving everything to me absolutely. Would I need to show them?"

"Tell me," he said. "These storage fees, how much are they?"

"Five hundred francs a year," I said.

"And ever since your husband's death, did you make those payments in your own name?"

I said, "Of course, though I'm afraid I have no receipts for them."

"There is no problem. You don't say anything, you just go to Chiasso and take the crate out. How long is it since your husband died?"

I said, "Three years."

He said, "That's perfect," and he laughed faintly.

"But there's another problem," I said. "There will be customs duty to pay once I take it out of bond."

He said, "You won't take it out of bond. I'll take it out of bond. I'll take everything out of your hands. Don't worry. I'll do the worrying."

I said, "But how can I get hold of you so that you can do the worrying for me?"

He said, "I'll write you a letter. I'll drop it in the post tonight."

I said, "Thank you," into a void. He had rung off.

I was again conscious of the beating of my heart, not as

jumpy as before but slow and strong now, giving me signals
of warning in the way that opinionated people do in serious
conversation, putting a heavy accent on every word.

IT WAS NOW THURSDAY in the first week in January,
and it had been before Christmas that I had gone to Monte
Carlo, to the Palace of the Sporting d'Hiver, on the viewing
day of one of those stupendous auctions put on by Brentford's several times a year. I was living in Bordighera, a cul-
tural desert, and I looked upon these shows as banquets to
make up for my periods of starvation.

It was a warm, brightly sunny afternoon, on which one did
not remark because one took it for granted. The main hall,
with its display of early-nineteenth-century French paintings,
starring names like David, Géricault, and Legros, was densely
crowded, and, seeking an interval of repose, I wandered off
into a narrow adjoining room, brilliantly lit, and lined with
glass cases filled with silver. This, too, I learned, was part of
the display; the auctioning of the rare silver was to follow
that of the paintings, the next day.

Here several young women of the staff were standing
about, all cast in the same mold—blond, tall, flat-figured,
thin-lipped, their straight hair fastened in ponytail fashion
with black velvet bows. They were old-maidish despite being
in their early thirties, and I wondered whether Brentford's
had a preference for their kind or whether their kind had a
preference for Brentford's.

It was only then that I noticed that there was one man

present as well. He had been hidden from my sight before, standing in a corner, and now he was coming forward to meet me. It was he who triggered and set in motion the fateful events that were to follow, not only because he was in charge but because of his aristocratic looks and large brown eyes with no glimmer of feeling in them. Seeing him, I decided to enter into the game of teasing pretense.

He came toward me in a leisurely way, obviously undecided whether I was worth his customary "May I help you?"

I said in French, "I have an Odiot tea service."

The effect of my words was remarkable. Halting in front of me with flattering abruptness, the young man said, "Oh, yes?" And soon I had a chorus of thin-lipped, ponytailed maidens around me, shrieking with pleasure at the news that I had a case with sixty kilos of silver in deposit in bond in Switzerland for which payments had been made over the past thirty years. Their merriment grew so loud that another of their ilk came in from the main room, telling us off because we were making such a din.

The young man gave me a card with the Paris Brentford's address, asking me to let him have further details and giving me to understand that my obstinacy in holding on to the silver was both ridiculous and wasteful.

When I got home, I was still in the mood of provocative teasing, wanting to find out what the silver might be worth, without the slightest intention of putting it on sale. I wrote him a letter. I gave the overall weight of the Odiot, which was made up of a stand, a teapot, a milk jug, a cream jug, a sugar bowl, and a cake dish. I gave the weight of the pair of candlesticks as roughly nineteen pounds, and described them as being two-branched figures of nymph and faun. I wrote "nymph & faun," feeling that the entwined ampersand made the letter look more businesslike. I addressed him not as "Dear Sir" but by his name on the card, Du Cross–Lafalaise, noting with satisfaction that I had been right in judging his looks as aristocratic. I put my name and address at the head of the letter.

And now, still sitting on the edge of my bed, and recalling the scene in Monte Carlo, and running through in my mind the wording of my letter to Paris, and feeling the signal of my emphatically beating heart, I suddenly felt like gasping for breath.

The man from Brentford's in Geneva, whose name I did not know, had called me on the telephone. This meant that he had gone to the trouble of finding out my number after reading my letter, which had been forwarded from their Paris office; that he had not intended to write me a letter, which I might throw away; that he had meant to apply shock and surprise tactics; that he meant to force answers out of me for which I could not have prepared myself beforehand; that he did not mean to let go. And recalling his laugh, and his looks, which I felt sure I knew, I thought how like Gordon he was, in invading and taking possession before one had time to defend oneself.

When I had first met Gordon, in the late afternoon of a mild, gray-skied day in June, he had picked me up in a pub in

Mayfair, where I had gone on the off chance of meeting one or several groups of my friends who used to gather there almost daily. Without my being aware of him, he had suddenly stood behind me, taken the glass I was holding out of my hand and placed it on the windowsill, grasped my wrist, and said, "Let's go somewhere else." And I, as though rendered senseless by the pressure of his hard thumb against my pulse, had found myself outside with him before I could gather my wits. He violated me on the bench in the garden of a house in Kensington where he was living in rooms. He had taken me there to show me the grounds, and I had agreed, believing that as long as we kept in the open air there could be no danger of any amorous advances. I had gone on believing it while strolling with him on the graveled paths of an ill-kept Edwardian garden, with tall old bedraggled trees, and shrubs whose foliage had been blanketed by the sooty London air. I was listening only halfheartedly as he told me of his disgust about his years in the navy, when he stopped in front of a bench. Halting in midsentence, Gordon threw me backward onto the bench and, remaining upright on his feet, showed me without any words how mistaken I had been. On that day in June, just like the man from Brentford's in Geneva, he had been nameless.

It was four days after the telephone call that I received the promised letter from Geneva, if letter it could be called. There were two cards in the envelope, both printed, the larger with Brentford's Geneva address and "With compliments," the smaller the card of Brentford's Mr. E. Byrnes

Forbes, with the same address and his direct-line telephone number. He was a Brentford's man, then—I hadn't been certain—but was acting on his own in our transaction. He had written a large scrawl on the bottom of the bigger card—his signature, done in a few slanting dashes, in which not even an *E,* or a *B,* or an *F* could be made out. I now sent him a letter saying, "Let's do it at once," as though harping on our intimacy and wishing to disguise the meaning to anyone else who might be reading it. Then I added, "At your earliest convenience," to mask my feverish desire to meet him.

He rang me up three days later, saying, "Mrs. Richardes," in his precise pronunciation, and without giving his name.

I said, "I wrote you a letter."

He said, "I've just got it. I've been looking at my diary. Would the first of February suit you?"

I said, "And what—"

He said, "It's a Thursday."

We both repeated, "Thursday, the first of February," in unison.

He said, "And where shall we rendezvous?"

"At Rosecrans," I said, "because they are in charge."

He said, "How will you get there?"

I said, "By train. I haven't got a car. There is, I think, a train at a ghastly hour, something like seven in the morning, I'm not sure, but I think, I think. It's via Milan and change there. I think I'll get to Chiasso by one o'clock."

He said, "I'll fly to Lugano. That's near Chiasso, isn't it?"

I said, "You know, I've looked up other lists I found since. There is more silver, unspecified. Dishes and ewers. And three rattles. Children's rattles. It sounds crazy."

"Oh, yes," he said, unperturbed. "Do not worry. I'll take everything from you."

"Even the rattles?" I said.

"I will," he said. "The Odiot and the candlesticks I'll take with me to Geneva, and the rest I'll throw into Zurich. We have a place there for this kind of stuff. Don't worry. That's definite." He added after a pause, "I'm looking forward to meeting you," and I, to disguise my eagerness, rang off with a hurried good-bye.

I blamed myself after this. I must have sounded quite scatterbrained to him, with my senseless "I think, I think" about the train times. And why did I have to bring up those crazy-sounding rattles, as though the uncertain number of dishes and ewers had not been sufficient to get him exasperated at my disordered rambling? And I thought with bitterness how meaningless his formula of politeness, when parting, must have been.

I SHOULD AGAIN make it clear that my negotiations with Forbes about the silver had nothing to do with money, at least on my part. Neither of us had mentioned a price for the Odiot and the rest, but I knew, as he did, that the sum in question could be in the thousands if not the tens of thousands of pounds—a considerable sum but not one that I was required to draw upon at that time in my life. This had not always been the case, or what I believed to be the case, about the state of my fortunes. My husband, who often said, "A life without servants is no life," had in the last years of our marriage moved us from a great villa in Estoril, in Portugal, to the small flat in Bordighera, on the western Italian Riviera. Servantless owing to this move, I had accepted this change in our lifestyle without a question, taking for granted that it was due to our reduced means. I knew all too well his frequent laments about his investments, and his telephone calls to his banker in Zurich, which he always started, disdaining to give his name, like this: "How are you? . . . Fine . . . Same here. Now, look—do I have any money? How much? Oh dear, oh dear. What am I to do? Because I've had this idea. I've been thinking—" At which point I always ceased to listen, for what followed made no sense to me, except to reinforce my conviction that his finances were in a precarious state. Ignorant as I was of his wealth, I did not know that he could have easily rented an opulent gentleman's residence, as had been his wont up till then.

I did all the housework. And though he often claimed to regret that I had to do it, his demands and rules did not diminish: a colored tablecloth for breakfast, a white damask cloth for dinner, butter curls in silver shells at each meal, and a separate tiny silver saltcellar with a minute salt spoon in front of each cover. He liked to say that not one day passed without his reading in the news the name of someone he had met and known. It would have been unforgivable if now, believing him to be impoverished, I had denied him his comforts—a man of his distinction and eminence, a man who had been a king's physician and who had given up, after the King's death, all medical practice, saying that he could not, after all, advertise in the *Times* for another royal patient.

In Bordighera, during the last year of his life, he had developed a quirk that I found increasingly hard to bear. He was by then in his eighty-third year, and growing steadily more enfeebled. Although he still managed to get dressed and go to a coffeehouse at night, he used to spend his days alternately lying down and sitting in our drawing room. Forced to save his strength, he avoided moving about, which meant that I had to fetch and carry constantly. Most tiring for me were his continual demands for mineral water, which he took with tiny sips of whiskey. The mineral water had to be ice cold, so I had to go each time to the kitchen, take the bottle out of the refrigerator, and then return it. The constant jumping up and dashing to and fro, the lifting and carrying of the heavy bottle, was for me a backbreaking fatigue.

It was at this point that the quirk would show itself. After his usual request for mineral water, just as I was on the threshold of the room, on my way back to the kitchen, he would call out to me to stop. "Here, come here and take this ashtray with you—it's full," he would say. And I would return to the marble-topped table in front of his easy chair, take the ashtray, and return in time from the kitchen with the water and the emptied ashtray. Very soon thereafter, almost each time, he would stop me just when I was in the door and make me retrace my steps, with an order, say, to pick up a dropped handkerchief and put it into the laundry basket, or to remove an empty glass, or to retrieve a fallen newspaper, or suchlike.

After a few days I remonstrated. I said, "Please don't keep calling me back just when I'm halfway out. I'd much rather do one errand and then another."

"But I'm only doing this to save you labor," he said. "As you know, I'm sorry for you, having to do so much, now that there are no maids. I'm only trying to spare you."

I found this reasonable. And yet, after a few more days, his "wishing to spare you" became increasingly obnoxious. And when I complained once more, saying that I'd rather not be stopped in my tracks, he said I was ridiculous to object. I did not argue anymore after this, but, ridiculous or not, I did not feel cared for by him, but on the contrary, choked, hobbled, strangled.

His obsessive halting me and delaying me he practiced, too, every time I got ready to go out to do the shopping. Just as I was about to open the front door, he would call me back two or three times running: "Don't forget to look in the mailbox when you get down," or "Do look in at the chemist's for my order," or "Do look in at the newsagent's for the *Herald Tribune*." And when I said that I never forgot to look in the mailbox, or that the chemist had said the medicine would not be in yet, or that the newsagent could not possibly have the *Tribune* because the foreign papers never arrived till four in the afternoon, he would say, "Never mind, you can always try. And with the mailbox you might forget, just this once."

Each day, my going out grew into a desperate battle to leave, but I kept silent. As my resentment smoldered and simmered and felt harder to keep under control, my sense of guilt increased. He was on the point of death, and I reproached myself for not being utterly fond of him.

It did occur to me, of course, that what he pretended was benevolent care was in fact disguised malice. I thought that he had started to hate me for my shortcomings, such as my past unwillingness to supervise the servants and to restrict their wasteful habits. I knew also, though he never blamed me outright, that he held me responsible for the fading and the ultimate cessation of his love life, due to what was, for him, my amorous ineptitude. On the other hand, in my case there had never been any love to bury; Gordon had remained within me forever, even after his suicide.

Perhaps to show me that he had been successful in his relationships with women before our marriage, to the point of gaining their enduring affection, my husband took to inviting his former mistresses to come and stay with us, for two or three weeks at a time, when we were living in plentiful ease and space in Estoril, in our fake fortress of a villa, with a tower and crenellated roof, a cloistered walk, parquets of flowers in front, and a pinewood in the grounds at the rear. I could not plead the excuse of being incommoded by their presence in a house with six bathrooms, a laundry room, an ironing room, a boiler room, and a gardener's and chauffeur's quarters. But on these occasions he would reproach me for not showing heartfelt pleasure toward our guests, then saying, "I do not mean this to be critical. It is just a statement."

And when those guests, and other people, too, exclaimed at our *grand seigneur* style of life, he would brush it aside, saying that the house was only rented, that Portugal was ridiculously cheap, and that for the rent he was paying in Estoril he would not be able to afford even a two-room flat in London.

These visits from my husband's women had tapered off when we moved to Bordighera. But then there came another occasion. About six weeks before his death, he was rung up from New York by one of his former mistresses. That evening, while we were sitting in a coffeehouse, we talked about her, and my husband said, "*On revient toujours à son premier amour.* We have been lovers ever since I first knew her."

I said, "But that's way back."

"That's true," he said. "We didn't meet often, but whenever we did meet we picked up where we left off. Lugano and Estoril."

I looked at him, speechless, and he said sharply, "That's none of your business."

Neither of us referred to her again. As is my way, I did not show that I was stunned. What had actually gone on between them the last time she visited Estoril, when he was well into his seventies, I did not want to guess. I did not believe that there had been many of Cupid's arrows left in his quiver. I was amazed at my benightedness, at my not having noticed what must have taken place on all those visits. But what wounded me was that he had felt compelled to make his disclosure gratuitously. This shattered me, for what it came from was his wish to bring my inadequacy home to me. Marriage is the tomb of love.

NOW, IN THE LAST WEEK in January, as I prepared to meet Forbes in Chiasso and found myself filled with a fierce desire to bring about what he had called our "rendezvous," there came a setback that promised to be disastrous. A series of railway strikes, which would block my journey, was announced. I was so desperate at the news that I asked a taxi driver how much he would charge to drive me to Chiasso, and he said it would come to half a million lire, or two hundred and fifty pounds. Miserly though I am (a quality once much appreciated by my husband), I did not flinch. Never did it occur to me to put off the meeting with Forbes to a later date. At this same time, my hairdresser, who had never yet canceled an appointment during all the years I had gone there, turned me away not once but twice, owing to some sudden unforeseen trouble with her staff. These incidents had no connection, to be sure, but determined as I now was to defy my husband's wishes about the silver, for no other reason than to meet Forbes, and feeling guilty about it, I began to imagine that my husband was stretching out ghostly hands from his grave, trying to delay me, to choke me. It was much the same sensation I had had many times in the last year of our marriage, when he had hectored and exhausted me with his demands, delivered from his easy chair behind the marble-topped table in the drawing room.

As I have said, his seated figure was habitually encased there in a thick, unwieldy dressing gown of Turkish toweling, which made him look like his own graveside monument—a Greek stele, with the head and shoulders of the deceased sculpted and set upon a square, tapering column. He made me shudder.

And then, on the Tuesday, as if Forbes had been wrestling with my dead husband and at least loosening the grip of his hands, the obstacles went away. My hairdresser had a cancellation and fitted me in at the last moment, and news came also that though the railway chaos would continue for at least ten days, there would be one clear, normal day of service in the midst of the strikes, because the various factions of the strikers could not agree among themselves. I rang up Forbes at once, to tell him I would be traveling the next day. I said, "I'll take the later train from here, at eleven. It is a through train, which will get me to Chiasso at five. I'll stay there overnight. And I'll be at Rosecrans on Thursday, before they open in the early afternoon."

After I rung off I was amazed and annoyed with myself, thinking over what I had been telling him. What did he care which train I took, and when I would get to Chiasso? Why tell him I would be staying in Chiasso overnight? For all he cared, I could have slept in a ditch. But soon after, my irritation with myself gave way to shame. I understood that what at first I had taken for scatterbrained, superfluous rambling had been a simple, strong cause. By delivering to him minutely precise information, I hoped to bring about what I dearly wished. I had a vision of alighting in Chiasso on

Wednesday at five. I saw myself standing on the platform, haltingly, amid the first rush of passengers speeding to the exit, and then a tall, blond, lean man in his early forties come walking toward me. He was wearing the same smooth, sleek, navy blue topcoat, with a narrow velvet collar, that Gordon had always worn. Stepping up to me with a smile, he wordlessly took out of my hand the small suitcase, the dark blue one I had chosen from among my other cases to be in keeping with his navy blue Crombie coat.

Then he would say, "Let's go, shall we? I've booked rooms in a hotel, just a step across the station square." I am ashamed to admit that my conceit did not stop there. I saw myself and Forbes, after dinner, walk along the corridor and stop in front of my door, and I saw him take the key out of my trembling hand. He opened the door for me.

The next time my husband's ghostly hand reached out to me, signaling me not to defy the wishes of the dead, came during the journey—the actual train trip, not the one in my dreams. About half an hour before we got to Genoa, one of the passengers, a man, returning to our compartment from the restaurant car, said, "There's a man next door who's just died. Not remarkable, considering he was eighty-three."

Taken aback, I said, "How do you know he was eighty-three?"

"His wife said so," the passenger replied.

I said, "My husband died at eighty-three, too."

"It's quite a good age to die," he said consolingly. And after giving me a swift, telling glance he added, "And he got the best of it, what with having a young wife like you. I bet you were taken for his daughter."

"It did happen," I said.

He said, "Nice—for him, not for you."

When we got to Genoa there was an ambulance on the platform, with two white-coated attendants lounging about. There was a further delay, and we were told that the train would not depart at the proper time.

"Why is this?" I asked, upset. "What are they waiting for?"

"They are waiting for the carabinieri," the same knowledgeable man told me. "Whenever there is a sudden death the police must be called." He laughed and said, "Don't forget, his wife was with him. She may have helped him on the way."

The train started at last, after only a half hour's delay, and once more I realized it had been as though my husband had been calling me back from the threshold.

Then there was a further delay—a breakdown before Como—when we stood for forty minutes amid fields and pastures. I was flooded with anxiety, for we would now arrive in Chiasso after six, when the money changers' booths in the station would be closed, and I had no Swiss money. But when we did get there at last, an off-duty ticket collector, seeing me lingering by the now deserted passport counter, accosted me and then walked me to the very door of a nearby first-class hotel. There, the reception clerk laughed at my offer to give him my gold watch as a guarantee for some Swiss francs until the next morning. He told me that I could pay for my dinner in Italian money and receive Swiss francs in change. And while I was sitting at dinner he even made a point of coming to my table to ask whether I found my room to my liking.

On Thursday morning a chill rain was falling—so thin, so steady and densely threaded, that it looked like a motionless shroud of mist. The elderly, morose driver of the taxicab looked at me with disapproval when told I wanted to go to Rosecrans, grumbling with bad temper that it was far out and out of his way. But I did not care by then, for I no longer felt the touch of my husband's delaying grasp. The new Rosecrans offices were in the last of a row of new-looking, low buildings oddly set in a stretch of barren countryside. The glass-walled entrance took me into a reception area, subdivided by many doors. At the far end of the hall there was a counter flanked by shiny black chairs. Deserted and soundless, the place made me feel like a trespasser entering a nightclub at midday. Yet as I reached the counter there appeared behind it a plump, smiling woman. She took me in at a glance, seemingly approving of my old coat of Scottish cloth, handwoven and homespun in greens and blues, and made up by a man's tailor who worked only exceptionally for a few favored women clients; my dark blue cube of a suitcase; my black crocodile handbag; my pale gray, hand-stitched pigskin gloves; my unmistakably non-English look, accentuated by my tweedy, understated, typically English way of dressing.

I said, rushingly, full of misgivings, fearing barriers of denials, towers of refusals, "I've come here—it's rather complicated, I wrote ten days ago—I've got a trunkful of silver stored here. That's to say, not here with you but in bond."

She said, "One moment, please," and returned almost at once accompanied by a young man, who in turn seemed to accept my appearance without question. He was sloppily dressed in sandals, creased flannels, and a lumpy gray roll-collar pullover. His countenance was grave and gentle, and a narrow, dark beard framed his cheeks and chin. By the looks of him I decided he was a pacifist, a nonsmoker, a vegetarian, a teetotaler, and a devotee of Tantric Buddhism. Though I am usually contemptuous of this sort, I was glad to see him.

He took me upstairs to a bare room with a deal table, where we sat down on two old wooden chairs. I pulled out the sheaf of my correspondence, which was encased in a folder of transparent cellophane. He said, "As soon as I got your last letter I went round to the bond place and made sure your crate is still there. It's in perfect condition."

I said, "How marvelous. Over thirty years."

He said, "Madam, that's what we are here for."

When I told him why I had to wait till the afternoon, he was incurious, perhaps on the defensive. He inquired at last about the stack of letters on the table, and I slid the folder over to him. I knew that by doing so I was giving away the only proof of my claim to the silver, and was even providing him with arguments for delaying the transaction, since the letters made it clear that the silver had been my husband's property and not necessarily mine, but I was indifferent to these misgivings. I recalled a shred of my first talk with

Forbes, when I had told him that I did not even have any receipts for the storage payments. "So you see how dicey it is," I had said, and he had given his faint laugh. "I do indeed," he said. "Don't worry. When I get there, I'll wipe the floor with them." And it was his laughing voice that had brought me here, nothing else. I had used the silver as bait to make Forbes meet me.

It was not yet midday, and there was nothing more to deal with till Forbes's arrival, which he had told me would be at around three. When I asked where I could have a meal, the young man was astonished. "But there is no need for you to wait at all," he said. "Why should you? Just write out a delegation of authority for him, for this man, and let me have it." And he took a paper from the table drawer, wrote out a receipt, and passed it over to me.

I said, "But I'm going to stay. I want to be with him."

He looked disconcerted, and waved his pen to and fro across the table. Convinced as he must have been that my decision to part with the silver had been forced upon me by straitened circumstances, he had wished to spare my feelings by inducing me to be absent during the handing over. I knew that the truth was quite otherwise, though I had no wish to explain myself to him. Clear in my mind at last, I thought, Why should I hang on to the silver? I'm not going to leave it in safekeeping for God knows how many more years and then after my death have it be taken to where he wanted it to go—to those nephews, his sister's boys, in Australia. It's Forbes against him, and Forbes must have it.

But then I reached out for the folder and the receipt and,

taking the pen from the man's fingers, said, "You are right. I might just as well. You never know what's going to happen. I'll write out your *plein pouvoir*."

The young man could not guess my reason for this hint at the possibility of my sudden death. An instant before, as I watched the pen moving in his hands like the ticking of a metronome, my imagination had put in my mind an engraving of Dürer, in which the hooded figure of Death, bearing a scythe and an hourglass, rides a skeletal horse, speeding for the graveyard. But the man was relieved, and he slid the papers into the transparent folder with an air of satisfaction, as though he had gained a point against the imminent man from Brentford's. It was obvious that he had acquired the conviction, though confusedly, that Forbes was nefarious, that he was taking full advantage of me, that I was a victim and should be defended against him. Whatever happened, now he had a document that would protect his firm against my own willful innocence.

Our business done, we were now kinder to each other. He drove me a few hundred yards across rough country to what he told me was the only inn nearby, apologizing all the time for the chill and the rain; for his small, shabby car, which did not run well; for the lack of a better accommodation. I saw him looking at me more closely—at my well-worn, expensive clothes. As is my custom, I wore no jewelry. My white pallor and the gloss of my black-brown hair, my Egyptian-looking greenish eyes, and the curve of my black eyebrows, which appear to have been brushed on with a stroke of India ink, would look garish if I were to add ornaments.

He was not quite sure what to make of me. He probably thought of me as being hard up. Before he let me out, he gave me his name and telephone number, written on a chit torn out of his notebook. His name was Cortona. If I called him anytime after two, he would come and fetch me.

The inn was a humdrum wooden chalet, enclosed by openwork galleries, with the obligatory scarlet geraniums in window boxes. I ate quickly, and had a glass of wine. After lunch, I asked the way to the lavatory. It was in the cellar, and while I groped my way in pitch darkness down a steep flight of narrow stairs, with no rails on either side, I dwelled with bitter satisfaction on the *plein pouvoir* I had written out for Forbes. It had not been an exaggerated precaution after all, and if I broke my neck Forbes would now be in posses-sion. Putting out a toe to find the next step, and perhaps a bit drowsy from the wine, I saw myself—even as I jeered at such a notion—as the sleeping princess in the fairy tale, waiting to be roused and delivered by the prince. And as I thought of the sympathetic commiseration I had sensed from Cortona and the plump receptionist, it occurred to me that they might be right, after all. Forbes might be prince or robber, or both.

ONCE I HAD RETURNED to Rosecrans, I was led to an office on the first floor, glass-walled and so vast that I could not see the end of it in the farthest shadows. I was in-stalled at a table near the door, and the kind, plump woman brought me a local newspaper and a cup of amazingly good, strong coffee. It was by now twenty past two.

Reading the paper, I heard a swift, swishing rustle behind me. Then silence. By the time I looked around, he was there, standing by the wall, sidewise to where I was seated. Dazzled as I was at the sight of him, as though by the flare of a fork of lightning, I could see only dimly, planted in the open door, the figures of Cortona and the woman, humble and reduced in size, like the figures of donors in old sacred pictures.

He was gazing straight ahead, as though unaware of my presence, and yet he must have been taking me in upon entering. He was, of course, exactly as I had known he would be. I would have been able to pick him out in any crowd— in the foyer of a theater, at a vernissage, in a lecture hall— among all the other men dressed in similar style.

Nettled by his silence and his refusal to look at me, I fought down the nervous laughter rising in my throat, and the temptation of a sarcastic "Together at last" or "Mr. Forbes, I presume." At the same time, I took advantage of this pause to trace him line by line, tint by tint.

He was fair, with the same faded, bleached, washed-out fairness as Gordon's. He was as tall and lean as Gordon, but more heavily boned. His ash-blond hair fell in strands, untidily, to the edge of his forehead. He had pale skin, a short, blunt nose, and a hard-looking face, with strongly marked bones of brow and cheeks, and a square chin. He was standing relaxed, with his legs slightly apart, and his magnificently broad shoulders and splendidly wide, deep chest hinted at a menacing strength, yet for me it meant protection.

His topcoat of cinnamon-brown herringbone tweed was wide open, to reveal a suit that could have been Gordon's: a pinstripe of dark, black-tinged brown, like bitter chocolate or black coffee. It was a three-piece suit, with a waistcoat—the dress of a man in the professions. His brown tie glittered with a pattern of tiny silvery half-moons.

I saw that he was smiling—a tight-lipped smile, as if to say, "Here I am. I might just as well look pleasant, while I'm about it, but if you don't find me to your liking, too bad."

Still more unsettled by the unspoken arrogance of his bearing, I said, at last, "You've made it earlier than I thought you would. Do you feel like the dog's dinner? Did you have to get up at some ghastly hour to get here?"

"Not at all," he said, looking me full in the face for the first time, and changing his smile into one of harmless cheerfulness. He had crossed to the table where I was sitting, and stood in front of it. "I got up at eight this morning, my usual hour. And I've put in a lot of work on my way," he said. "I had a meeting in the airport in Lugano. Then I went to see a client there. Then I drove across the lake to see another client in Campione. Then I came here."

Facing him from so near, with only the table between us, I was overwhelmed by the presence of this young man of less than thirty—who could have been Gordon's younger, stronger, tougher brother. I was in a state akin to drunkenness, in which one listens to oneself uttering remarks that are forbidden. I said, "But you are so young."

He seemed disconcerted, as if I were doubting his expertise, his competence. "I'm sorry for being so young," he murmured.

And I, still flooded by recklessness, now said what could be taken as relating to our business, but what was, in fact, something quite different: "I am in your hands now."

Forbes straightened to his full height, and looked at me at length. A few heartbeats later he said in a low voice, "Yes, you are in my hands now."

He now abandoned his stance in front of the table, and murmuring, "They don't overwhelm you with hospitality, do they?" he took the only chair in sight, turning it to face me.

I said, "The Rosecrans man, you know, when I told him there'd be a gentleman from Brentford's coming to help me, he hadn't an earthly what I meant. Never heard the name. Unbelievable."

He said, "Unbelievable."

"I didn't tell him, though," I said. "Why should I? Brentford's is Brentford's."

He said, "Thank you."

I said, "You know, when you called me, I liked your voice on the phone. If I hadn't liked it I wouldn't have come."

"You wouldn't have come?" he said, with his indulgent, smiling voice.

I said, "No, I wouldn't have come."

"Are voices important to you? Do you judge people's characters by their voices?" he said in the same light tone.

"No, not on the whole," I replied. "Not really. Or, perhaps, yes. Though I've never really thought about it." And something came to me suddenly that I had never known before: that I had not liked my husband's voice on the phone. It had sounded weak and querulous.

Feeling that I had run into a cul-de-sac, and aware of how increasingly foolish I must appear to Forbes, I said, hurriedly, "A voice can be fateful, though. Now, take Sibyl Hunter, the wife of Sterling, they had the flat above me when I was still living in London, in Hunter's Lodge—"

He said, "Where exactly was that?"

"In Hammersmith, on the towpath," I went on. "I lived beautifully in a Queen Anne house, the garden giving onto the towpath. The house was Fine Arts and Monuments."

"You mean under the protection of the Ministry of Fine Arts and Monuments?" he said.

"Yes, and Sibyl—she told me, you see—was in publishing, and she rings up the *Architectural Review* and there is this man on the phone, and he says he'll mail it to her—the stuff she has been asking for—and she says, 'Don't, I'll come over straightaway and fetch it myself,' and slams the receiver down because she's fallen for him on the spot and is dying to meet him, and that's how they got married, and because Sterling was Daisy's cousin, and Daisy owned Hunter's Lodge, they got the flat above me."

"Remarkable," he said, in his smiling voice. "And how did it turn out?"

Together, starting with "the dog's dinner," we had slipped into a trifling, bantering way of talking—a form of exalted gossip that we both knew very well. I said, "Mr. Smith, the plumber, he comes down to me one day and he says, 'I've just been to the Sterling Hunters up above, their sink is blocked, and, if you ask me, that marriage is going down the drain.' "

He said, "Remarkable. And would you have said Mr. Smith was to be trusted?"

"The trouble with Mr. Smith was that he was so devastatingly handsome, though he was a bit long in the tooth, but that's what saved him with Daisy. She couldn't stand men, but you've got to have a plumber, and his getting on in years made him more digestible to Daisy, if you see what I mean. She used to say, 'Mr. Smith is simply devoted to his face. He can't pass a glass without stopping and having a look at his face.' And once when Mr. Smith is in hospital with his heart, Daisy goes to see him—she was very good that way, with servants and workmen—and she comes back and says to Caroline and me—Caroline was a cousin of hers, just staying—so Daisy says, 'My dears, you know how handsome Mr. Smith is, but, my dears, in bed he's simply heaven.' And we were both in stitches, Caroline and I, because Daisy didn't know what she'd been saying."

Forbes said, "And what was this with men and Daisy?"

"That's from when Daisy was a young girl and she went to stay with friends in India, and there is this major and they fall for each other, and he has this sick wife, and it's understood between them they'll get married as soon as. And then Daisy gets back to London, and she learns—not from him, mind you, but from friends—that the major's wife did peg out, all right, but he upped and got married to someone else. But I never did believe it—I mean, that Daisy got off men altogether because of that. I mean, it's a bit too easy, isn't it?"

He said, "I agree."

"For me it was lucky," I said. "What with being a woman on my own, and out of the top drawer, as Daisy said. Even with foreigners like me, you can tell straightaway, so I got the flat. But before me she'd had a colonel from the War Office, with his wife, in that flat, and when the wife goes to the nursing home to have a baby, the colonel puts on his wife's clothes at night and goes out on the towpath and then he tells the Sterling Hunters what divine adventures he's been having—not that they'd let on to Daisy, heaven forbid. But you see, she did take it out on men—just think of little Harry. She took him on as a tenant because she was pally with his mother, who was a Lady in her own right, and little Harry—he wasn't little, really, just a grown-up little boy, if you get me—he puts red-checked curtains on two of the front windows when he moves in, and Daisy gives him notice and he has to leave, because it's demeaning to the character of Hunter's Lodge, and out he goes. And after this, there was one more man, who didn't last out the first stay of his week, even."

"Why was that?" Forbes said, encouraging me, either out of politeness or genuine interest.

"He moves in on the Monday, and on the Tuesday a woman comes and she stays the night and she leaves soon after six, but Daisy is up and watering the garden, though it's pouring with rain—you wouldn't expect it, would you?—but you don't know Daisy. Then Daisy gets on the phone to him, and she says, 'Sir, when I let you have the flat I understood that you were a bachelor.' He says, 'That's true.' She says, 'How then can you explain why you had a female person staying with you last night?' He says, 'I'm a bachelor, that's true, but I'm not a monk.' She says, 'In that case, will you please put a month's rent on the table in the hall downstairs and the keys, and leave this day.' And after that there were no more men, and Caroline got the flat, because she wanted to be in London to study the piano."

Forbes said, "And you stayed there for how long?"

I said, "For five years, till I got married."

He said, "Those were the happiest years of your life."

I did not reply. Then I said, "Caroline stayed there, too, till she got married, but, mind you, even though she was a girl and a Hunter, there was a time when things looked very dicey for her, too."

"How was that? Do tell me," he said.

"It's like this. Daisy is what one calls 'being so very brave,' not having got any live-in servants and making do only with charwomen, and this morning she cooks her breakfast and carries it into the dining room and trips over an odd foot and stumbles and nearly comes crashing down with her tray, because there is a young man on the floor, in evening dress and fast asleep. Daisy gives him a kick between the shoulder blades, and she says, 'Young man, I don't know who you are and I don't want to know, only I do want to know how you got here, but I'm going to have my brekkers first.' Now, wasn't that wonderful of Daisy?"

"Wonderful," he said. "But do go on."

"It turned out Caroline had brought him home from a do," I said. "A dinner dance and then the Bag of Nails. He was seeing her home in a cab, and by the time they'd got to Hunter's Lodge he'd passed out, and the cabbie refused to carry on with him. He follows Caroline inside and shoves in the body before she can slam the door on him, and that was what saved Caroline, really, from being thrown out by Daisy—his being on the floor downstairs and fully dressed. But even then it was touch and go for Caroline."

Forbes said, "And you, yourself, you always kept out of trouble?"

"I always minded my p's and q's in Hunter's Lodge," I replied. "But still, I did have a very awkward moment once, and it really wasn't fair of Daisy—it wasn't as though she'd ever told me before, and so how could I guess?"

Forbes said, "I'm sure it wasn't fair of Daisy, and you couldn't possibly have known if she hadn't told you before. And what exactly was it? I think I should be told in case I meet Daisy, too."

"It was to do with Caroline's admirer—she'd asked him over to tea, and you couldn't fault him, because he'd stayed at Sandringham and Osborne—he had been in the Buckingham Palace crowd when the Queen was still Princess Elizabeth. The tea was in Daisy's drawing room, downstairs—Caroline couldn't have had him in her own rooms, naturally—and there I was in my own living room, reading the *Sunday Times,* because when I moved in, Daisy said she wouldn't tolerate my having the *Observer,* it being liberal, practically Bolshie, and it'd give the house a bad name."

One more glance at Forbes made it clear to me that he knew I didn't usually babble on in this fashion, and that he and I were speaking in a private tongue, almost a code, that we had both learned long ago.

"In he comes without knocking," I went on. "This young man, like carved-in-one-piece-out-of-an-oak-trunk-looking, and he says, 'Excuse me, is this the loo?' And I remember Daisy's got some unmentionables she's washed that are now drying in her bathroom, and I show him the way to my own. And next time I see Daisy I remark on it, and Daisy stares at me, wide-eyed, and she says, 'You don't mean— You let him use your own bathroom?' And I say, 'But Daisy, what on earth, you wished him on me, didn't you?' And she says, 'How ghastly preposterous. How could you ever let a man use your bathroom?' That's why she had sent him out of the house and to the garden loo—we did have one in a wooden hut in the rear, with a stone figure of a cat perched on the roof to make it more wistful-like, not crudely looish. I'd never given it a thought. I thought it was only for persons, not for people—persons like the window cleaner and the gardener, and suchlike creatures, if ever. Later, the oak trunk said he was longing to meet me, and even Daisy couldn't object, and he took me out a lot after that, mostly to parties given by ladies-in-waiting, till I got married. He got married, too—actually to a lady-in-waiting to the Queen."

Cortona came in, passing between us, raising both hands in a gesture of apology and shaking his head, giving us to understand that he was not yet ready for us. When he'd gone down the long room, Forbes said, "That fellow was creeping round before, too, taking a peep at us, but you didn't see him—you've got your back to the door."

We both kept silent, following Cortona with our eyes till he was out of sight in an adjoining office. I was sure that though he had not quite heard Forbes's words, he had felt the contempt in them.

Forbes said, "So you were with Daisy for five years, weren't you, till you got married? And then you left London. Why was that?"

"My husband didn't like snow in the winter," I said.

"And then you went where?"

I said, "First, six months in the south of Spain. Then two months in London. Then—oh, twice—summers in Salzburg, then twice in Lugano, six months each time. Once we took a house in Lausanne. Then three winters in Bordighera."

"And Portugal," he added. "You told me this—the English lawyer in Lisbon, last will and testament."

I said, "Yes, that was when we were in Estoril. There we stayed longest, because there is no snow and lots of servants."

"And you were always renting places—you never did own a house, did you?"

I did not reply.

He said, "So much shifting about, why was that?"

I said, "Because my husband didn't work. He gave up work before I met him."

"Even if he didn't work, why didn't he settle down?"

"I don't know."

He said, "Look, you were talking so charmingly a few minutes ago about Daisy, and the loo with the stone cat on the roof, and Caroline being in stitches, and Mr. Smith who was devoted to his face. And as soon as we get to your husband you dry up. Why is this?"

I did not reply.

He said, "Look, I want to get to the bottom of this." His voice, lower than before, had lost its smiling indulgence.

I drew a sharp breath to stifle the sob that was rising in my throat. I had now been with Forbes for less than half an hour, and already he had put a finger unerringly on what I had never been conscious of before—that I had never dared to ask my husband why we could not settle down for good, anywhere, just as I had never dared to question any of his other decisions. And I knew now that the choking and strangling he'd made me undergo in the last year of his life had merely been a continuation of what had gone on before.

Not only this. Forbes, in this short span of time, had shown more interest in me than my husband had done during all our years together. In the beginning, whenever I had wanted to tell him about my family and my background he had always cut me short with, "Who wants to know what your mother said to Clara, your parlor maid? Who wants to know what the cook said to your grandmother, and why your mother and your grandmother had a row about it afterward, and what Clara said to you? Who cares about the time when the Hungarian count first came to dinner and didn't leave a tip for the maids?"

Forbes now said, "I ask you, and you say you don't know. Or you don't even reply. Why is this?"

"I can't reply, because I've never thought about it," I said.

He said, "Do you want me to believe that you never gave a thought about the way you were living, that you never thought it odd?"

"I didn't let myself think," I said. "My husband was a great doctor. He was so distinguished, so superior, and I'm so inefficient, even with servants."

He said, "What you are really telling me is that he made you feel inferior all the time—is that it?"

I said, "Yes, even— I've got some good qualities, too, you know. He'd praise me, like saying, 'You do make an excellent pot-au-feu, I'll say that for you,' but it was backhanded praise, as though it were astonishing that I could ever do anything well."

"So that was how he kept you down," Forbes said. "An old man with a beautiful young wife. Quite systematic, wasn't he, in running you down?"

"And he was jealous," I said. "He didn't love me, but he was jealous."

Forbes said, "Jealousy lasts longer than love."

We both kept silent for a while. Then I said, "Yes, it's all true, but it never occurred to me before. And you give me the creeps."

"Why do I give you the creeps?"

I said, "You are living in Geneva. How long have you been living in Geneva?"

He said, "Two years."

I said, "Then you must know. You can stay in Geneva for weeks and see nothing spectacular, and then one morning you look across the lake and there is Mont Blanc, with its monumental crown of snow, the highest peak in our part of the world. It's been there all the time and you never knew it. And this gives you the creeps. Do you understand me now?"

He gave his faint laugh. He said, "I do, indeed."

CORTONA CAME IN at last, getting between us, stopping and nodding his head. We both got up. As I rose from behind the table he came hastily forward and helped me into my coat and picked up my suitcase, looking pointedly at Forbes all the while, to show that he, Cortona, was more caring and attentive than Forbes was. And Forbes met his eye with his tight-lipped, arrogant smile. I waited till Forbes was beside me and then I let Cortona precede us. I could tell that this annoyed Cortona, who would have wanted me to walk with him, with Forbes tagging behind.

As we walked out, I remembered something I had once heard about the Maharaja of Nepal, who had an anteroom in his palace in Kathmandu where visitors who came with petitions and demands were required to wait. The room was lined with distorting mirrors, convex and concave, diminishing or enlarging, but always rendering the beholder as a grotesque monstrosity. The room, though apparently designed to amuse those who waited there, was calculated to make them feel ridiculous and humble before they were admitted to the presence of the princely ruler. And while we went along the landing and descended the stairs I thought that during all my marriage I had seen myself as reflected by my husband, as inadequate and humble, and had taken it for granted that this was my true image, so I had no right to expect his interest and esteem.

Outside, Forbes and I stopped while Cortona went to his car, and he looked at me for a long time. "Are you still thinking of Mont Blanc?" he said at last. I did not reply. I noticed for the first time that his eyes were brown and not pale gray like Gordon's, which had reminded me of stale ice on a wintry river.

Cortona drove up and stopped before us. "The car doesn't run well," he said again, getting out.

"But you'll soon get a new one," I said. "That's good."

He said, "It's not good, because the new car will be just as ugly as this one." And we both started to laugh. I was glad of that, for his sake—happy to share a joke from which Forbes was excluded.

Cortona held the rear door open, and Forbes got in and sat in the backseat. I knew I must not get in with him. It would be unforgivable to let Cortona be alone in front as if he were our driver. Forbes ostentatiously leaned back in the far corner, filling all the space available with his diagonally outstretched legs, and making no move to close the door. Cortona slammed it shut under his disdainful glance.

I got in front, and as we started off I said to Cortona, "I was given such excellent coffee in your office. I was quite amazed. Was it brewed, or out of an urn?"

He said, "Out of an urn. Reserved for our special clients." He looked pleased. It occurred to me that Forbes had not been served with coffee. I had been speaking Italian with Cortona, and I wondered whether Forbes had understood. It came to me, of course, that I was being attentive to one man in order to disconcert the other. I looked over my shoulder at Forbes's sarcastic countenance, and I said, in English, "I was just remarking that I got such excellent coffee at their place."

"Why did you say that, slap on, about my being so young?" he said abruptly.

"But you *are* young," I said.

"That's no answer. Why did you say it?"

I said, "I can't possibly tell you."

He said, "If you think that our chap here understands a blessed word of what we are saying, you are mistaken."

I said, "I wasn't even thinking that."

"I want to know," he said.

"Don't be silly," I said.

"I am silly, and I want to know."

I said, "It's to do with your voice on the phone. It's— I made a mistake. I couldn't tell your age from your voice. I thought you were older. Forty-two or so."

"I'm beginning to see. But not quite yet."

"Let it be."

He said, "You were trying to figure me out. What I looked like."

"Yes."

He was silent. I said, "No, I wasn't trying to figure out what you looked like. I didn't have to. Because I knew."

He said, "You are telling me you knew what I looked like? Before meeting me?"

I said, "Of course I did."

"And do I look like what you knew I'd look like?"

I said, "Of course, but——"

He said, "But younger. That's it."

Startled by his astuteness in penetrating me, I said, "But your eyes are wrong. They are brown. They should be gray."

"I stand convicted for being young instead of forty-odd and for having brown eyes instead of gray," he said. "Not Dr. Richardes redivivus, was it to be? Hubby?"

I said, "Don't be beastly."

"Who was it?" he persisted. "How long ago? Hunter's Lodge vintage?"

"I can't possibly tell you," I said again.

He said, "You can possibly tell me. And you know as well as I do that you will tell me in the end if I keep at it long enough."

I said, "That's true, you have not only his looks. You have—the same way of torturing me."

For a while we were silent. Then I said, in a louder, brighter voice, for Cortona's benefit, "*Lascia perdere,* as the Italians say. Let it go."

Looking at Cortona, I saw that he was pleased. He seemed

to have gathered that Forbes had been tiresome and that I had snubbed him.

WE STOPPED AT LAST in front of a shed and Cortona, with attentive speed, came running to my side of the car to open the door for me. Then, seeing that Forbes made no move on his own, he opened the rear door as well. Watching Forbes get out without a sign or word of thanks, and then straighten his magnificent shoulders and throw out his wide chest while he looked into space, I thought that in Cortona's place I'd have hit him.

We entered the windowless shed. It was bare and brick-walled, with a stone-paved floor smeared with damp earth and streaked with grease. There was a long trestle table in the center of the room, and an old-fashioned slope-fronted stand-up desk in one corner.

Forbes said, "There's our reception committee," raising his chin toward a group of elderly, morose workmen, per-haps half a dozen of them. Some were lounging against a table, some leaning against one wall. In the gloomy twilight, with their earth-colored, muddy-looking clothes, they could have been posing for a picture by Cézanne. None of them moved. They were pretending not to have seen us.

"Bright-looking lot," murmured Forbes, and Cortona, crossing over to the desk in the corner and placing on it a ledger he had brought with him, cast him a resentful look, guessing the nastiness of his remark.

"How do you speak to him?" I said to Forbes. "Have you

spoken to him yet? Does he speak English? I suppose he must have some commercial English?"

"How should I know?" Forbes said. "He does believe that he speaks English. His very own brand."

There must have been a door in a hidden space at the rear of the shed, because now I saw a crate being carried in by four of the men and put down lengthwise on the trestle table.

The workmen stepped back, and two others came forward. The crate's lattice of wooden laths was hammered at, splintered and broken, and flung on the floor. The sacking beneath it was ripped off. There stood revealed a beautifully made tin trunk, about five feet long, undented and glossy, with the black-painted metal shimmering red and green like the backs of some beetles. One of the men said to me, "I'm telling you, this chest is valuable. It's worth more than anything you have inside it."

I would not have been surprised if Forbes had been thinking in the same vein, suspecting me of having lured him to Chiasso on false pretenses, now that he had prized out of me what I had never intended him to know.

I said, "You know, I've seen only snapshot pictures of those candlesticks. But I do remember them as being filthy black."

"Oh, I like it black," Forbes said caressingly. And I saw myself with Gordon, standing in front of his door, saying what I had been saving up to say all evening, in the pub and during dinner, and looking forward spitefully to his being disappointed: "It's no go, tonight. I've got the curse." And how stunned I was at his reply: "Oh, I like women with the curse." I said, "You mean, you will?" And he said, "Of course I will."

One of the men, crouching by the chest, had been hammering with his fists at the hinges, and now said to me, "Have you got the keys for the padlocks?" I shook my head. I recalled the two cigar boxes, in a drawer in the desk at home, filled with keys, with purposes unfathomable to me, but each known and meaningful to my husband, who had disdained labeling them. The man rummaged in a bag on the floor by his side and took out a long, clawed metal bar. We listened in silence at the grinding, squealing, and screeching as the locks were burst open.

Forbes gave a short laugh, hard and bright. The man who had been crouching was now on his feet, with one hand clutching the other.

Still laughing, Forbes said, "Look, now he's hurt himself. He's bleeding. Now he's running outside. Now we've got to wait till he's stopped bleeding. What a nuisance."

Disconcerted, I raised my face to his ironic, knowing smile. I smiled, too. I felt myself blushing. I knew I should have shown distress and concern. It was like a duel between me and Forbes. He was forcing me, wordlessly, to admit that I was not nice—that I cared as little as he did. I saw his hard smile change into one of indulgent amusement, and I seemed to be once more with Gordon, who, after torturing me to make me admit one of my ugly, shameful secrets with his relentless questions, disregarding my reasonable explanations and finding the true meaning behind my senseless and foolish remarks, would then be delighted and take me to his bosom. Forbes said, solicitously, in utter contrast with his former hardness, "But aren't you getting cold, standing here on this damp stone floor?"

We both looked down at our feet, standing so well-behaved side by side—my pretty white boots, with the sheepskin forming a white, frothy rim above my ankles, next to his dark brown, laced leather shoes, and I was flooded with deep gratitude I had not felt since Gordon's death. We did not speak again or look at each other till the chest was prized open and the lid raised.

I HAD EXPECTED to see a layer of wood shavings, or that synthetic straw used by professional packers, or sheets of corrugated cardboard. There was, instead, an expanse of linen—white, fawn, pale blue, and all creased and tired-looking. Forbes said to me, over his shoulder, "Someone's shirts and pajamas," perfidiously reminding me that he knew I was violating my husband's wishes. He kept his eyes on me a few heartbeats longer, and then moved to the rim of the chest and swept off the swaths of linen. I saw him bending over some tightly packed rows of woolly nests—brown, black, gray—which I suddenly recognized as my husband's rolled-up socks. Forbes did not seem to be taken aback. Bending low, he delved speedily among the socks, bringing some out and unfurling them unhesitatingly. His wide shoulders were blocking my view.

I went and stood close behind him. On the ledge of the

table, near the chest, there was the silvery glitter of flat, square, and oblong cigarette cases, already a half dozen or more, each different. While I tried to count them he kept unrolling one sock after another, each time yielding one more case. I stopped trying to count them.

I picked up one of the pieces, worked in a pattern of basket weave. "Oh God, look at this," I said in dismay. "All this modern rubbish. It's nothing—just its weight in silver."

"And who are you to cast contempt on this glowing example of patients' gratitude toward their beloved doctor?" he said, with mock solemnity. Then, in his ordinary voice, he said, "Don't worry," and again gave his faint laugh. "I told you I'd take everything." He went on digging and probing in the depths of the woolly nests, with a calm greed that made me shudder. I watched his hands—pale and lean, with long, bony, square-tipped fingers—and sensed that my shudder came from the voluptuousness of a forced surrender. I felt Gordon's fingers probing and penetrating me, and I heard Gordon say, "I never go myself where my hand has not gone before."

Trying to hide the tears I felt welling up, I turned away, dabbing at my eyes, and then slid out and replaced a few of the tortoiseshell hairpins that were stuck in the twisted strands of the chignon on the nape of my neck.

"Now," I heard Forbes say, and he drew in his breath sharply. Then, in a very low voice, "I've got the Odiot."

When I turned to Forbes, he was standing motionless and upright by the table. As though for my pleasure, he had swiftly placed the teapot on its stand and had grouped the jugs and bowl around it like a wreath. In one glance, I took in fluted, bellied curves and embossed garlands of leaves and dog roses. A rage of disappointment flooded over me. Instead of the austere swanlike elegance of the Napoleonic silver I had been visualizing, I was met with the cozy prettiness of some opulent merchant's tea set. There weren't even the engraved initials that would have told us it had been manufactured to order.

"Not even a crown, or a coat of arms," I said.

"You thought your—"

"No, no," I said brusquely. "It came to my husband from his sister. She bought it, God knows where."

He said, "As an investment, obviously."

"What on earth did my husband imagine he'd got?" I said. "Empire, my foot."

"It's 1860," he said without hesitation. "You won't get more than fifteen thousand francs for it."

I said, "So what? It's not the— You understand."

"Yes, yes," he said, soothingly. "But it's quite pretty, really. Look, it's got that plug on the chain attached to the stand, with the hole on the side, you see. That's for keeping the tea warm on the stand—now, isn't that nice?"

I said, "Don't be beastly. My uncle had an oil sketch by Rubens, but when he took it to Christie's they said it wasn't; it was by a contemporary of Rubens. But that's different, whereas here a child of five could have—"

He said, "It happens all the time."

I went over to Cortona, at his desk. He pointed to the

cover of one of the files, and said, "I see the payments are all from a trust account and signed with your name, but with no initials."

Greatly relieved, now that I was safe from any quibbles, I said coldly, "Oh, yes, didn't you know? I took it for granted you knew." And I showed him my credit card, on which my full name was printed. It bore a hologram picture of a man, which disappeared when the card was moved, like a fold of *changeant* taffeta, which shifts color with each change in the pleating.

When I returned to Forbes, he was considering a pair of tall candlesticks he had brought forth in the meantime. He seemed more upright and at leisure. "They aren't Renaissance, they're Victorian," he said. "You can't pretend surprise over this. You had a jolly good intuition—you told me on the phone, you'll recall."

We stood silent, gazing at the blackened silver: the square, down-tapering columns, two feet tall, topped by head and shoulders of figures—one nymph, one faun—each with upraised arms, bearing rings to hold the candles. And reminded of my husband, robed in toweling, already in his own stele, I seemed to be looking at his face modeled in tarnished silver. But another feeling arose in me as well—a revulsion against an ancient, bawdy joke. As we know, nymphs and fauns are not to be held in awe. They are minor rural deities, given to frolicking among wooded grounds. As painted and sculptured through the ages, the faun leers and the nymph looks frightened. The faun is forever the chaser and the nymph the victim, and though the outcome of their encounter is certain, their amorous situation feels both transitory and nasty.

"They are not really done in the manner of Renaissance grotesques," Forbes said. "I'd say they were realistic portraits—an old boy and a girl."

"Ghastly," I said. "And they'll be even more repulsive-looking once they are cleaned up."

"Their very ghastliness makes them intriguing, don't you see?"

"The girl doesn't look so bad, though," I said. "She's just a teenage floozy—a salesgirl behind the jewelry counter at Woolworth's. A thin young vixen, and anemic. She's never had enough to eat. And they've gone all out on her hair—lots of work there, all those curls and waves and tendrils and loose wisps down the shoulders."

He said, "And yet you are terribly upset. And disgusted. Why is that?"

I did not speak.

He said, "The nymph doesn't look like you, so she is inoffensive. Shall we go a bit further? Shall we say that it is the faun who is the trouble, because he looks like someone you know, doesn't he?"

"It's just that he is so old," I said, avoiding his eyes. "He's about sixty, and I thought fauns were young."

"He is about sixty," he said. "Shall we say he is about the age your husband was when you got married?" He waited and then went on. "He does look rather like your husband, doesn't he?"

I said, "But my husband never had this revolting goat's beard. He was clean-shaven."

He said, "Very well, but let's get to the bottom of this. What is it that reminds you particularly of Dr. Richardes?"

I said, "The superior leer. The way he raises his head—I can just see him saying to someone, 'You are an ignoramus, you have no right to discuss this subject.'"

"That is not what hurt you in particular, though, was it?" he persisted. "What is it that you find so shattering?"

I said, "The spite and malice. But smiling always, pretending he was being humorous and kind. It's a hidden malice, like when he made out he was impoverished—and I believed it. And he did it so as to take this miserable tiny flat we had at the last, and to make me work. Fifteen hours a day I was on my feet looking after him, and not even a char or a part-time nurse to take over."

"An old man and a young wife," he said. "It was his way of tying you down, to make sure you didn't walk out on him. 'Till death us do part,' don't you know."

I put both my hands over my eyes. I said, "Don't torture me."

He said, "It's all over now. Look at me."

I looked up at him with trembling lips. He said, "You are in my hands now. I'll do what I want with him. I'll sell him down the river, the way he never wanted to be sold. I'll get rid of him once and for all. I'll take everything away from you, and there is nothing to worry about. My shoulders are wide enough."

Looking up at him, I recalled Gordon, after he had made

me surrender one of my shameful secrets, saying, "My sweet child, you don't know the pleasure you are giving me." And then, as so often happened, after I had tried perversely to evade what I was longing for and had made him obtain it by force, he would say, when I returned from the beyond, "That wasn't so bad, now, was it?"

FORBES TOOK a small magnifying lens out of his coat pocket. "My loupe," he said, and, bending over the faun, he gave a swift scrutiny down one side of the face. "I can't help being intrigued by him," he said, shaking his head. "Very fine, delicate work here, all this crosshatching, and the wrinkles."

I said, "I wonder if his sister— Maybe she bought the candlesticks as a joke, because of the likeness, to make him stand up on the mantelpiece, holding the candles. They didn't get on, you know."

He said, "How did your husband get hold of the candlesticks?"

I said, "She gave them to him, with the Odiot, to settle a debt."

He said, "But he left you his heir, entirely and absolutely, of all he possessed, didn't he? You told me on the phone."

I said, "Yes, of course."

I went and stood at his side as he drew out of the chest, with contemptuous speed, a salver and two jugs. "This one is only plated," he said, after barely glancing at it. "Now we are scraping the bottom of the barrel, and here are your rattles, three of them, just as you told me on the phone. Flimsy, and poor workmanship. 'Behold the child, by nature's kindly law / Pleased with a rattle, tickled by a straw,' I don't think. Away with them to the rubbish dump in Zurich!"

I went out and stood beneath the eaves, staring into the curtain of rain, and I thought of Gordon, greedy to penetrate my thoughts and my body. Gordon the sailor, the slinky, slippery, slithery fish, who had slipped into his watery death in the bathtub, his blood mingling with the water, and had drowned before the blood had ceased to flow from his wrists. And I thought of Forbes the agent—the sliding go-between, the delver, the searcher, the finder—seizing, unwrapping, and disentangling the silver others had worked and fashioned, and then letting it glide through his bony, grasping fingers, passing it on, letting it go.

When I went back inside, the table was blank and empty, and the chest closed. Forbes and Cortona were standing by the desk, bending over some files, talking. Forbes came to me, saying with contained anger, "The fellow wants such a high insurance." Cortona joined us, and we watched the workmen seal the edges of the chest with transparent tape. Cortona handed me a pen and asked me to sign my name in two places, across the tape, and as I did, Forbes, smiling arrogantly, murmured, "You wouldn't believe it—these precautions. That fellow will wet his pants next."

When we left, Forbes again seated himself in the back of the car and made no move to close the door. Cortona shut it with deliberate slowness, as though just having caged a dangerous beast and wanting to make sure it was safely locked up.

Cortona got in and said, "Where do you want me to take you?" and I said, "To the station, please." He did not ask Forbes. The hostility between the two men was such now that I was convinced that had I not been present Cortona would have driven off, leaving Forbes in the desolate country, in the rain.

In front of the station building, Cortona handed me my suitcase with a gravely deferential bow, and I thanked him with heartiness and repeated my good-byes, as though finding it hard to part with him. Forbes stood a few paces away from us, pointedly aloof, gazing into space. I glanced at him sidewise, then turned and stood facing him and lifted my gaze to his. Our eyes met. His lips twitched, sardonic, triumphant. He did not speak.

I raised and lowered my shoulders, and went through the glazed station doors, which slid open at my approach and slid closed behind me.

MY RETURN JOURNEY WAS unremarkable until after the halt in Como, when the doors of my compartment were wrenched apart by a young man, thickset, with black-rimmed glasses and an inquisitive, canny, impertinent air, bearing a strong resemblance to an Italian journalist I had recently met. The intruder, waving a cigarette in front of his face, said, in English, "Anyone here who can give me a light?"

It was a nonsmoking carriage, and the passengers, all elderly, small-town northern Italians, looked at him as though rendered speechless by some obscenity he had uttered. I opened the jaws of my handbag, saying, "Here," and held my lighter out to him. He took it and enclosed it in his fist.

"How many languages do you speak?" he said unexpectedly.

I said, "Five."

"So do I," he said. "Five or six."

"That's fine," I said, wondering whether I'd ever see my lighter again.

"What are you?" he said, still standing before me.

I said, "Never mind."

"Where were you born?"

I said, "In a bed."

"You are utterly fascinating," he said. "Tell me what you are."

I said, "Light your cigarette and begone."

He said, "I shall not light my cigarette till you tell me."

Though no one in the compartment had moved, and none were glancing at me, I could feel their concerted pressure on me to get rid of the intruder, who kept looking at me with his fleshy face creased in an impertinent grin.

Forbes, too, had made it plain, in the unspoken dialogue between us, that he had been intrigued by me. He, too, had wanted to find out my birthplace and my background. He had tried to find out my age as well, though it must have been plain to him that I was almost twice as old as he. But, not getting any farther, since I did not volunteer any of this information and he could not demand it, hemmed in as he was by his upper-class breeding, he had penetrated instead into the crooked and involuted paths of my inner maze, where everything was dark, bewildering, and mostly shameful. And now I was faced with this stranger, an emissary sent by Forbes to ask the questions Forbes had wanted to ask, and to extort my answers.

"Very well," I said. "I was born in Prague. And Prague is in Bohemia, so I am Czech. And that is the last you will get out of me."

He stepped into the corridor, lit his cigarette, and came back and gave me the lighter with a delighted grin.

All the other passengers in my compartment got out at Milan, and I was then joined by a youngster, who, reading "Richardes" on the label of my suitcase, fell at once into excellent American English. The trouble with foreigners, he told me, was that they all thought he was Italian. But he was not Italian—he was Milanese. The worst of all foreigners were the young girls, because they spoke stupidly and made impossible romantic demands, wanted a Latin lover and all that rot. For the rest of the journey he kept telling me why he was not going to commit suicide.

Acknowledgments

I wish to express my deepest gratitude to Roger Angell, the fiction editor at *The New Yorker,* who was the first reader of most of these stories, and who possessed an almost telepathic feeling for what it was I meant to say. His intelligence and care as an editor have been invaluable to me over the years.

I also wish to thank my agent, David McCormick, for his devotion to my work and his good sense.